5442 4915

W9-CCF-103

A Distance to Death

Also by Holly Menino

Murder, She Rode

Calls Beyond Our Hearing:
Unlocking the Secrets of Animal Voices

Darwin's Fox and My Coyote

Forward Motion: Horses, Humans,
and the Competitive Enterprise

Pandora: A Raccoon's Journey

A Distance to Death

Holly Menino

MINOTAUR BOOKS

A Thomas Dunne Book

NEW YORK

A THOMAS DUNNE BOOK FOR MINOTAUR BOOKS.
An imprint of St. Martin's Publishing Group.

A DISTANCE TO DEATH. Copyright © 2014 by Holly Menino. All rights reserved. Printed in the United States of America. For information, address St. Martin's Press, 175 Fifth Avenue, New York, N.Y. 10010.

www.thomasdunnebooks.com
www.minotaurbooks.com

The Library of Congress Cataloging-in-Publication Data
is available upon request.

ISBN 978-1-250-04649-9 (hardcover)
ISBN 978-1-4668-4676-0 (e-book)

Minotaur books may be purchased for educational, business, or promotional use. For information on bulk purchases, please contact Macmillan Corporate and Premium Sales Department at 1-800-221-7945, extension 5442, or write specialmarkets@macmillan.com.

First Edition: August 2014

10 9 8 7 6 5 4 3 2 1

For Frances,
friend for the long haul

A Distance to Death

1

Stories like this usually start out with a body, the form that holds the person in his or her last earthly state—God knows what comes after that, I don't. I could show you this body, the arrangement of the head, neck, and the arms and legs, the location of the wounds or the lack of them and the details of blood and semen, the juices that keep our species viable. But if I started with the body, you would miss half the ride.

Ride is what the people who rode the horses called it, but the Tevis Cup was really just a race, a very long race with strict requirements for staying in it. As the miles passed under the horses' hoofs, a lot of information would come with them, information that should help you understand what happened to her and why he died. So let's leave the bodies for the time being and start out with the bang at the beginning.

The trailer ramp crashed down, and the sound reverberated from the barn and corrals and the edge of spruce forest that descended into the meadow. After five days on the road, the springs that let the ramp down had gone slack, given up, and it slammed down loud enough to wake the dead. But apparently there was no one here, dead or not, to disturb. I looked around

2 • Holly Menino

in road stupor. Three thousand miles with only one overnight stop. Isabel and I took turns driving and sleeping until we came to this barn at the end of a driveway high in the Sierra Nevada not far from Truckee, California. I was woozy from the altitude and fatigue.

The scene could have been a photo shot in black and white and then tinted with pewter and green. The sandy soil was gray with outcroppings of lighter rock, and the spruce trees that stood back at a respectful distance were a dense blackish green. The weathered wood of the barn and corrals needed no tint. The little ranch was an establishment called Farrell's, just up the mountain from the flat rim of land that surrounded Donner Lake. The Donner party, coming from the East through Utah, had met starvation here just a couple of years before the Gold Rush, when the prospectors and miners stampeded in from the West. After the gold petered out, a fat vein of silver was claimed by Henry Comstock, and then fifteen years after the Donner party's ordeal, two haphazard miners came in from the West in search of silver. They found gold, and the Squaw Valley rush was on.

When I read those facts aloud to Isabel Rakow as we came in view of Donner Lake, she said, without giving thought to what it must have been like to start in chewing on the hide roof over your head in the middle of winter or to strike it rich by accident, "Eighteen sixty-three? Four years after *Origin*," referring to Darwin's book on evolution. Isabel had a trick of the mind that sent many topics boomeranging back to Charles Darwin or to endurance riding. We had spent the last five days confined to the cab of a diesel pickup where the noise of the engine was constant and conversation not. Occasionally Isabel would make a brief comment. It would seem to come out of the blue, but it didn't. Her mental life was something intense, and her remarks were what boiled up from it. "You know, he," she might say—was there any doubt about who *he* was?—"gave a mirror to a female orangutan in the London Zoo?"

Why would I know something like that? I had never really considered Darwin's importance or the importance of the theory of evolution. Although I had no objection to being edified, as far as I could tell from Isabel's sporadic commentary, Darwin's life was pretty dull, and when I said something like this, Isabel said, "Read the *Beagle*," as if I would ask her to stop the rig at the very next public library so that I could comply. So far as I had been able to determine, Darwin was the only man she had ever allowed in her life.

If Isabel was as highway-addled as I was, she certainly didn't show it. The little veterinarian looked as snugly put together as usual. She was tiny and plump, with dark hair and bright blue eyes. Everything about her radiated energy—and control. Her hair was a curly black cap. She never let it grow, and she never let her lipstick wear off. She was inclined to be aloof and keep me at a respectful distance. But over the months I had spent training with her on the trails, she had become what I would consider a friend. With me at least, if not with her pet-owning clients, she was candid about the fact that she ministered to cosseted dogs and cats because that produced enough income to keep her in horses. Although she never actually told me this, I had the impression that she had grown up without much money, and I think she kept up appearances to fit in with her well-heeled clients—also maybe because she wanted to hide the highly intelligent mind behind her carefully maintained face.

What betrayed the quite deliberately composed Isabel was her voice. When she opened her mouth, what came out was startling: a thin, penetrating call ushered by a heavy New Jersey accent. This voice sounded just now as she was looking around.

"Wonder where Farrell is."

The ranch we had driven into was at seven thousand feet, a bed-and-breakfast that had trail horses to rent out, and we had come out a couple of weeks before the Tevis ride to let the horses adjust to the thinner air. Way back in April we had reserved beds for ourselves and stalls and turnout for the two horses on the trailer. I took a look inside the barn and found two empty stalls freshly bedded with shavings.

"He may not be here," I reported, "but he is expecting us."

We turned our attention to the horses, Darwin and Owen. In the trailer Darwin's round brown rump was aligned side by side with Owen's remarkably bony gray backside. It was time to unload the horses, and I went forward to the door at their heads.

"Watch him, Tink," Isabel warned, but I knew exactly what to expect. Owen was a phenomenally competitive trail horse, and competitiveness made him envious, and envy made him tricky. If Darwin was asked to back out of the trailer before Owen was, the gray horse would explode backward, tearing out pieces of the trailer and anything else that came between him and his little margin of victory. Owen had to be first, and he was always invited out of the trailer before Darwin. Even so, he usually made a big, thumping, rattling deal about it.

I snapped a long lead rope to his halter and took a step toward the ramp, where Isabel was standing by. The horse began scrambling and launched himself with a backward leap. This ballet was standard operating procedure, and I gave him enough slack in the rope to let him make his move. Probably too much slack, because he immediately took advantage of it. He stood straight up on his hind legs and, bracing against his backward momentum, threw one gray foreleg over the rope and bolted. The lead rope ripped out of my hand, and the horse galloped free, speeding past the barn to the nearest corral in search of other horses. What Owen was expecting after so many hours on the road was a ride camp inhabited by endurance horses and their riders. He was well accustomed to what ride camps should look like, and this place did not meet his expectations. He sped along the corral fences, and evidently determining he was not in the right place, shot out of sight looking for the kind of camp he had in mind.

"Little cheat," Isabel commented levelly as I ran past her on my way after the horse. Sometimes aloofness is a form of graciousness.

Owen had got the jump on me, and he blew by the last corral, charging down the lane toward the steep road we had taken to get to the ranch. His bony backside flew down it and out of sight, giving us pitiful humans a farewell salute with a flip of a silver tail. Owen was barefoot like so many of the horses that run endurance these days, and without the definition of a steel shoe, each hoof left only a rindlike impression.

When I got to the paved road, I stopped running because I could see there would be no gain in it. I couldn't run and follow Owen's tracks at the same time. In fact, I could barely run at all. The high thin air stole my breath. My legs felt oddly weighed down, and the road and the gray-green mountainside spun unsteadily before my eyes. It was the altitude and our fast trip up to it that day.

The sudden climb up to Donner Lake on Interstate 80 began a few miles east of Reno, where the Sierra Nevada stood up abruptly from the desert. The mountain range was a daunting prospect, offering nothing to an approaching traveler but challenge and hardship. From a distance it was hard to imagine a way over or through the steep, dry mountains, which held out no promise of sustenance for humans or wildlife. As the truck and trailer turned up the interstate, making easy work of our passage, I thought of the Donner party laboring to get their wagons up into occasional high meadows. It must have taken real fortitude to even contemplate, let alone undertake, a crossing. Every face of every mountain was steep, sometimes sheer, and when we left the interstate and the roads were narrow with no shoulder, I couldn't figure out whether it was more scary to look down into a breathtaking drop-off or up at the heights still ahead of us.

"This country," Isabel commented, "is enough to make you believe in God."

"Or at least pray," I suggested even though I knew she didn't do either, believe or pray. "I can't figure out how people got here in the first place or why they stayed."

"I think once we are on the horses and moving over the ground stride by stride, the mountains won't look so tough."

To Owen the terrain hadn't looked tough at all.

A half mile downhill, at a break in the enormous spruce trees, Owen's tracks stopped. He seemed to have lifted off the road into the bright sky above the trees. I stood at the edge of the road and looked down. The sunny mountainside was steep and covered with stone rubble until it met the same road I stood on as it switched back across the grade. Straight down would be the shortest way, but the footing in the loose rock would be terrible. So I discounted this possible path and tried to clear away fatigue and think.

Owen wasn't my horse. He belonged to Isabel, like this whole endurance enterprise. I was a newcomer, introduced to Isabel and her sport by my friend Frankie Golden. People who knew Isabel and Frankie said things to me like "You're riding the Tevis? Wow, that's a tough ride. How many rides have you finished?" Only a few, just enough to amount to the three hundred miles necessary to qualify for the Tevis. I was a green, green gringo, but this ride, the Tevis Cup, was important. More specifically, finishing this ride was important. The motto of endurance riding is To Finish Is To Win, and the finish line a hundred miles west of where I was now was something I had fixed on like a man overboard fixes on the ring buoy at the end of a line. So, okay, now I had managed to lose the horse that could carry me to the finish. I thought of Charlie and Stephen, my husband and stepson, back on the farm south of Philadelphia. Right now they were probably situated comfortably in Charlie's study, which over the past couple of months had become a cheerfully messy war room. Charlie's reading matter had been cleared from the sofa to make a place for Stephen and the rubble on the coffee table relocated to the rug nearby to allow space for a laptop. On weekends, I would find them there, Charlie hunkered down in his armchair and Stephen hunched over, poking at his laptop, deep in contemplation.

Charlie's venture company, Halefellow, was involved in what he called a protective buyout of a small company that somehow turned protein into medicine, and he wanted to put Stephen in the middle of the deal. Which I thought was very sweet and also smart. It was a friendly kind of merger, and we had begun a friendship with the aging scientist who owned the company. He had turned to Halefellow for help. He knew exactly what kind of help he needed, and he had turned to the right investors. While Charlie understood the money and the statistics of research and development, he had no experience with the computing part of the biology. Stephen did.

James Grant-Worthington was a molecular biologist who was on the faculty at Stanford University and, working in a lab there, had developed an innovative method for rapidly and accurately producing artificial proteins. Why was this important? he asked rhetorically when he made his presentation to the Halefellow board of directors. Because some of the proteins that had resulted from this laboratory breeding—recombinant proteins—had powerful therapeutic capacities and they were of intense interest to the pharmaceutical industry. Grant-Worthington had started a small business to exploit his process, AccuGen. Then two of the proteins Grant-Worthington had developed had proved themselves effective weapons in the fights against AIDS and hepatitis, and this had led to the little company's rather explosive success. It was clear to Grant-Worthington that he could not manage the company's future on his own, and this is what he told the Halefellow board of directors. He was—as everyone in the boardroom could see—getting up in years, and he wanted, first of all, help in restructuring the company as a publicly held corporation with a plan for stable succession of management. Next, there were some aspects of the company's production process that were beginning to limit its growth. These were primarily computational—Charlie had pounced on this like his cat Greenspan on a mouse—Stephen! Here was a role tailor-made for Stephen.

What followed was the happiest time of my life. Stephen or Stephen and his girlfriend Alex were at the house constantly. Charlie went into Philly and New York only when absolutely necessary. And I was starting to get back on the horse. Not young stock, nothing spooky, no fences. It was just Owen and just enough to keep me looking ahead to competition.

Stephen dug into research on generating recombinant proteins and the computational requirements for sorting through the myriad proteins that resulted. He glowed from the effort, and Charlie, designing the Halefellow reorganization of Accu-Gen, basked in his new role as mentor. He had lost his own father at the age of fourteen and had never had children of his own. Stephen kept the surname of his father and my former husband, Frank Elledge, and although Charlie had always had a warm relationship with Stephen, working together had cemented something almost biological between them. In his own way Charlie too needed this deal to come along.

About a month into their evaluation of the company and its prospects, Charlie invited Grant-Worthington for his first visit to the farm. When he mentioned the scientist would stay for dinner, I panicked. My cooking skills and repertoire were decidedly limited. But Charlie said, "Don't worry about what you fix. If I read this guy right, he'll be happy with scrambled eggs."

In a way, Charlie was right about the scrambled eggs, but what actually happened is that Dr. Grant-Worthington sensed my apprehension and joined me in the kitchen to take over operations there. "No need to be proud, my dear"—in British-inflected English and as if I were in junior high—"this is my idea of a vacation. You know, not answering questions about the balance sheet." All of us—Alex, Stephen, Charlie, and I—benefited at the table, and somehow Grant-Worthington managed to shift the credit to my side of the ledger. It was the first of quite a number of visits. Sometimes we went out to dinner. Sometimes James cooked.

It wouldn't be long before James would be doing the cooking again. My friend Frankie Golden, who had suffered a number of defeats in tennis at the hands of James, was on her way out to these mountains to help with the horses during the race. The plan was for Frankie and Isabel and me to meet him in Palo Alto after the Tevis ride. We would leave the horses in Truckee for a few days and converge near Stanford with James and Charlie and Stephen for what James called "a real celebration of our new arrangement." Although Isabel had met James only briefly, I had a pretty reliable hunch that her interest in Darwin and evolution and James's intimate knowledge of DNA would instantly put them on common ground.

Standing in the steep road that led to God knows where, I only hoped that at the end of the day Isabel would still be on common ground with me. Her horse was gone, quite gone, and no doubt about it, the fault was mine. What in hell was I doing chasing somebody else's homely horse in these godforsaken duotone mountains? I had no business way out here. This wasn't my sport. I belonged back home eventing, running at cross-country fences, flying, and I was only doing this endurance race because when Charlie agreed that I could start riding again after a fluky accident and a year of physical therapy, he said, "But no *jumping*. . . ."

I missed him now, missed him looking after me, trying to keep me out of predicaments like this. I was wishing myself off the mountainside and back to the farm and Charlie and Stephen when I looked down over the scree that tumbled far below to the switchback and noticed something there. The round rubble rocks were decorated with dark pearls. Manure.

This was hard to believe. Why had Owen careened down this steep rock-strewn slope when any ordinary horse would have taken the easy way the road offered? The answer, I feared, was because he was an Arabian. I started down carefully, sometimes dropping back on my butt to skid more safely. How could the horse have navigated the grade and the rocks without hurting himself? He might bang his legs up badly enough to put us out of the race before we even made it to ride camp for the start. After hauling two horses across the country and being attached to Isabel and the specter of Darwin for two thousand miles, this would be pretty hard to take. I wasn't getting any younger, and I was aware of rust settling in. I had been out of competition for more than a year, and I needed this ride. While I was pretty sure Owen would have been able to go the hundred miles, I wasn't at all sure I could. But to try to get through the miles and be reassured about that was an almost physical need.

Thirty yards from the road, the flat, green-brown spheres of manure led in a curve to the left. I followed Owen's turn, followed the road into a narrow valley between the mountain I had come down and the one rising next to it. Now the view along the road was a straight shot, and there was good visibility for almost a mile. No horse in sight. Evidently Owen had already started his own race.

I was struggling for breath. My lungs seemed to take a long time to fill up. And I was losing heart. Often a horse that finds itself loose becomes frightened and disoriented, and it will run until it is exhausted and then wander lost and spooky until death claims it in one way or another. Could be a semi or maybe just a broken-down fence. There would be no way to make up the loss to Isabel. It wouldn't be a simple matter of paying for the horse, because she hadn't paid for him, and she hadn't bred and raised him the way she had Darwin. She had inherited him from a client whose Blue Heelers she treated and who was a friend and challenger in endurance racing. When Owen's owner was diagnosed with an aggressive cancer and she had to stop competing, she told Isabel, "I want you to have my little mare." Isabel agreed but only reluctantly because there wasn't anything special about the mare. Sometime later, however, when her friend's death was in plain sight, Isabel said, "Why don't you give me your good one too? Be better for him." This gift was a compliment, and it made Owen irreplaceable. A priceless little bastard.

Owen's tracks followed the dirt shoulder of the road down the mountain for about half a mile then veered into what was an obvious trail. For the horse this seemed to make sense. Trails, which were usually forgiving underfoot, were preferable to the hard asphalt road, and when he was under saddle his rider often made this dirt-over-pavement choice for him. This particular dirt thread was a rollicking, up-down passage that continued to carry his hoofprints until it met another road. The new road was just gravel, but it had the curious appearance of being well cared for. Evidently Owen had found this a promising avenue, and I trudged along dutifully in his wake until a quarter mile on there was a metal sign embossed with the message PRIVATE ROAD—AUTHORIZED ACCESS ONLY.

The road was a level track cut through spruce trees on the floor of a narrow valley between the mountains. I could see the horse's hoofprints cutting into the gravel far ahead. I considered turning back. But I had no idea how far from the ranch I was, and no idea how far this mighty endurance horse might run before he tired. Even so, whatever the distance, the fastest way to get back to the stable was on the horse's back. Then again, if I stuck to the gravel road and someone challenged me, I couldn't pretend I couldn't read. I would have to plead forgiveness— borrowed horse, valuable horse, no harm intended. While I deliberated, Owen was gaining time. So I kept going, kept passing spruce trees. I passed plenty of spruce trees. When I had started after Owen I was road weary, and now I was genuinely tired. My feet, although in sensible grippy trail shoes, hurt, my back hurt, and my legs wondered why the hell they were trying to stand between my back and my feet.

Remorse was setting in. I'd pulled a fast one on Charlie to get him to let me ride and compete. What I'd said was, "Compared to the jumping, to the speed of a three-day event? Charlie, this is a walk in the park." Some park—2,500 square miles of unbelievably dry, boulder-strewn mountains. Too far from Charlie and Stephen and the horses in my own barn. I was ready to retire from the chase when the trees lining the road receded to offer a grassy, mowed berm, and the berm opened out to a carefully landscaped mountain meadow. At the far end of the meadow, against the dark green backdrop of spruce, was a remarkable building, churchlike but too large for a church and not large enough for a cathedral. Its spruce timbers lifted huge facets of dark glass skyward. Except for this glass, every piece of the building was direct from nature. I was struck by the structure's ethereal reach, by its perfect accommodation to its ragged mountain setting, and by how much it must have cost. Very expensive, and very private. I was an intruder, and my weedy, rack-hipped horse was now trespassing on the lawn to one side of the parking lot, making free with privately owned grass. There were two cars in the lot, and if anyone who had arrived in them was even close to the glass walls, there was no way that person could have failed to see me approaching the horse. He was still wearing the halter and lead rope, and I put a big smile on my face because to the horse you must always seem to be the same welcoming, powerful person.

"You conniving little piece of Arabian shit," I told him sweetly, when I actually wanted to break his legs one by one. Then, just as abruptly as he had left me, Owen came forward to put himself in my hands. He dropped his head against me and breathed in to get my scent and then let out a long sigh. I looked over his legs, and miraculously, the only marks on them were a few places low on one hind leg where the hair was scraped off. Owen was what is called flea-bitten gray, which means only that he was old enough so that his coat was sprinkled with chestnut freckles. Grays change color from the moment they are born black or some other dark color until they die white. Right now it was hard to tell exactly what Owen's color was. His sweat had dried, and his freckled gray coat was caked with dust from the mountainside.

My sweat hadn't dried. My T-shirt was splotched with per-spiration, and my breathing was still quick and ineffective. But Owen wasn't breathing hard, and his ears stood at attention. I realized I didn't understand these Arab horses the way I un-derstood my Thoroughbreds at home. However harebrained an Arab might act, the horse always assumed great intimacy with you. Now alert and curious, he lifted his sweetly shaped head way up so that he could focus better on me, and he as much as said, "So where is camp? I need to get to camp—and when does this race start?"

The main door of the glass and timber building opened and two men wearing sport jackets and carrying computer cases started toward the cars in the lot. Spotting me, one of them, a young, square-chested guy with an unruly thatch of blond hair, started in my direction. He was smiling and at the same time coming toward me with big, bounding, I-belong-here-you-don't strides. I stayed put, wary and uncomfortable at being appre-hended. He set down the computer case and put out his hand rather forcefully. "Josh Untermeyer," he said with good humor. "What are you doing here?"

There didn't seem to be anything unfriendly in this, but I was on the defensive.

"Horse got away from me," I said in case this man didn't understand that Owen and I had just reunited. For a moment, my attention wandered to the other man, who was just now sliding behind the wheel of his car. He was older than this Josh by a good bit, tall, with not much hair and a pair of dark glasses riding his shiny crown, and he looked a little rumpled, newly disheveled. But even after he settled his glasses back on his face, there was something almost familiar about him. I couldn't define what it was. But I didn't think about this any longer than it took for him to back his car around, send an absentminded wave in our direction, and drive out of the lot and down the gravel road. I dismissed him and responded to the younger force confronting me.

"You ride in here?"

I could see that he wasn't really all that young, maybe early thirties. It was his energy, barely under wraps, that was youthful.

"No, he ran, I walked." I said. How could he see my sweaty shirt and not believe that?

"Okay, you walked," he said in a good-natured way. "Who are you?"

"Tink Elledge."

"Tink. That's not your real name, is it?" Without waiting for me to speak, he drew what looked like a cell phone from the pocket of his sport coat and raised it close to his face. I saw that it was in fact a radio. He pressed a button on its side and spoke into the static he raised. "Kurt? Kurt?"

He reached only static. He smiled and shook his head at this, then turned the unit off and stowed it back in his pocket.

"Asleep at the switch. Was there anybody in the booth at the gate?"

"I never saw a gate."

He shrugged. "That's why they didn't ring you in, then."

I couldn't tell what his intentions were. He was hard to read because he was both aggressive and friendly. Maybe he was just trying to piece in the backstory. I tried to help with that. "I started up at Farrell's ranch, this horse ran off, and I ended up here."

"Do you know how to get back to Farrell's?"

"Not a clue. Where am I?"

"The Institute for Biology and Higher Mind, about ten miles from Farrell's. Educational foundation," he explained. I wondered where the students were, why the parking lot held only two cars. And if this place was here to educate the public, why was it so intensely private?

At that point this Josh Untermeyer seemed to go off duty. His interrogation ceased. He went into his laptop case for a pen and a small portfolio with a pad. He drew a map. Looking at the lines he had made for the gravel road and the paved ones that connected with it, he said, "Are you going to have to walk all the way back there?"

"No, he is. With me on his back."

"Pretty easy to get lost out here." Josh's concern seemed genuine. This guy was a bundle of mixed messages. And all of them came on strong. "Do you want me to go inside and phone Todd Farrell? He could come down here with his trailer and pick you and the horse up."

"No thanks. In a couple of weeks, this horse is supposed to go a hundred miles, so he better be fit enough to go back over the mountain today."

He registered this and said, "Oh. Out for the Tevis?"

Like everyone else I had talked with, he didn't bother to add *Cup* to the name of the race, *Tevis* was all that was necessary. Short name, long race.

I was eyeing one of the boulders that ringed the parking lot. It looked like it would make a good mounting block. I folded the map into my jeans pocket. Then I was up on Owen. No bridle, but his run between the mountains had smoothed off any edginess so that I could steer him with my legs and the lead rope attached to his halter. For an Arab, Owen was long-legged and angular, with higher withers than most of his breed. Ten miles with Owen's slat-sided body bumping up and down between my legs without the buffer of a saddle could leave quite an impression.

Josh saw I was about to ride away, but he wasn't going to be put off. "I'll just drive up and let Todd Farrell know where you are, tell him you're on your way."

How could I stop him? This guy was a little overwhelming. "Very thoughtful of you—if you really don't mind. My friend— the woman who owns this horse—has no idea where he is or whether I've found him."

As his car pulled away I realized I hadn't given him Isabel's name or cell phone number. No doubt he was as wired in as everyone in business was these days. Wouldn't it have been simpler to just phone ahead?

When Owen and I headed out the private road, I looked back at the remarkable structure. The place radiated some kind of awareness. I had the sense, completely without grounds, that my departure on Owen was being observed. I knew there was no one inside, but the glare off the huge windows made the building appear watchful.

When I slid off Owen near Farrell's barn, Josh was still there, leaning back against the fender of his car and talking to Isabel, who took our return as a matter of course—what goes up must come down, Arabs that run off must come back to the tent. When I made a vague apology about not offering a cell phone number, he turned briefly from his conversation with Isabel to say cheerfully, "They're no good up here. Not enough towers, too many mountains."

He directed his attention back to Isabel, and tired as I was, I could see that it was, in fact, his full attention. I turned Owen loose in his stall, offered him water, and when I returned to the conversation, Josh Untermeyer was still focused on Isabel Rakow. This guy was a force of nature; a positive, forward-going force of nature. Apparently he wasn't put off by her voice or her cool intensity. Maybe he was a match for the intensity.

I heard him say, "Oh really? I know quite a bit about Darwin." I thought this was an obvious lie made to impress her. But it caught Isabel's attention, and she offered a cautious interrogation, evidently trying to plumb the depths of the knowledge Josh claimed to have. He was carrying most of the conversation, and only occasionally did Isabel's voice keen over his.

Although Isabel didn't appear to see it, there was something going on inside Josh Untermeyer, and that something was about her. It was a little improbable. Pretty, bright-eyed, but sober-sided Isabel—and Josh, very friendly, a little too pushy, and trying to control his wiry blond cowlicks with an occasional swipe of his hand. I was embarrassed without exactly knowing why. It was as if I had blundered into something very private, as if I was present at a moment of creation that nobody else recognized.

Todd Farrell rescued me from this discomfort. He drove the dirt lane very slowly, probably because his pickup was fifteen years older than the one that had carried Isabel and me across country. Even at a crawl, the truck came on with a sound track of rattles and clangs, and when he pulled up to the barn and stopped, a gong sounded somewhere in the drive train. He had a dog with him, a red-brown Border collie that jumped over him and out the window before he could open the door. The dog raced toward us, low belly, butt high, like we were sheep to be cut from out of the flock and penned.

Todd emerged from the truck, a sturdy, barrel-chested man in jeans. Under the shade of a cowboy hat, he wore a chestnut beard that framed his muzzle, and the white hairs growing into this beard gave it an odd pinkish cast. He strode after the dog hollering. "Baby, quit that! Baby! You hear me?"

Evidently not. What stopped the dog was Isabel. It circled us newcomers warily, growling and gradually homing in on Isabel.

Todd Farrell laughed. "Must be a vet. Baby knows one as soon as she sees one." Then he remembered himself. "Hey, girls! You got here. I'm Farrell." This greeting put me off because we were definitely not *girls* any longer. But it wouldn't be long before I would get used to this term for us, and its power to offend would disappear. Also, I would soon discover *Farrell* was the way everyone in these parts referred to him. I shook his hand, and Isabel turned politely in his direction.

To Josh he said, "Hi, kid. Still doin' God's work?"

When Josh didn't respond immediately, Farrell looked from Josh to Isabel and realized he might have stepped in the middle of something. He said, "Anyways, it's always nice to have riders here. Horses all in one piece? Mind if I take a look at them?"

I followed him into the barn. "Maybe this seems nosy," he said to explain his interest in seeing the horses, "but sometimes people will haul all the way across country and never bother to check whether their horses are acting right. Sometimes they're not. Don't want to drink and eat right. Then before you know it, I have to get the the vet out here in the middle of the night."

He looked over our horses, the new manure in the straw and the level of the water in the buckets, and said, "Bay looks pretty good. But this gray"—he stroked Owen's shoulder with a sunburned hand—"doesn't haul very good, does he?"

"Oh, he hauls just fine," I assured him. "He just didn't like where we unloaded him. Took off."

"He did? These Arabs can pull some really funny stuff."

"If you think walking miles in strange country is funny."

"Which way did he run?"

"I don't really know, but I ended up way the hell off and gone at this amazing building."

"The Institute," he deduced. "And that's how come Josh is here."

I could see that this corner of the Sierra Nevada might look vast and endless to me, but to him it was just his little hometown. Now he turned his offhand hospitality to me.

"So how about you? Got the brain fuzz?"

So there was a term for this debilitated state. "Definitely. And slow. I'm really slow."

"Give it a few days," he advised. "It'll go away—now how about your rooms? Want to see them?"

On our way to the house, we passed Josh and Isabel, still talking. The red-and-white Border collie was still menacing Isabel, crouching behind her and making little dives in the direction of her heels. Isabel, who spent her work life dealing with serious biters, paid no attention. Farrell snapped, "Baby! Didn't I tell you to cut that out?" but not really expecting Baby to mind this command, moved on.

Without hurrying, Farrell crossed from the barn to the low, rambling plank-sided house. I trotted back to Isabel's truck to rescue my purse and then caught up with him. In the front face of the house there was a door, but it must have been largely ceremonial, as there was no path leading up to it. We used the back door and came in through a hall, where a telephone perched on a small oval table, passed the entrance to a large bright kitchen, and went through the dining and sitting rooms to arrive in a long hall on which the doors of the guest rooms opened.

"You can take any one of these you want. Bathroom's down the hall. Fix you a drink?" He turned to go. "I'm fixing one for myself."

The five guest rooms were identical, and looking around the one I settled in assured me that Farrell's place was the genuine article. The walls were plain plaster without any Wild West tchotchkes or phony Native American gewgaws. The big window offered the room's real ornamentation, the mountains rising and falling, rising and falling until their outline met the sky.

I took off the trail shoes and stretched out on the double bed. The dramatic view made me a little homesick. I was used to the roll and gentle camber of the fields in the Brandywine country, and I was used to being with Charlie and to having Stephen and Alex in and out on weekends. I hadn't seen Charlie in five days now. This was the longest period we had been separated, and I hadn't talked to him since the morning before we started up into these mountains. I had told him, "There's no point in you coming along. It's not a spectator sport, and you won't see anything, Charlie. You might be able to watch me ride two or three fifty-yard stretches if you're fast enough between the holds." Now I wished I hadn't said any of this. I rolled over to retrieve my purse from the floor and dug out my cell phone.

On the little screen, the roaming symbol lit up. Higher charges. But what the hell? I was very far from home. I needed to talk to Charlie, and I had never been very good about money. Which was one reason—there were others, of course—why Charlie was my third or, depending on how you counted, my fourth husband. The tiny wireless charges were nothing compared to what I would have been spending if I'd been at home with my own horses. And these, my own horses, were another cause for homesickness.

Speed dial brought up Charlie's number and then in a punctuated burst of tones transmitted. The ringtone sounded. It rang and kept ringing. I looked at my watch. Five-thirty, which meant that Charlie should have been getting ready for bed. Thinking he might be out with my terriers, I hung up, waited for a few minutes, and then worked the speed dial routine again. Again, the phone rang through willingly. No one picked up. I was a little troubled but not worried. So I left the phone on my pillow and went in search of the drink Farrell had promised.

I found Farrell in the kitchen. Without the cowboy hat, which was a bit of a shock. The beard around his muzzle was the only hair on his head. Thoroughly modern cowboy, he had shaved the rest of his head. Also, my sexism had led me to expect to find someone else, specifically a woman, in the ranch kitchen. But evidently Farrell was the sole proprietor here. He swept a welcoming arm toward a stool parked near a spotless counter and then brought out a glass.

If Farrell's truck was a rattletrap, his kitchen was a starship, a technological marvel. Evidently all the rust on the Farrell ranch had collected on the old pickup. In his kitchen the long counters and several sinks gave off antibacterial glints, and a line of restaurant-grade appliances marched along them. There were machines here whose purpose I couldn't guess.

"This is beautiful," I said after a swallow of scotch.

"You like? So glad. I love this room, live in it. I always dreamed about having a place like this"—this passion for a kitchen was something I didn't expect from a man—"planned for it, but couldn't make it come true until I got her out the door."

"Wife," I suggested.

"Right. I had to buy out her half of the ranch. But"—he smiled, his eyelids closing self-consciously—"you're probably not interested in that old story."

"Oh, I'm very interested," I contradicted. "I've been through three divorces myself, so I know every one of them is hard but hard in a different way."

He regarded me seriously now, looking me over carefully. Finally he decided, "You seem to be doing okay. I mean, you're out here to ride the hundred and you must have a little bit of money somewhere."

"A little bit. And I'm fine," I assured him. "Better than I've ever been in my life and with the best man I've ever known."

"I had to fight for every inch of this place."

He forgot about not wanting to burden me with his story. He'd started it, and now there was no way he would hold back. Farrell was going to be a talker. I thought I'd try to help him segue to the end and said, "So how did you finally come up with the money for this place and this amazing kitchen?"

"Borrowed it from a friend—or actually through a friend—she was doing business with a real estate guy who liked to invest."

"Your friend—is she that special kind of 'friend?'"

He laughed. "No way. It wouldn't work. I've given up finding somebody else. I'm not young, you know."

I laughed. "Neither was I."

"How'd you meet him?"

"Charlie? At a benefit dinner—silent auction."

"Haven't tried that." But he was giving the idea some thought.

"Give it time." I advised him about women as he had advised me about brain fuzz. "She'll come along."

Isabel, pulling along both of our suitcases, came into the kitchen with the Border collie driving the suitcases from behind, herding them. Isabel looked around and said, "Wow."

"Wow yourself," Farrell responded and went into a cupboard for another glass. Skulking past Isabel, Baby took up a position on her cushion under the end of the nearest counter and sat, lids half-closed on her gimlet eyes, observing the veterinarian who had invaded the kitchen. "The way Josh was acting, you must be giving off pheromones. You know what they are?"

Isabel gave our host a fixed look and said, "Of course."

"Well, I didn't until I heard this thing on the radio about insects and most other animals giving off these chemicals to attract a mate. Josh was acting just like that, wasn't he?" Farrell laughed. Isabel looked a little startled and, trying to change the subject, said she'd rather have wine. She wasn't really into whiskey, she'd rather have just a little wine. Without halting his conversation, Farrell obediently drew a bottle of white wine from his enormous stainless refrigerator. "Just like he caught a big whiff of something and was stoned on it."

"He is a little appalling," Isabel commented.

"Josh? He's all right. Maybe a little forward, but he's a good guy—and part of his job is being forward."

Isabel did not appear to be interested in this, so I took the bait.

"What does he do?"

"Public relations." He stressed both words of the term as if we might not understand it. "Consultant. Does some work for the Institute. So how he is fits in really good with what he does."

"He didn't mention any of that." Isabel was trying to turn the conversation.

"Course he didn't!" Farrell hooted. "Those pheromones you were giving off were so strong he couldn't think. Maybe you could bottle some of the stuff and give it to me."

Reflecting on the conversation she had just escaped, Isabel said seriously, "He did seem to know something about Darwin and evolution."

"Sure," Farrell said as if we should have seen something this obvious ourselves. "He's working for the Institute."

"The Institute." Isabel had no idea where I'd been that afternoon.

"Evolution is what they worry about." Our host was going for another drink.

"Why should anyone worry about evolution?" I wondered and then, remembering the Scopes trial and the textbook fights, felt idiotic.

"I don't know, really. Seems like maybe it's against their religion."

"Not if it's what I suspect it is." Isabel suddenly understood what Farrell was alluding to. "I think what you're talking about is intelligent design, and it's true that people who believe in intelligent design believe in that for religious reasons. See, when Darwin published his theory of evolution, it was pretty scandalous because it held that changes in plants and animal species came about over very long periods of time and that man was just another animal who came on Earth through the same process. It contradicted what the Bible taught about creation— you know, the seven days and all—and the bishop and the church crowd really didn't like that. There are still people who want to stick with the Bible's account of how the world came to be, the creationists. But then there is the intelligent design crowd. They believe evolution is okay. But they want God to be involved. So they believe that God created the world and everything in it, including the process of evolution."

"If they believe in evolution, then why can't they believe anything else they want to believe?" I said this because I could just hear liberal old laissez-faire Charlie saying it.

"The problem with it is," Isabel plowed straight ahead, "that it is scientific bullshit."

This was the first cussword I'd heard her utter. It caused me to revise my notion about what Charlie would have thought. If it was scientific bullshit, he would try in his gentle, genial way to dissuade anyone of that opinion.

"Where is this institute?" Isabel asked as if she was looking for directions so she could go there and straighten out the people who ran the place.

"I don't know, but I was there this afternoon."

"Well, in case you might be thinking of heading over there . . ." Farrell teased Isabel and launched into directions to the Institute if she were going to drive.

"Thanks," Isabel cut in, "but it doesn't sound like a place I'd be interested in visiting."

"Never say never." Farrell glanced over at the two suitcases Baby was harassing. "Now, is this all of you? I thought you made a reservation for three."

"That's right. Frankie is driving up from Sacramento tomorrow." Frankie Golden was my oldest and closest friend and, ultimately, the person who had arranged to get me out to these mountains with Isabel's horse.

"She'll probably find you sitting right here," Farrell predicted. "Supposed to rain like hell tomorrow."

"We'll be sitting on horses in the rain," I advised him.

Using his term for us, which I was still finding annoying, Farrell remarked, "You girls are serious, aren't you?"

"They won't call off the Tevis if it rains, will they?" Isabel asked pointedly.

2

The rain did, in fact, come in. It woke me early the next morning, pelting the big window in my room in long, steady waves. It draped the mountains in a dense gray heavier than any fog. The rain was impenetrable, and it had moved in for the day.

Even before I shed my pajamas to dress and go off in search of Farrell's coffee, I retrieved the cell phone from my purse. I was hoping to catch Charlie early in his day. I let the phone ring a long time. He didn't answer. I was puzzled until I remembered Josh Untermeyer's comment about cell phones in the mountains. I pulled on breeches and a T-shirt and headed to the kitchen to ask Farrell about how to call home.

I found him peering into the oven. Unlike any number of women I knew who had made big investments in their kitchens, Farrell justified the expense of his. The night before he had laid out plates of beef bourguignon for Isabel and me and then, ignoring the usual protocol of professional hosts, settled with his own plate at the table with us, passed a basket of bread and a bowl of salad, and poured red wine. Delivered without fanfare, Farrell's dinner brought unexpected pleasure. Now he waved me in the direction of the coffeemaker.

"What'd you girls do to deserve to ride in this shit?"

I squelched the urge to advise him that I was no longer a girl. "Farrell, what is it about the phones out here?"

"It's good shit," he continued, "but it's still—you're not trying to use a cell phone out here, are you?"

"It rings," I explained to justify my attempts.

"Somewhere out in the ionosphere. Damn things are useless out here. Use the phone in the hall. It's a landline."

His phone reported the ringing on the other end of the line with reassuring authority. But it too failed to bring a response. Charlie didn't pick up. This worried me a little. But it was midmorning in Philadelphia and Charlie might have gone off to some appointment or other. I dialed the phone again, this time using the number for Stephen at his office in the modem company. Stephen would know what was going on.

But his buddy who answered reported that Stephen wouldn't be in that day. In fact, he didn't know when Stephen would be in. This was a little more alarming than Charlie being out of reach, because Stephen's discontent with his job and his restlessness anticipating marriage had been worrying me for the last couple of months. I hoped he hadn't done something rash like quitting, but at such a great distance, nearly the span of the continent, there was nothing I could do about it. Feeling cut off from my stepson and husband, I meditated on the steam rising from the cup Farrell offered me, hoping there was a dirt-simple explanation for the silence from home.

"Problem?" Farrell inquired.

"I guess not."

"Rain makes everything harder," he suggested.

"No kidding!" Isabel arrived for coffee with her rain suit over her arm, signaling the impending necessity to mount up and jostling me out of my worries.

If there is anything that can douse your enthusiasm about riding, it is not your last fall from the back of a horse or your last visit to the emergency room, it is a good rain. Even in the finest high-performance rain gear, your body becomes as slippery as an amphibian. Every inch of leather or biothane becomes slimy. Every effort you make to communicate with or even just stay with the horse slides away into the damp.

That said, I certainly wouldn't beg off riding or putting in the necessary miles before the Tevis. I hadn't competed on a horse in any sport for almost two years, and I had come all the way out here to do just that, compete on a horse. I had no delusions about winning or even placing in the Tevis Cup, but in this sport whose motto is To Finish Is To Win, I intended to finish. In order to finish, you have to start, and in order to start, you have to ride, even in the rain.

From the oven Farrell withdrew a baking sheet that carried a flaky, delicately browned ring of coffee cake. He considered his work critically, turning the baking sheet to search out flaws. Then he said, "Now there's one thing that's gone right today, anyway."

"Well," I said by way of a nosy compliment, "whoever she is who invested in your kitchen knew what she was doing."

He smiled.

"You sure she's not that kind of friend?" I teased, partly just to flatter him and partly because the night before, on my way to the kitchen for a glass of water, I'd passed him in the hall. He was talking on the phone, apparently in extended conversation.

The pastry had a raspberry filling, and Isabel and I lingered over it while Farrell briefed us on the local trails. Our plan was to ride a slow twenty miles that day, then use the following three days to ride the hundred miles of the Western States Trail from Robie Park to Auburn in three sections. Frankie Golden would come to chauffeur us with the horses to the starting and ending points each day. When we told Farrell this, he offered Isabel and me a pearl of endurance wisdom. "The Tevis trail runs generally downhill from eight thousand feet to about twelve hundred. So why don't you get the advantage of working uphill? That'll make the race feel easier. For each piece of the trail, you could drive south and then head back up in this direction." After that, the horses would rest for a week.

Apparently Farrell, who didn't seem to have the passionate attachment to horses that Isabel and I had, thought of his horses the way I thought of my little John Deere tractor, a tool to get a specific job done. In the case of my tractor, the job was to spread manure. In the case of his horses, the job was tourist income. Because he regularly took groups of tourists out on horseback, he carried Lake Donner geography and geology in his head. He drew a series of maps on napkins, marking important features like water crossings and treacherous footing. "Keep in mind, girls, that this whole area west and south of us, what we call the Divide—on the maps it's the Foresthill Divide—is littered with old mines left over from the gold and silver rushes. Some of them are actually still in use—but in any case, it's not a good idea to go exploring by yourselves."

"We won't be off the horses long enough to do that," Isabel promised him.

I was trying to pay attention to the lines Farrell's pencil was etching into the soft paper of the napkins. But I was a little distracted by worry about Stephen and Charlie. I wished the phone in Farrell's hall would ring. But the sound that came from the hall the next moment was a voice, with a high edge, tight with urgency.

"Farrell?" a woman called. "Farrell!"

He turned just as she came into the dining room.

"Oh good. Here you are." She looked around a little frantically, without taking notice of Isabel or me. "I need to talk to you, Farrell."

"Sure thing." He waved at an empty chair. "Sit down."

But the woman didn't do that. She went on, "I'm sorry. I know you have guests, Farrell—"

"Sit down, Celeste," he said more firmly. "These girls are Tink and Isabel, Elledge and Rakow."

Celeste didn't respond to his instruction, in fact, didn't respond at all. She was a tall, slim person in urbane clothes—gray slacks sharply creased and a short-sleeved sweater with swashes that crisscrossed from her shoulders to her waist—that seemed at odds with the rustic furnishings of Farrell's dining room. Her shoulder-length dark hair turned under in a carefully sculpted bob, and she held it back from the sides of her clear, fine-featured face with combs. Her wide cheekbones were set at a classical angle, and if her eyes hadn't been nearly bulging with anxiety, her face and her person would have been attractive. As it was, her eyes sought Farrell from behind a bleary red mist, their color hard to define. Maybe gray, maybe hazel.

"Farrell, please." Her hand went to her temple, and she struggled for composure. "I need to talk to you."

It was an awkward, uncomfortable moment. I knew that Isabel and I shouldn't be witness to this stranger's distress, but by unkind happenstance we were. We should leave the room, I decided, and allow the poor woman her privacy. I tried to get Isabel's attention.

Then Celeste spoke again. "He's gone, Farrell. James has gone."

Farrell seemed to shake himself and come alert. "What do you mean?"

"He was just lying there," she reported, "and he wouldn't wake up."

The awkwardness now multiplied. We were submerged in an intimacy that had nothing to do with us. Yet how uncaring it would look if we stole away.

"You sure?" Farrell rose to take Celeste by the arm, maybe to support her, maybe to guide her to a chair. "Has someone come for him?"

"No, I couldn't—" then, still oblivious to Isabel and me, she managed, "I was so upset—I haven't moved him."

"We can't have that." Farrell pulled a chair away from the table and settled her in it. "You know that."

I found his assurance comforting. I hoped Celeste found that too.

"Wait here," he instructed, and this seemed to include everyone in the room. He went through the hall to the telephone.

I heard him say, "Todd Farrell, and Celeste here was with him. Thinks he's died." After a pause he said, "Yeah, that's him. Comes out here all the time from the university." Then he said, "Right. How long you think you'll be? . . . Meet you there."

Farrell returned to the dining room. "Sorry to take off like this, girls. But I need to drive Celeste back to the Institute." He had her by the arm again. "Hardly fit to drive the way she is."

This much was quite evident. In fact, I wondered how she had managed to get to Farrell's on her own. Isabel watched through the glass in the back door as the two of them made their way out through the rain. There was a gold Hummer parked haphazardly where the driveway curved up from the barn.

"Poor lady," she said. "So sad and I felt somehow, you know, that it wasn't right for us to be here."

"I know exactly what you mean," I told her. We cleared the table, and as we were pulling on our rain suits, I said, "The only good part is that Farrell really knows how to take care, doesn't he?"

As soon as I had folded the napkin maps into an interior pocket of my rain jacket, we braved the rain. This first twenty-mile foray on the trails was to let Darwin shake the travel stiffness out of his legs—after Owen's self-guided tour the day before, the gray horse hardly needed this.

The red-and-white Border collie, bristling with fear and hostility, trailed Isabel and me as we walked out into the rain. I was surprised that, dense and heavy as it was, the rain was soft. There was no wind. Even so Owen ducked his head and pinned his ears back evilly as soon as I led him out of the barn. Darwin, something of a Boy Scout if you don't count the remarkable spook he had developed, stood watching and wondering at the rain.

Just as Isabel and I mounted up, Josh pulled up next to the barn door. Checking his image quickly in the rearview mirror and taking a swipe at his unruly hair, he pulled up the hood of his rain parka. As he left the car and headed toward us, Isabel, who now knew enough about this guy to consider him slightly feebleminded, let out a long, impatient breath. But Baby, who had seen enough of Josh to find him socially acceptable, trotted up to him expectantly, and when he stroked her head, she wriggled against his knees. This dog, who had a strong aversion to veterinarians, had a strong affinity for men who didn't smell as if they were in that profession. In a moment, the dog was belly-up at Josh's feet.

"We're going out," Isabel said the obvious to head off a time-consuming encounter.

Josh grinned and said what was equally obvious, "I see."

Isabel said nothing. Owen milled restlessly, his coat already soaked, but Darwin, the soul of equine patience, stood in the rain without offering to help Isabel escape.

Josh persisted. "When will you be back?"

There was another awkward silence. I finally broke it. "Why don't you come back midafternoon, Josh?"

"Oh." He brightened. "You'll be out all day? Why don't I meet you with some lunch?"

"We don't do lunch," Isabel said immediately, and I nodded. It was true. Until we returned there would be nothing but the rain and the two beats of the trot, steady trotting broken only to let the horses drink. Truth to tell, I wasn't looking forward to it. It wasn't only the rain that dampened my enthusiasm or the fact that Farrell was having to deal with a dead man and a grieving woman. Concern about Charlie and Stephen and why I hadn't heard from them revisited me every few moments, and even before we rode out of the lane, I was longing to return to the ranch house, where a telephone would be within easy reach.

Riding when you really don't want to ride is essential to endurance racing, and I'd been conditioning for racing long enough now to accept that. Riding when I wanted to hover by the telephone and really all of this—conditioning for races, nonstop journey to the California mountains, worrying about Charlie and Stephen while I was slip-sliding in the saddle on top of a bony gray horse that belonged to somebody else—was ultimately Frankie Golden's doing. She had provided my introduction to Isabel Rakow. Frankie owned two French bulldogs, small, rather useless but adorable dogs whose punched-in, wide-eyed faces could have been Japanese anime. Useless, but I can tell you these fellows were an improvement over the dachshunds, which became perfect cylinders because Frankie couldn't keep her hand out of the treat jar.

Isabel took responsibility for the Frenchies' health care, and spotting a potential trail buddy in Frankie, she'd pestered her to start riding. This was somewhat self-serving. Isabel kept two competition horses because in endurance a spare is essential, but she didn't have time to condition more than one of them. Frankie took Owen out for a test drive and phoned me as soon as she got home.

"I need some help, Tink. I need to get out of this riding deal."

"Why?"

Frankie could ride. She wasn't great but, mainly due to my indoctrination, had workmanlike skills. She said, "I play golf, but I don't play endurance golf. I can ride, but I don't want to ride endurance. It just goes on and on. It's going to take up so much time—my tennis will go right out the window. And this horse—I can't tell Isabel this—but I hate him. He just will not quit."

This piqued my interest. "Sounds like he was custom-made for his job. Who is this Isabel person?"

At the time I had spent more than a year in rehab for neurological damage from a freak accident in which the promising filly I was riding sent me headfirst into a fence post. The rehab was slow going because it involved retraining nerves. I was sticking with it, but frustration had set in early on, and I was at the boiling point. I wanted to ride, and I wanted to compete. But I had made an agreement with Charlie, who had been badly scared by my accident. About my return to the back of a horse, he was adamant. It was too soon, he kept saying month after month, to get back on the horse with the goal of eventing.

Without mentioning it to Charlie, I paid a call on Isabel and found Frankie's veterinarian a small person with a sweet face and a cool head. I rode Owen, and this was the first time I'd swung my leg over a horse in sixteen months. On that first day Owen was not exciting. He was not a horse I would've picked for myself. He was narrow-bodied and slat-sided—"That's the way we like them," Isabel reported about the preferences of endurance riders, "built like a radiator, so they disperse heat"—but he had a pretty face and ears that turned in toward each other. More important, he liked to go. Apparently go was all he knew.

I hadn't even dismounted before Isabel said, "I'm taking him and Darwin to California next summer. How would you like to get him fit and then go out with me?"

The abruptness of this request caught me off guard. I never would have offered a horse of mine to a rider I didn't know and who had been on his back only once. But she had seen I could ride, and what she needed was another rider. She was quite determined to have that, so I could understand why Frankie had opted out. I said, "I don't know anything about your sport."

"Best time over the distance," she gave me the elevator speech, "And every time the vets check the horse, he has to be fit to continue. You know, survival of the fittest."

I recognized this phrase, of course, but had no idea it was the key to Isabel's riding ambitions or that Darwin the historical figure was a passion equal to endurance riding. In fact, the nineteenth-century scientist's ideas about competition and survival were the reasons for her attraction to a sport where surviving a distance and besting others were the goals. Although I didn't know it when Isabel proposed the California ride, I would hear a whole lot more about competition and survival in the days ahead. I would learn the story of Darwin whether or not I wanted or needed to, the way kids learn stories from the Bible without being offered the choice not to. Isabel wasn't ordinarily a talker. In fact, she would be quite taciturn until either Darwin or horses got her started, and with me as captive audience, she would make use of our hours on the trail to dispense sizable chunks, unrelated by chronology or science, of her knowledge of Darwin and evolution.

I tried to dodge her question about California. "He's pretty green," I suggested. She said, "He doesn't need schooling. Nobody schools. So don't try to teach him anything. Forward is all he needs to know."

If forward was all it would be, I realized, Charlie might go along with this. No running at big cross-country obstacles that didn't come down. He might be talked into it. Owen might just be my ticket back into competition. I looked him over more carefully. He had nice big feet—I couldn't understand why he wasn't shod—and his legs were really pretty good, set correctly under him with no jewelry, no bony bumps from injury. His dark eyes were large and soft and steady, an indication of intelligence and honesty. He might hold up over the long haul.

I said, "Okay, this horse is your understudy. Suppose I ride him for the next six months and then your bay gelding—what's his name?—goes lame. Who rides Owen? And who goes to California?"

Isabel had to think about this. "Very good question. Maybe the fair thing would be that, depending on when Darwin went out of commission, we could both compete Owen but not at the same rides. Then if Owen looked good to go to California, we would lease a horse out there. You know, there are guys who keep a string of distance horses fit so they can lease them."

That did seem fair. I wanted to spend the time with someone else's horse only if I were assured of competing him. The opportunity to ride in competition and, along with it, the chance to win with a horse would certainly brighten my horizon. If rehab and its stultifying repetitions were the stick, endurance riding just might be the carrot.

"Okay," I decided, "let's talk about the conditioning schedule." What I planned to do was to invite Charlie to take me out to dinner, put on a dress, and lay out a plan for this terrific opportunity that could not be turned down. But what I did was to walk back into the house in my riding breeches. Charlie, my brilliant, affable third husband stared—hard.

"Yes?" he said in as cold a voice as I had ever heard from him. "What is this, Tink?"

I was unprepared for his reaction. He felt betrayed. "Wait a minute, Charlie. Could you? It's not what you think."

"It *is* a trout in the milk."

"I'll only ride on the flat. No jumping. No high speed. And I am able right now to sit on a horse. You know that, don't you? Charlie, you have to let me do this."

"Even though you go behind my back, you break our agreement?"

Eventually Charlie, who is a liberal and more forgiving than God and who is fond of saying "Forgive but don't forget," calmed down. Because he is a businessman and businessmen like to do things by committee, he said, "We will meet with the occupational therapist and get her assessment."

The upshot of the therapeutic consultation was that I must keep working at the rehab assignments and I could start riding. "But," Charlie decreed, "no jumping. Ever." I didn't take *ever* very seriously because I knew I would recover fully. I had come a long way and didn't have that far to go.

We sought out a new trailhead Farrell had indicated on one of his napkin maps. The openings to these trails were frustratingly similar, the napkin was turning to pulp, and the first trail we sent the horses up dead-ended at the base of a bluff after a couple of miles. We turned back, maintaining the same long trot on which we had ridden in. This was according to Isabel's training system. No matter the late start, then the false start, she wouldn't hurry the horses to make up the time. She wasn't racing now, just building the capacity to race. In this sport time stretches with the distance, and the name of the game was to keep the machine—the horse's body—in working order. We rode with heart and body-temperature monitors whose displays we wore like wristwatches and whose sensors fit under the saddle girth. What endurance riding required was patience, but now I was decidedly impatient.

Asking Owen to move up a big grade, I lifted myself out of the saddle to let his body work more freely under me, and after a couple of minutes the heart monitor showed a slower pulse rate. At a wide passage farther up the trail, Isabel, bumping up from the saddle occasionally, brought Darwin alongside Owen. The gray horse pinned his ears.

I said, "Determined to be vile this morning, isn't he?"

"That's the way he expresses himself," Isabel said. "Just like Owen, the real person."

I knew I was supposed to ask the question, even though I also knew it would automatically send Isabel back to the middle of the nineteenth century, geology, species, and whatever. "Okay, Isabel, who was Owen?"

"One of the first fossil scientists. Looked at dinosaurs. Darwin thought he was a friend, but he stabbed Darwin in the back."

"Literally? Stabbed him?"

"Nope. In those days you could publish a book review without signing your name. Owen had a mean streak in him, and he saw how Darwin's ideas about species and evolution were putting Darwin in the public eye. He was jealous, and so he wrote an anonymous review of *Origin*. Scathing, a real shredder. Darwin wasn't fooled. He knew right away who the reviewer was because Owen had praised the work of 'Dr. Owen' in the review. Made Charles mad, made him sad. Betrayed by his friend."

"This horse isn't mean," I defended the paleontologist's equine namesake.

Isabel smiled sympathetically. "No, he's just a determined old bird who will make you work for every steady step you get out of him."

This may have been true, but there were other aspects of his personality, and I said, "He wants to get there first. He wants to win—so why aren't you riding *this horse* instead of Darwin?"

"Because I don't think he's tough, at least not tough enough to take care of himself on the trail. A really good horse has to be conservative, has to assess how much effort to put out at any given time."

"But he"—Darwin—"spooks," I pointed out the hole in her argument. "That's a waste of energy and distance right there. You could save yourself some mileage if you could fix that."

"It'll fix itself." She turned her wrist to look at her heart monitor. Her hands were pale and shriveled from the wet. My hands were equally pale and shriveled. Gloves wouldn't have helped, because once they were soaked, they would only accelerate the pickling process. "As soon as he gets past the start, he'll get down to business."

We rode on. The more often I thought anxiously about getting back to Farrell's telephone, the more our twenty slow miles stretched out to become some of the longest miles I'd ridden. I said, "Sometimes I feel like I'll never get off this horse," and Isabel just nodded.

When we finally put the last stretch of the ranch lane behind us and dismounted, there was a car parked by the barn door. His cool reception that morning hadn't deterred Josh. He waited behind the runoff from the barn's eaves and went immediately to Darwin's head. We led the horses inside, and as I settled Owen for the evening, I was in lower spirits than I had started the gloomy day in. Isabel was suffering Josh's attention politely while she looked after her horse. Eavesdropping shamelessly but morosely, I hurried through such errands as flakes of hay and damp saddle pads. I learned that the Institute for Biology and Higher Mind was Josh's best client and that the people there were cool. Then I heard her call his attention to the bay. "Do you know who this horse is named after?"

"Let me guess—Charles Darwin?"

I would have laughed if I hadn't been in such a leaden mood, and I wondered whether Isabel even smiled. But something, a smile or something else, seemed to be encouraging Josh. So long as he didn't interrupt her riding and didn't mind Isabel's eight-word responses, they could talk as long as he wanted. She might have been irritated if it were not for the fact that he was interested in—at least he said he was interested in— Darwin and evolution. He knew enough about this to keep her responding, and that at least, made him an improvement over me. Occasionally I heard a sharp question from Isabel challenging him—"I mean, how can you put those two ideas in the same sentence?" Josh was managing to engage her, and he seemed to be taking this as conquest.

The freshly sponged-off Darwin chewed on a pile of hay, and the two of them lingered to talk. I didn't intend to linger any longer than strictly necessary, and as soon as I had hustled through the evening chores, I left the two of them in privacy and sloshed to the house to ask if there had been any word from Charlie or Stephen. Farrell shook his head.

"That's frustrating," I admitted, trying not to betray the depth of my disappointment and, especially, not wanting to inject self-pity, given the chore with Celeste he'd had to take care of. "How did things go for you at the Institute?"

Farrell shrugged sadly. "Sorry to say it, but it was just about the way Celeste expected. The old man was dead. The squad came, and there's lots of arrangements, you know. Called the lawyer right away, then other folks connected to the Institute."

"Did you know him well?" I asked gently.

"About as well as a guy like me gets to know an honest-to-God genius and gentleman. For someone in his position, he was pretty humble. You know, an old shoe."

"How old was he?" As I myself got older, I found myself asking this question more often about someone who had died. Maybe just to compare the answer with my own age.

"Grant-Worthington? I'd say he was maybe seventy, maybe a couple of years past that."

My mouth had fallen open, I guess, because I had to will myself to close it. Will myself not to make any exclamation or outburst. I was stunned.

"Why are you looking like that, Tink? You know him?"

I couldn't absorb this news as fact. I knew that Farrell was reporting it as fact, but I couldn't accommodate it as such. James, such a powerful intellect, just wafting passively into death? I stammered a little, editing my response as it came out. "Well, if he's the scientist my husband does business with, I . . . I do know him in—indirectly. Works with proteins?"

"Right. So your husband does, what?"

"He's a businessman," I said, trying not to sound too dodgy, even though I was dodging Farrell. I didn't want to say *capital* or *investor* because I didn't want to reveal the nature of Charlie's dealings with James. I was off balance, sad and bewildered by what seemed to be the facts—and defensive. James had been out here, not at Stanford, and he had been coming out here often. Did that change who James was or our relationship with him? Being truly muddled, I guarded my own knowledge of James while I tried to sort out the facts of his death and what it had been like for him.

"Was he alone, Farrell?" I asked because this seemed the very worst way to leave the world.

He looked at me blankly. Then he said, "No, of course not. She was there. Celeste was."

"She was his . . . partner then?" I asked.

He nodded, smiling a little. "Yeah, that's what they call it now, isn't it?"

None of it seemed to jibe with the James we knew. He may have been getting up in years, but—what was it they were saying these days, seventy is the new forty?—he hadn't seemed old to me. He was too vigorous. And for him to have maintained a relationship with a woman? He and I had had any number of quietly personal conversations, and yet he had never mentioned her—or for that matter, this remote place in these mountains far from his lab.

To mask the noise in my thoughts, I said inanely, "Well, maybe that makes it not so bad for her then—I mean, if she was there."

"She was pret-ty upset," Farrell responded without actually disagreeing with me.

"What was he doing at the Institute?" I wondered.

This brought another blank look from Farrell. After a pause, he said, as if it were something I should have known, "He owned it, Tink. Or his foundation did. One way or another, his money bought it. Celeste ran it."

By now I felt like I had been turned upside down and shaken vigorously. But all I said was, "Oh, I see. How sad for her." And I meant that last. How terrible to be abruptly partnerless, to be carrying on alone. I didn't know Celeste, but that didn't keep me from imagining her pain.

I said no more to Farrell. As it was, the information he had given me thus far was too much for me to handle on my own. I found it difficult to believe that James had died the way Celeste and Farrell seemed to describe it. But then James himself— this *woman*? this *institute*?—had thrown a few surprises into the mix. I didn't know what to make of any of it. Charlie and Stephen were the only fix for this. And where were they when I actually *needed*—as opposed to *would have been reassured*—to see them?

I tried the phone in the hall again. Useless. Farrell came past to stand by the back door and watch out through the rain. He had his eye on a car advancing up the ranch lane. After a moment he said, "Nobody I know. This your number three maybe?"

It was. Without benefit of rain gear, Frankie Golden propped open the door of the rental car and struggled to open an umbrella without actually getting out of the car. She was locked in combat with the door and getting wet anyway. I headed out the door to rescue her, but Josh beat me to it. He had spotted her from the barn and rushed to hold the door while she forced open the umbrella. Then walking behind her, he rolled her suitcase down the walk. When she was safely delivered to me, he hurried back to the barn and his conversation with Isabel.

"Is that some of our competition?" she demanded about Josh. Frankie was a full-bodied redhead who liked clothes, any kind of sports contest, especially prizefighting, and pulp fiction. With creamy, freckled skin and a thick fall of auburn hair, Frankie was a beautiful, voluptuous woman, and she was looking ahead to the race. Being as competitive as I was, she asked the question about Josh because she was already scouting potential rivals.

"No," I said shortly and waited impatiently for her to collapse the umbrella and step out of her pumps, which were soaked. Ditto for the dark green citified slacks.

Frankie was typically more sensible than her clothes or her voluptuousness would indicate, and with her I could always come right to the point. I didn't say "How was your flight?" or "Any trouble driving in this downpour?" I said, "We need to talk," indicated with a nod the direction I wanted her to take, and trolleyed her suitcase through the dining and sitting rooms, drawing Frankie in its wake to my room.

"Have you talked with Charlie or Stephen? I haven't been able to get hold of them, and I really need to."

"You do?" she said cheerfully, and this not so much a question, just encouragement to say more.

"It's pretty bad, Frankie. Grant-Worthington has died."

She blinked, her lids closing emphatically over deep brown eyes, and then straightened a little and regarded me quite seriously. "You're right. Bad."

"He died out here." I began giving information out of any logical order. "He had a woman. And an institute he founded."

She squinted a little, trying to make sense of these items, and said, "I can understand the woman, why we didn't know about her. But what's the institute?"

"It's about science and Christianity, I guess. A few miles south of here."

Her eyes widened. "Well"—she was a little indignant—"we should've known about that, shouldn't we?"

"Exactly. I don't know what to make of the Christian part." But now as I encountered Frankie's puzzlement, I began to recognize that what we knew of Grant-Worthington was only one side of the man. As I thought back to his visits to the farm and the growing warmth of his friendships with us, I saw now that he and I had had a number of conversations in which he could have easily included his pursuit of questions about biology and the life of the spirit—or even mentioned his woman friend—but he had held back.

In fact, on one of his early visits to the farm, he made the only reference to religion I could pull from my memory. James, as I had been instructed to call him, seemed comfortable with Spit and Polish, my two terriers—when Spit bounced off the floor to the center of the table, James's conversation never missed a syllable—so I invited him to see my horses. When he stepped up to my young mare, whose accident had caused my layoff from competition, he started laughing. I was mildly appalled. No one laughed at my horses. They were serious forces in their competitive realm.

But it was just a memory of horses that had made him laugh.

"My mum," he said, "was quite the rider. Tally-ho and after the hounds, you know. And she was of a mind that horses and health were intimately linked. Riding in the open would strengthen the weak and fortify the others. So from the time I was four, every afternoon there we would go—bump bump, bumpity. Of course, I adored her, but I dreaded those afternoons. I prayed that the horse would die and I would be allowed to forget the face of Mum's groom and to go back inside to put my feet on the grate and nibble on cookies."

Then James gave my filly an honest going-over and said, "Quite lovely—I'm sure Mum would have coveted her. Horse people, you know, always covet the horse that belongs to another—but none of the Ten Commandments goes against that, does it?"

We could have talked further about the commandments if I had only picked up on this religious reference. But I'd failed to do that, and now I couldn't remember another remark that touched even as briefly on Christian belief. Why had he kept this part of his person out of sight?

"Why did he hide this religious stuff? Was he afraid we would think he was less of a real scientist or maybe a crackpot?"

"Slow down, Tink," Frankie suggested. "Grant-Worthington had enough social polish to cover up just about anything—and maybe he was just intensely private. Lots of people hide their private lives."

No doubt this wisdom came from one of the mysteries she read. Still, the point was valid.

"How did you find out that our very private friend died?"

"His woman friend—Celeste—is a friend of Farrell. She rushed over this morning looking for help."

"So the part about the woman is probably true." Frankie was starting to come around, to accept some of the same information that was so hard for me to accept. "But I keep thinking of the tennis. He seemed so fit."

"I've thought of that, too."

Tennis, it seemed, was another physical pursuit that James's mother thought promoted health, and as soon as he figured out it would free him of any obligation to spend time around horses, he began to develop his game. When he'd mentioned this to me, I—intent on being a good hostess—had offered to play.

I made no claims about my tennis game and was not surprised when, on his next visit, James quietly thrashed me at tennis. That is, he was quiet, I was panting, grunting, running all over the court.

"That was no contest at all," I accused him. "You never even broke a sweat."

"I don't like to do that."

"Let me fix you up with my friend Frankie. Her game is much more up to yours than mine."

But that didn't turn out to be the case. Frankie was still red in the face when she and James returned to the farm. "How can a person win at tennis without moving his feet?" she demanded.

"But I do move my feet," James protested mildly.

"I was too busy to notice," Frankie protested in return.

Now I said, "He seemed so fit."

Contemplating this, she agreed with my assessment. "Quite fit. But let's face it, he was also getting old—and he knew he was getting old. That's why he came to Halefellow and Charlie in the first place. Maybe a heart condition was just one more thing he was keeping from all of us. So I don't think we should leap to any conclusions."

"Right," I said and returned to my most immediate worry. "Charlie. I need to get hold of Charlie, or Stephen—or both. They have to know about this."

"Of course they do."

"I've left messages for both of them."

Frankie thought about the dead end in communications and made an inspired proposal. "You have a girl taking care of your horses, right? Why don't you call her?"

I explained that we would have to rely on Farrell's landline and said, "He knows I've been trying to reach Charlie, and he knows Charlie has done business with Grant-Worthington. But until I talk to Charlie, that's all I want Farrell to know. We didn't know as much about Grant-Worthington as we thought we did, and we know absolutely nothing at all about the people he had around him here—Celeste, this guy Josh who's trying to latch onto Isabel—"

"Oh, is that what's going on out in the barn?"

"—or even Farrell himself. So please, nothing about Accu-Gen or the buyout."

"Course not," Frankie snapped. "James may have thrown both those things into question."

I was glad she mentioned this before I did, because it seemed crass to worry about a business deal at the moment of a friend's death. But it was precisely this worry that made it so urgent that I locate Charlie and give him the news.

"As far as anyone else is concerned," Frankie said, "I know nothing. Not James's death. Not Charlie's deal." She took up the handle of her suitcase to steer it out of the room. "You go call your horse helper, and as soon as I can park this, we'll see what this place has to offer."

Like everyone else who entered Farrell's, Frankie was drawn to his kitchen. She padded into it barefoot, carrying the wet pumps. Her toenails were painted a rich wine color, and she had retrieved the soggy shoes from the hall. Farrell took them and set them over a hot-air register. Now he would have his social event because to Frankie there was no event that wasn't social. She was a hugger, she sometimes gushed, and she could flirt. She *loved* this place, she told Farrell. "Tink and Isabel tell me you are a fabulous chef."

Farrell blushed. The color surged up from his flannel collar to cover his shiny head. She had him. Talk about pheromones.

I could see why men were attracted to Frankie, because I loved her for some of the same qualities that drew them. We had remained close confidantes through five divorces, three of mine and two of hers. The reason that my total was one higher than hers was that she had a different perspective on marriage than I did. Frankie loved men, and she loved romance. But marriage was the business end of romance, and having been financially successful in two such businesses, which as marriages failed, Frankie had cashed out her winnings and gone out of business. She wanted to keep the fun in what romance stopped by, and the door was always slightly ajar.

Farrell brought out the scotch and the white wine. Frankie gazed at these happily. "You wouldn't happen to have fixings for a martini, would you?"

Farrell couldn't believe his luck. Isabel and I were used to Frankie's magic, but our host was innocent. He applied himself assiduously to a shot glass and a cocktail shaker. In the midst of this production, the girl who was taking care of my horses at home returned my call from the phone in my barn. There was no one at the house, she reported. No sign even of the dogs. The house was locked, and there was only my car left in the drive. My head was pounding.

Farrell poured the results of his mixing into an honest-to-God martini glass and presented the precious product to Frankie like a gem on a velvet cushion. I tried to hide my anxiety about the situation at home, but I blurted it out.

"That's good news," Frankie said immediately about Charlie. "That means he planned his exit, the dogs are taken care of, and maybe Stephen is with him. You'll hear from him, probably sooner rather than later, and in the meantime, there's nothing to be done but ride. That's what we came out here for."

"You're out for the race, too?" Farrell said. "I hope you brought some different shoes."

"Right, sure. Boots. I'm crewing," Frankie told him, and this brought a quick glance from him. Farrell was in for some surprises. At earlier distance rides, Frankie had demonstrated her aptitude for competition crewing. She ran a tightly organized support operation and was ferociously competitive.

"Crewing," Farrell repeated. "I don't know how that works back East, but in the races out here, it's a tough job. Very competitive."

Frankie sent him a little smile over the rim of her glass. "I *know*."

3

I passed the night in bad sleep. When sleep came, it was only sporadic, and in the morning, my headache, which had never let up, only intensified.

The noise of the television drifting down the hall from the ranch house's big sitting room irritated me. It was the national news, and Isabel and I found Farrell watching it, squatting on his heels as if he hadn't intended to stay in the room very long and momentarily would have to leave to return to his routine in the kitchen.

He glanced up at us, then returned his attention to the television and said, "Unbelievable. Four people. Just up the road."

"Killings?" I hoped he wasn't talking about that because I didn't think my head could take the graphic gore that televised news offered up anymore.

"Four," he repeated. "Since yesterday. Those two are on a rampage."

Mercifully, because I was drawn into the broadcast, the television was dwelling at the moment on interviews at the scene of the crime, rather than on the details of the shootings. Farrell began supplying information one piece at a time. "Guy from Canada—tourist probably. Two bank tellers, and cop in Reno."

"Do the police know who killed them?" Isabel wondered.

Farrell couldn't seem to look away from the screen. "Yeah, they're on the run. It's a local guy and his girlfriend—calling themselves the next Bonnie and Clyde."

"You know the guy?" This possibility seemed quite tantalizing.

"Sure—he's a kid, really—he used to work for the Institute." The broadcast cut away from the crime scene and was fixed on a license number.

"Better write that down," Farrell instructed himself, and went out to the hall, where there was a ballpoint next to a little pad. "Four—oh—oh—one six—SL. Brown jeep. Celeste had to fire him. That's what she told me, anyway. But I don't know a thing about that girl he's got with him." Farrell returned to the sitting room for the remote and punched off the television. "Maybe I'll hear something."

No doubt he would. Farrell was hardwired into the local network, and eventually someone would phone in with whatever information was lacking. But the news had bothered him. He hovered over a skillet of sausages and every few moments gave his head a quick shake, like a horse when a fly lands on its ear. By the time he turned off the heat under the scrambled eggs he called his fluffies, though, his agitation had disappeared, and as he's set out our plates, he explained himself. "It kind of gets to you, doesn't it, when evil jumps up and sits right beside you?"

He sat down at the table with us, more to speculate out loud than to eat. "I hope these two don't make it as far as south as Sacramento before the cops catch up with them—all hell will break loose all over again."

The couple on the rampage seemed to disturb him, as if by knowing one of them he was somehow responsible. I might've paid more attention to this breaking local news but I was too preoccupied with my own small-scale drama, the question of where Stephen and Charlie were and the sharp throbbing of my right temple.

My patience for Owen and his big ego was short that morning, and I was irritated to see the indefatigable Josh drive in again. Fortunately, he didn't have enough time just then to wear thin with Isabel or me.

"Just want to say hey," he told Isabel. "Got to get to a pretty serious meeting."

I didn't bother to absent myself because he wasn't expecting to stay, and also there was someone else in the car, the man I had seen leaving the Institute building when I first encountered Josh. Even though the man's head was bent over something in his lap—probably a computer—and I couldn't get a good look at him, there was still something I recognized about him. But I couldn't put my finger on exactly what it was or why it was familiar, and this should have been a signal.

"Who's your friend, Josh?"

"Paul Savage," he responded amiably. "Nice guy. Did real estate for Grant-Worthington."

I knew both those names but didn't pay any attention to the mention of Grant-Worthington's or Josh's use of the past tense for the man's real estate. I was too astonished. I hoped I didn't show my agitation. I hoped Josh would return to his dogged interest in Isabel without noticing that the travel mug in my hand was waggling or that as soon as I could set it down, I went straight to the ranch house and my room at the back of it. I was rattled—no, I was disturbed—and shamed. Thirty years earlier, when Paul Savage had a full head of hair, he had been my first husband. I hadn't made things easy for him, and this is an understatement.

I hoped Paul hadn't noticed me and, especially, that Josh hadn't mentioned me by name. I was ashamed to think what Paul's opinion of that name must be and horrified to think it was possible the two of us might be put in a situation where he might have to use that name. I hadn't spoken to him in almost three decades. He was ten years older than I was and a business protégé of my father's. That, I feel certain, was the reason my parents had encouraged the wedding and the two little girls—Paul's daughters from a previous marriage—who came with it. Paul and I had been polite and considerate but primarily physical—our two bodies locked together, I thought at the time, fulfilled my obligation to him. We lasted almost two years. Then he and the girls were gone, and I was a disappointment to my parents. Although I tried to keep up with the girls and their progress through school, their birthdays and graduations, I never made any attempt to contact him directly. I didn't have any idea how to commence a new kind of relationship with this man. So I didn't try.

Now, as I thought back over my two subsequent marriages to the same man, Elledge, I realized that I hadn't done any better with him. I may have done things differently but not better. After he left for the second time he became *Elledge* the way Paul had become *Savage*. I referred to each man the way a sportscaster refers to a player in a ball game. Now I feared that I might have to reencounter Savage with his full name, the real person as he had emerged from our divorce. I couldn't believe he would think much of my person as I had emerged from it, and according to my scattershot thinking at the moment, he had as many reasons to want to avoid an encounter as I did. No way, I promised myself, would I ever ride anywhere near the fantasy Institute building again. This was a promise that shouldn't be hard to keep, because I suspected Isabel's aversion to the place would be just as strong.

I heard someone in the hall. I hoped it would be Frankie and not Isabel because I could explain my sudden departure and upset to Frankie. Having helped me through that first divorce and my shame, she knew all about Savage. Whoever it was, I needed to pull myself back together quickly, cover up any traces of disturbance, and mosey up the hall as if I were just returning from the bathroom. I turned the doorknob quietly and took a stealthy step out into the hall. My foot tripped Charlie. He lurched sideways, rebounded from the wall, and recovered himself upright.

"Hi, baby." His arms came around me. "How's the horse holding up?"

I was crushed against his solid paunch, flabbergasted.

"Got a hug for me?"

I couldn't make my arms do what they ought to. Here he was, the tall, amiable man I'd been longing for, then half-frantic about. But my arms hung at my sides because I was overcome now with a second wave of shame about Savage.

"Hey," he said like he was trying to wake somebody up. He reached for my hand. "Your hand is shaking."

"Goddamn it, Charlie! Of course it is."

He studied me with concern, which made me feel worse. Charlie has the most impossibly warm gaze blue eyes could ever drop on a woman. This, and the fact that he never judged me, never made a critical comment, snide remark, or even a joke—of which he made many—at my expense. His gaze was how, when I was sour and done with men, he had caught me up. He looked the same as ever now—tweedy, slightly rumpled, and taller than me, well fed, with slightly overgrown chestnut hair and a slowly expanding shiny spot on the crown of his head. He was always unassuming, and although no one would ever accuse him of trying to hide anything, his manner masked the most brilliant, the most comfortable, most amiable genius. He said, "Why *of course*?

"Where the fuck have you been? And where the fuck did you leave Stephen?"

"Stephen is here," he said calmly, and to my continuing discomfort, folded me back into his arms. "He's outside talking with your friend Isabel."

"I've been trying to reach you—and him—for *days*!"

"That's probably been hard," he agreed. "We've been on airplanes, then on the road."

"You could have at least called me," I kept up miserably.

Dropping one hand to reach into the pocket of his sport jacket, he brought out his cell phone and said, "Dead spot."

Of course. I had to drop the charges.

"Kiss?" he asked, and when I complied, he looked into the open door beside us. "This our room?"

"*Our* room?" I followed him into it. "Charlie, what are you doing here?"

He closed the door and slid the bolt against anyone who might come along. He was serious now. "We have a problem."

"Yeah? You and Stephen?"

He sat on the edge of the bed and patted the place beside him. "Grant-Worthington has died," he told me as if the implications of this news would come to me instantly in full-color 3-D.

I nodded sadly. "I know, Charlie."

"How?" His question was wary. "How do you know?"

"Well, the woman he was keeping out here—"

"Woman!" He was startled and shot the word back at me. His surprise confirmed my sense that Grant-Worthington had intentionally kept this relationship out of sight from us.

"I know, Charlie," I said again. "It doesn't seem like James, does it?"

He sighed. With him, this was a sign of frustration.

"She runs his institute."

Another sigh. "So you know about that, too. This wouldn't be one Celeste Fuertes, would it?"

"Yup. That's her."

This news seemed to have a discouraging effect on him. He sat looking at the floor, rubbing his forehead. I patted his knee to get his attention.

"Charlie? What's this going to mean?"

"Beyond losing a friend? I haven't had time to get any details. As soon as we got the phone call yesterday, I put the dogs in the kennel, locked the house, and picked up Stephen to go to the airport. But this institute could be a problem. Even the woman might be a problem. Because the deal wasn't done yet."

"But you *signed*," I protested. "Stephen signed, and James signed."

"The preliminary agreement, which was really just a letter of intent and was pending on due diligence and final formation of our new corporation."

I tried to think around this problem. "He had lawyers, Charlie. Couldn't they just take over and make this thing happen?"

But I knew it couldn't be as simple as that, and I began to sort out the possible damage. It started with uncertainty about the Halefellow buyout but quickly shifted to my stepson Stephen, whom I doted on to a nearly neurotic extent and who for many years had been the only focus of my life—if you don't count the horses. With me, it was just Stephen and the horses until Charlie came along ten years ago. Although Stephen now shared me with Charlie, our relationship was more settled and more intuitive than the newer understanding I had with Charlie.

Stephen wanted the Grant-Worthington deal to ease the restiveness and unhappiness that had overtaken his work in the past year.

The first signal of this came when he arrived at the barn early one morning and found me in the tack room. I was sorting through bits, looking for a snaffle with a roller link I'd put away years earlier. I looked up from the tangle of metal. "Going in late today?"

He took the chair next to the rolltop desk where I filed the horses' paperwork. "I'm going to quit."

The bits clanged as they returned to their heap. "How can you quit, Stephen? You're an owner—and you *invented* that modem."

"Well, I mean, sell out."

I was thrown off balance, a little alarmed. Stephen had done so well for himself, tamed the mad inventor streak in him to develop a practical creation, a high-speed modem, and working with a group of friends, had gone to market with the Tear-Ass. There was a girl he was passionate about, planning to marry. Everything seemed so settled for him. Now this.

"But why?"

"Why not?" he jibed. In hindsight I realized that he had been even quieter than usual the last few months.

"It isn't Alex, is it?"

"In a way it is, Ma. I want to be married. I want to settle in with Alex. Long-term stuff. But I can't commit to that if it depends on me staying with the modem thing."

"Why not? I thought you were happy." This was almost an accusation. "What is this, a case of cold feet about a wedding?"

Stephen didn't answer this. He said, "I'm not making anything now."

"Except a shitload of money," I pointed out.

He sat looking down at his hands. "I mean, I go in there every day. . . . Ma, I thought you would understand."

"I'm trying to. Can't you just tell me what the problem is?"

"It's beans. I'm not *making* anything. I'm counting beans—or I'm watching other guys count beans."

Why hadn't I seen this? I knew this kid. So why did I congratulate him when he joined management? For some people, working was showing up at a job. For others like Stephen, it was taking raw ingredients and solving technical problems to create something new.

"Okay, you're right. You need to make a change. But don't do anything right away. Let's talk to Charlie when he gets back from New York tonight. He really knows this stuff and can help you be smart about making things change."

Here, in so many words, is what Charlie told Stephen: Do not sell out. Keep your share of the business but become an inactive owner and accept a commensurate cut in compensation. Then start looking around for a new project.

But Stephen hadn't even had time to work through the first part of this plan when the new project fell into Charlie's lap. James Grant-Worthington came looking for what Stephen and Charlie had to offer, computing savvy, expertise in statistics, corporate know-how, and, by way of Halefellow, capital.

Usually I tried to steer clear of involving myself in Charlie's business because in the history of our marriage, this had proved the one topic that was likely to ignite a fight. No marriage is without its sore points, and for the most part I was fairly uninterested in Charlie's business dealings. But with Stephen and his career involved now, the old tension surfaced between us again. I was stretched out on the sofa in his study as usual, propping my feet on the end of the sofa, and I said, "Charlie, what income will Stephen get from this deal?"

"Stephen will be hired by the new company, and he will make a salary."

"And what will you make?" I asked this because the two of us, according to Charlie, had enough income and I wanted to be sure that Stephen had enough to be as comfortable as he was now when he and Alex were married.

"What I will make is whatever I am due as a proportion of Halefellow's share in any—notice, Tink, that I said *any*—profit taking."

"So Stephen is an *employee*? Charlie, he's the brains Grant-Worthington is counting on."

"We are aware of that, Tink."

"*We are aware of that*." I threw it back in his face. "Is Stephen *aware*?"

"Of course, Tink. Of course. We don't need to go in to this any further."

This command-and-control response lit my fuse. "Well, *you* may not need to go any further into this. But *I* do. Stephen is my son, or the closest thing I will ever have to a son."

"Stephen is an adult," Charlie said stiffly.

"Charlie, do not mess with me. I *demand* to know the details of this. We are not talking now about money I might waste on horses"—a clear reference to his earlier worries about me—"we are talking about Stephen. His well-being."

Charlie looked as if I had struck him. His genial poise was deflated. I think he was hurt by the thought that I might put Stephen before him—and it's true that in this case I would have.

He seemed to be looking at the leg of the sofa when he said, "I've never had a child, Tink."

"Neither have I," I came back, "but I'm going to look after the person who came to me instead. And you, Charlie, are not going to stonewall me."

Charlie dropped into a few moments of silence. Then he said, very quietly, as if negotiating a defeat in war, "Okay, Tink. But I have to give Stephen his authority in this."

"Absolutely."

"Should I tell him you would like—"

"I need."

"—to confer with him before he signs on?"

So it was over. Charlie hadn't recognized that a mother, even a stepmother, can be a ferocious contender.

Stephen came out to the barn with a draft of his contract.

"Charlie said it would be best if I talk to you about this."

"You're going to make a huge creative contribution to the company," I said, "and I want to be sure you are paid accordingly."

He said, "Ma, we're talking about Charlie."

"I'm not. I'm talking about you." I reached for the document, and after I had looked through it, I said, "You've got to be kidding!"

"What, Ma?"

"This is obscene!"

He looked baffled. "I thought it was okay."

I said, "Okay? I'd love to try to live off these six figures. Only thing is, Stephen, get Charlie to get the wording for an escalator clause."

He smiled and nodded. "Gotcha. Escalator clause. Where'd you learn that, Ma?"

From Charlie.

Now in the bedroom at Farrell's Charlie seemed to be telling me the promise the deal had held out was about to be snatched away.

"We didn't know about this foundation linked to AccuGen," he said, "although eventually Grant-Worthington would have had to tell us. And linked to the foundation is this institute. It's a big, expensive piece of real estate."

"Right," I said, "that goddamn church thing between the mountains."

"You know about that too, Tink? Have you been there?"

I told him about the wild-goose chase Owen had led me on, and I told him about Josh taking such an intense interest in Isabel. But I didn't tell him about Paul Savage. I couldn't make myself do that. Now that I was getting over the shock of meeting Charlie here in the Sierra Nevada, I was happy in his presence, and I didn't want to do or say anything that might blight that happiness. He would have to find out, just as he would have had to find out about the Institute. But that didn't have to happen just then and further confuse an already-confused situation in which nothing seemed to match up. Maybe after the Tevis would be a good time to let him know.

"Charlie, does it strike you that there's something about what's going on that isn't quite right?"

He studied me thoughtfully.

"I mean James's death. I mean, okay, so he's an old man who dies. But a person can be old and healthy, and if he had any health concerns—"

"He acted as if he had all the time in the world, didn't he?" Charlie promptly built on the point I was trying to make. "So how did he die?"

"And why? I wouldn't be so suspicious except there is so much we didn't know about James"—it made me sad to say this—"and the stakes are a whole lot higher than we ever thought."

"A whole lot of questions," Charlie summarized. "Maybe we'll get a few answers today. Stephen and I are due at a meeting there in a half hour. Grant-Worthington's lawyers, Celeste, the executive director of the Institute, and a couple of other people.

When I called Halefellow, the board freed up some serious funds. So it's entirely possible that this meeting will be all we need to redo the deal."

"God, I hope so, Charlie. This could be so hard on Stephen."

He shrugged to feign nonchalance and reassure me. "It's not the last possible deal Stephen and I could make. There are any number of high-tech and biotech companies he could help develop—*but*, if this meeting goes right, it would be nice, it would be really nice for us. Why don't I take everybody out to dinner after the meeting?"

We walked outside, headed to the barn. "We won't need to go out, Charlie. The best food in the West is right here."

"Great. All we need is a nice, slow sit-down meal." Charlie included Stephen in this statement of need, but that meal and its graceful setting were primary only for Charlie. Stephen could care less about either of these things. For two years when he was growing up, he and I lived on a steady diet of peanut butter sandwiches and orange Jell-O.

What he had grown to be was a slight young man with dark eyes as bright as he was and long shiny hair pulled back into a tawny ponytail. He was quiet but not shy, and candid. He didn't call himself an executive, but he told me that lots of executives in his high-tech line of work dressed in the same teenage uniform he wore—jeans, very clean, T-shirt ditto, and usually the shirt was the display field for a formula or a quotation from a famous physicist. Given his usual, I was astounded to see Stephen wearing not only chinos and a sport coat but a tie. He stood on the bit of lawn by the barn in conversation with Isabel—I could only imagine how sparse these exchanges were. In a moment I had him and the sport jacket in my clutches.

"Very nice." I stroked the linen and silk weave. "Very nice—but Stephen, have you lost your mind?"

"Only temporarily, Ma," he said sheepishly. "Charlie helped me pick it out in the San Francisco airport. I wanted something that was kind of serious, because this deal is getting kind of serious, you know."

"You look gorgeous—doesn't he, Isabel? And I'm sure that Charlie"—I started trying to jolly him up as if he were ten years old and trying out for basketball—"I mean, I'm confident that *you* and Charlie will get this done the way you want it done."

"No, you aren't," he said in perfectly good humor.

Although Isabel and Charlie laughed, I wasn't embarrassed. "Well, I mean, I am—"

"Worried," Stephen finished for me. "I know, Ma."

"Okay, okay." I was defeated. "It was probably just your new look that threw me off."

Stephen sent a knowing smile in Charlie's direction. Somehow, instead of easing their minds, I had just added another layer of worry, upped the ante.

Charlie checked his watch and said, "We'll need to get directions."

I probably could have been able to retrace the route to the Institute over the trails Owen and I had blundered along, but neither Isabel nor I knew which roads would take them there. I ushered Charlie and Stephen into Farrell's shiny kitchen, and the first thing he said after introductions was, "Right, the Institute—you hear the old man who built the place died?"

"We did hear that," Charlie said, and I noticed he did not acknowledge that was the reason for Stephen's and his sudden visit.

"In his sleep," Farrell volunteered without anyone asking. The mountains may have blocked cell phone signals, but obviously they had done nothing to short out his local hot wire. "Makes sense. He was getting up there." Wherever *there* was.

Charlie asked if he could manage two extras for dinner that night, and he said, "For the two of you? Hell yes. Love that, and love to have you bunk here if you want to. I still have empty rooms."

I watched as the rental car ferried Stephen and Charlie out the ranch lane and realized with an abrupt thud in the region of my heart that they were about to encounter Savage. But Savage is a fairly common name, and neither of them would expect that this particular Savage would have been anything special to me, would they?

4

It was coming up on noon, and we were finally tightening girths and getting ready to mount, when the rental car reappeared at the other end of the lane. Only an hour earlier, Charlie and Stephen had left for their meeting, and now, as if they had glanced off the air and reversed like a boomerang, they were back. Isabel, who had stripped off the saddles earlier that morning when my husband and stepson had arrived unannounced, sighed, put her foot in into the stirrup, and swung up.

"Sorry, Tink," she said, "but I really have to put in some miles on this horse today."

"Of course. I know you do." My attention was divided between Owen fidgeting, waiting for me to mount, and my family its second unexpected appearance that day. "I wonder what the hell has happened."

She nudged Darwin with her heels and headed out the lane. Owen watched them enviously because he watched everything enviously, and in a moment, I pulled the saddle off him again and left him standing befuddled in his stall—the second time that day he'd been all dressed up with no place to go. But I had to find out why the meeting at the Institute had ended so quickly.

"We couldn't get a quorum," Charlie said when I caught up with Stephen and him at the back door.

"The director, that woman Celeste, begged off," Stephen explained, "and the real estate guy was a no-show."

"But he left here with Josh. They were headed over to the meeting." I said. Actually, whatever the story with Paul Savage, I was relieved they hadn't met up with him.

Charlie shrugged. "Maybe she sent him home before we got there. The guy at the gatehouse relayed the message that she was sorry but she wasn't able to see anyone today."

I could certainly understand why just now she wouldn't want a group of men, including the ever-ready Josh, descending on her to transact business. "She's probably overwhelmed. I'm glad I'm not in her shoes."

"I'm glad you're not, too," Stephen made a little joke.

To my surprise, Charlie was not entirely sympathetic. In fact, he seemed a little miffed. "There are certain realities that she won't be able to avoid."

"Probably like the very realities she's having to deal with right now," I defended Celeste. "Notifying people. Memorials."

Farrell came out from the kitchen, drying his hands with a dish towel. "How's she doing?" he asked about Celeste.

"Apparently not well," I said.

Farrell nodded. "It a lot for anyone to handle."

"Yes, of course," Charlie said with a tight little smile. He wasn't responding to any of this the way I would have expected him to, the way he usually would.

"Going to be a service," Farrell went on, "and he's got family, some family, at least, even if he never had children. They'll have to be involved."

"Farrell," I wondered, "how did you leave things over there?"

"Well, of course, the emergency squad came for the doctor. Took him to be cremated. Celeste had two security guys with her, said her sister is on her way down from Vancouver, and like you just said, Tink, she was making a list of folks to call."

"Do you think there will be an autopsy?"

My question dumbfounded Farrell. He looked at me with a humorous half squint, as if I had just now fallen through the sky to land on Earth. "You know where you are, Tink? You are in the mountains. You are in old gold rush country. And out here we don't do autopsies just for the hell of it, just to find whatever bad spot a person's body had that might have made that body stop dead. We got to have something obvious that says wrongdoing, something like a gunshot wound."

Without being inhospitable and as if he were giving friendly directions to a passerby, he had put me in my place. Okay, I was an outsider, but that didn't answer my questions about Grant-Worthington. And it wouldn't keep me from asking more questions about him. But Farrell probably wouldn't be the person I would ask. I suspected he was tied to the locals with too much loyalty to give up good information.

"You'll probably get a call," he assured Stephen and Charlie, "to set up another time to get together."

"Sure," I said encouragingly. "Something will work out soon."

Stephen was eyeing me uncertainly. Charlie sighed his God-grant-me-patience sigh and said, "We'll have to rely on your landline, Todd."

Farrell was unused to being called by his first name. He glanced up nervously at that and said, "Sure thing. Sure thing."

Charlie, making a put-upon remark about twiddling his thumbs, meandered into Farrell's sitting room, where Frankie was camped out in front of the television, apparently waiting for updates on the local murders. She was taking advantage of her last day without horse duty and, after sleeping until mid-morning, was still in her bathrobe.

"How did it go?" she asked Stephen, who was settling into one of the old-fashioned armchairs to open his laptop.

"It didn't, really," he told her. "They didn't show."

Frankie took this in carefully, without comment. She had sensed the tension Charlie carried into the room. My genial, generous husband was in a surprising mood. He didn't seem to know what to do with himself and, without even glancing at the television stood gazing restively out the window. Ordinarily, good humor was a point of pride with him. But he turned away from the view complaining. "Mountains," he said. "And horses. That's all there is out here, mountains and horses."

"That's the point, isn't it?" Frankie reminded him brightly.

"It isn't *my* point."

I was caught off guard by this suddenly hard facet of Charlie's character, and I was a little annoyed that he seemed to be thinking only of business. "Have a heart, Charlie. The poor woman has lost her partner. She is stunned, muddled, maybe not even able to grieve yet."

"And there has to be some fallout over at the Institute"—Frankie nodded at the replay now showing on the TV screen—"from these murders."

Her remark pulled Charlie's attention to the television. He watched the account that had been repeating since the early hours of the morning, and Frankie said, "Farrell told me that guy used to work for the Institute and—"

"Now he's a disgruntled ex-employee," Charlie completed her sentence. "You're right, Frankie. That's probably the reason she—the director—couldn't make the meeting. She has a public relations brush fire to put out."

That, I realized, would of course involve Josh Untermeyer and was likely the reason he hadn't returned to Farrell's looking for Isabel. Would it involve Paul Savage, who had accompanied him in the car but apparently hadn't been at the Institute? Really, I vowed, I would explain Paul and his presence in these mountains to Charlie—and Stephen, for that matter—at my very earliest opportunity.

Having accepted Frankie's explanation for the aborted meeting, Charlie relented. He relaxed and seemed to prepare himself to bide his time. "Why don't we go to Truckee and look around? I'll take everybody to lunch."

"Charlie, I know you just got here," I began to excuse myself, "and I know I was worried crazy until you did get here. But I really need to put some miles on the horse today."

Charlie agreed—he would take Frankie and Stephen to lunch, and Farrell, if he wanted to join them—and he followed me out to the barn, where Owen, never suspecting that he would be saddled for the third time that day and then actually ridden, was stretched out on his side having a nap and issuing remarkably slow snores.

"I know you thought I was being very cold and unfeeling," Charlie suggested cheerfully.

"I was surprised at you," I admitted.

"It's just that I don't like being lied to," he explained, "and unless I have to, I try not to deal with liars."

"Who"—the saddle I laid on Owen's back was a surprise to him—"Charlie, who do you think was—"

"Ultimately, James. James Grant-Worthington."

So that was it, the reason for Charlie's uncharacteristic bad mood. He felt betrayed by James.

"We have just walked smack into a wall of his lies."

"Lies of omission," I pointed out to excuse James.

"Still," Charlie insisted, "lies. And at this point, with James out of the picture, there is not much we can do to establish what's true. Which is frustrating, very frustrating in itself. But I don't think it's only James who has lied. This morning, while the security guy was getting messages from Celeste and relaying them to Stephen and me, I had the sense there was something going on in the Institute, some kind of scrambling to come up with something plausible when they—whoever was at the Institute—realized we were at the gatehouse waiting for them. Whoever it was, somebody wanted to keep Stephen and me in the dark."

"Frankie had a pretty good explanation for that," I pointed out.

Charlie nodded. "It worked so far as it went. But there's a lot, especially about James, it doesn't explain."

Absolutely right, and although I didn't mention my destination on the horse because I knew Charlie frowned on me poking into things that didn't directly affect us, I hoped my ride would bring some explanations. If there was anyone who could explain James's reticence or—if Charlie was right—lies, it was Celeste. Owen would get his twenty miles—ten miles to the Institute each way—and I might gain some insight. Now, fully tacked up, Owen fidgeted impatiently, swinging his rump as I tried to finish my conversation with Charlie. The horse was still moving as I swung up, and my customary hug around Charlie's neck would have been too dangerous for him. I left him with a kiss blown off my fingertips and concentrated on settling Owen before we reached the slippery surface of the paved road.

When we came out of the ranch lane into the road, I stuck to its shoulder, and when the horse reached the head of the trail on which he'd made his getaway that first day, he turned as automatically as if he had been taking that trail every day for years. The trail looked remarkably different from the back of a horse than it had when I was scrambling after that horse on foot. It was much narrower than I remembered and the branches much lower. Ducking these and dodging tree trunks that threatened to remove my kneecaps, I rode down to the base of another mountain and followed its rise and fall. We came out into the grassy valley edged by spruce, and I knew immediately where I was. Because I now sat about five feet above the ground, I could actually see, a half mile down the manicured gravel lane, the small, dark roof of the guardhouse. I turned in the opposite direction, toward the Institute, and chose a route that paralleled the private road while hugging the edge of spruce trees.

I wanted to be able to move the horse quickly back into the trees if necessary. And in a few moments, this did turn out to be necessary. Josh's car materialized as it rounded a slight turn in the road. I urged Owen into the trees and turned him to face across the valley so that I could watch the car pass. Josh was driving, and there was someone else in the car. Savage, most likely. I hoped that meant that Celeste was alone.

The spruce trees came closest to the building at the rear. I picked out a tree and tied Owen to it. Then I walked around to the main entrance. On the other side of the trapezoidal glass door panels, the sweeping foyer was filled with light as bright as day. I located a buzzer discreetly embedded in the glass wall, and although when I pressed it nothing was audible to me, a moment later Celeste advanced across the foyer.

She opened the door with a distant, bemused expression. She was used to greeting the public and didn't betray that she didn't recognize me. While the general outlines of her appearance hadn't changed, the impression she made was overall quite different.

"Yes?" Her makeup was laid on precisely, pale persimmon lipstick making a sweet bow of her mouth, and her hair was freshly, professionally done.

I put out my hand, and she offered hers to be taken. "I'm Tink Elledge," I told her. "I met you yesterday morning at Farrell's. I'm a guest there."

"Oh, yes," she said uncertainly, as if she were trying to retrieve the memory of that encounter from inside a cloud.

"I'm out for the Tevis, and when Farrell heard I was riding this way, he asked if I would stop and look in on you."

"Oh, yes," she said again. "Please come in. I'm just making coffee. However did you get here?"

"I rode. The horse is tied out back."

"I see. You must not have passed the gate."

"I didn't see a gate," I lied and then added quickly, "Farrell asked me to find out if there's anything you need."

Indicating a hallway at the back of the foyer as the direction to proceed, Celeste laughed. "Oh, there's lots I need. But I don't even know where to begin." She led me into a kind of workroom where there was a very large printer, a copy machine making productive noises, and a coffeepot surrounded by a little crowd of mugs. She went immediately to silence the copy machine and remove its contents to a manila folder. I was impressed to find her working.

"Now, what do you take?" she asked about the coffee.

"No additives," I said primly, and this made her smile. She presented a full mug and said, "That couldn't be easier." In spite of the facts that the room had no windows—in contrast to the glass walls in the more public parts of the building—and was lit artificially—in contrast to the astonishing light in the foyer—there was something quite homey about it. Likewise, I felt unexpectedly comfortable with this woman who had encountered me only once, if she remembered it, and yet invited me in to talk.

"I'm not surprised that you really don't remember me, Celeste, because I just happened to be there when you got to Farrell's. But I know you've lost someone who was very important to you."

She let out a long breath and said with a certain amount of resignation, "Well, I certainly was a mess, wasn't I?"

I shrugged. "You were upset. And Farrell is, of course, concerned about you."

"He is good to me, and I have been good to him"—was it possible that she was the friend who'd loaned Farrell the money to buy his place?— "so when things started to spin out of control, he was naturally the one I wanted to help me."

"Taking care of people seems to be his talent—and his pleasure. If you think of something he can do that would help get things back under control, I bet he'd jump at that."

Celeste grew quiet then and, absently removing and reinserting one of the combs that held her hair, seemed to be taking stock of her situation. "In one sense, things are under control. James saw to that. I have a job. I'm paid by the foundation that created the Institute, and of course I won't be turned out on the street. But beyond that there is uncertainty, quite a good bit of it, in fact."

I immediately intuited what this uncertainty was—the ex-employee. But there was also the same uncertainty I would have faced if Charlie had suddenly disappeared from my life. "You mean what you will do with yourself, with your life?"

"Well, there is that." Her answer surprised me. "The uncertainty is James's company. He was a scientist, a very good one, and he started a company to make new kinds of medicines. It was very successful—in a way, too successful for James. He hated the day-to-day business of running the company, which, fortunately, was beginning to attract the interest of some outside investors. Too many of them—forgive me, why am I telling you all this?"

I didn't know. I lowered my eyes to stare into my coffee. I hadn't expected to hear and learn so much, and although I felt a little guilty about consuming this freely shared information, I wasn't going to do anything to cut off this sad, obviously still confused woman. I had paid this call to gain insight into James Grant-Worthington, and I certainly was gaining some of that.

"Anyway," Celeste said by way of summary, "now it's competing interests, and I have no idea what will happen to the company—or eventually, the foundation. It could get messy."

Quite messy. I struggled to manage the crucial information she had unwittingly delivered and still keep up my end of this cordial conversation.

"For now, though," I suggested, "it must be a real comfort to know he was trying to look after you."

"Well, yes," she said uncertainly, and this prompted the worrisome thought that maybe James had not provided for her in his will.

I said, "How long had you known him?"

"A year." Then she added, "And a couple of weeks."

Instead of sorting itself out, the situation with James Grant-Worthington was becoming further snarled. Apparently Celeste hadn't known James as long as we had. No wonder she was feeling vulnerable.

"You're probably wondering," she said, "about James and me. He tried to be discreet about us. But I know people talked. Because they wondered"—she was beginning to stammer—"I mean, Farrell actually asked me."

"About sex," I came to the point to relieve her discomfort.

"Yes," she said, and a sudden happy light crossed her face. "We managed," she assured me wistfully. Wistful because that would be gone now. "I think I made him happy."

She had cared for him, maybe even loved him. That fact lay unacknowledged for a few moments before I said, "I'm sorry, I'm truly sorry."

She looked up suddenly. "No. I should be the one apologizing. I've been going on and on. When you don't really know me and only came over because Farrell asked you to. How inconsiderate."

"People in your situation should be allowed some of that—at the very least." Accordingly, I made no effort to leave even though it was clear our conversation was ending but waited to allow her to say more if she wished to. When she rose, I said, "I better see about the horse. He likes to take self-guided tours."

She smiled a little at this and said, "I'm glad he brought you here. Please tell Farrell I really appreciate his concern and I'll keep in touch."

She was sincere, and although she hadn't meant to say as much as she had, I could tell she had been candid. I felt like a thief stealing away with the burden of someone else's feelings, but as much as she had explained, I still didn't understand James or his behavior in dealing with Halefellow or, especially, in dealing with Charlie and Stephen and me.

Like a thief, I couldn't wait to make off with my loot and examine it. As soon as I had settled Owen in the barn, I drew Charlie and Stephen into a conference in Charlie's and my room, where we sat face-to-face on the two beds. Charlie's displeasure at finding I had ventured alone to the Institute was quite evident. But I tried to brush that aside and move directly to my discovery

"Apparently," I told them, "Grant-Worthington had more than one offer for AccuGen."

Stephen's face took on the very neutral expression he assumed when he was trying hard to be objective and proceed logically. "Does that mean," he asked, "that James signed more than one letter of intent?"

Charlie was letting go of his disapproval even more easily than I'd expected. He said, "Tink, as long as you were going to sneak off to pump Celeste for information, why didn't you ask about that?"

"I told you, Charlie. I was just trying to figure out what was going on with James that he didn't tell us some very important things about himself."

"Things he didn't feel he *could* tell us," Charlie amended. "But you shouldn't have gone over there. You put the deal at risk. You put me and Stephen—"

"I did not. How was Celeste going to figure out I had anything to do with you? We don't have the same name, and I was right there with her in Farrell's dining room before you even arrived."

Charlie shook his head, finding something about me hopeless, and Stephen shifted uneasily. Both signs of distress made me regret my impulsiveness but not my discoveries.

"I'm sorry, Charlie."

"No, Tink, you're not." And he wasn't angry—usually the only thing I could do to make him truly angry was to put myself in danger. He was resigned to me being the way I was and to carrying on in good humor.

"Charlie," I said contritely, "what can I—"

"*Do?*" He anticipated me gleefully, and the touchy moment passed. "What you can *do*, my sweetie, is stay out of Stephen's and my business."

"James was just as much my business as yours," I defended myself. "And what I found out could help you two a lot."

"You're right," Stephen said. "Ignorance wasn't bliss. We already found that out."

Charlie actually smiled then. "Okay, let me be more precise. No more friendly gestures toward James's woman friend."

"Why not, Charlie? She might just need some female support."

"Not from you," Charlie concluded and gave me a playful smack on the knee. "Things could get messy," he promised, rather cheerfully echoing Celeste's earlier remark. "Very messy."

5

But that didn't happen right away. In fact, order seemed to be reestablishing itself. After dinner that evening, Josh called on the landline and asked for Charlie. Would it be possible to reschedule the meeting with Celeste and the other principals for Tuesday, the following morning?

When he came down to breakfast the next day Stephen had on the sport coat again, and I heard Charlie, who considered meetings a special art form, giving him his usual prefatory advice. "Before you go into a meeting, decide exactly what you need to get out of it. And if you can't decide, don't go." This advice was unnecessary now. They had decided, and they were going.

Just as they were getting into the rental car, Charlie said, "If nothing else, we'll find out if there is a competing offer on AccuGen."

If nothing else. But there was something else. Paul Savage. I was repeating my earlier error, letting my husband and stepson go off innocent and unprepared for an encounter with my previous husband. Why was I doing that again when I'd had every intention of cluing them in before what would be a troubling encounter? Because the moment had never been right. In Charlie's mind, and probably Stephen's, Grant-Worthington's death overshadowed all other considerations. Charlie's thought was fully occupied with why and how James had died and, above all else, what it would eventually mean for Halefellow and, hence, for Stephen and him. He was uneasy about the meeting, very uneasy, and this was what he wanted to talk about.

Here was where I made a positive contribution. Although I had failed to interrupt his preoccupation by drawing his attention to my own concern about Paul, I did manage a constructive suggestion. "What about Halefellow's lawyer, what's his name—Kravitz? He's irascible, but really savvy. Couldn't he attend by phone?"

Normally, Charlie would have told me how brilliant my idea was and then proceeded without adopting it. But he considered the suggestion seriously, nodded, and said, "Right."

Before their car was out of sight, Isabel and I were loading up the two horses. Frankie, turned hastily out of bed and nipping coffee from a travel mug, settled herself behind the wheel of the truck and spread a map across the dashboard. She hadn't been content with Farrell's napkin drawings and had paid a visit to the forest service headquarters. The map of Tahoe National Forest she returned with was exquisitely detailed.

A dotted line showed the progress of the Tevis trail. It ran through a long geological formation Farrell had called the Foresthill Divide. The Divide is a sharp ridge set in what is essentially a deep canyon bounded on the west and north of I-80 by a steep wall and on the east, the lower side, by Lake Tahoe. The Divide is sheer on each side. It juts up in parallel with the canyon's wall to subdivide the canyon. This ridge begins at Auburn and ends in a remote meadow called Robinson Flat, where in the early 1900s the U. S. Forest Service built a tiny cabin for a forest ranger. The ridge subsides then into the broader canyon, and the road along the top of the Divide ceases. It connects to nothing.

To go by road from Donner Lake or Truckee to any point on the Foresthill Divide, you must drive a hundred-mile circuit, first down to Auburn, then up the Divide. This is what we did. From Donner Lake we drove a lopsided half circle. Interstate 80 carried us down along one wall of the Divide as far as Auburn, and then we took a narrow road along the top of the Divide to the village of Foresthill. On either side of the ridge, canyons plunged down to different branches of the American River. As Farrell had suggested, we were riding the race trail backward. We had chosen this middle section of the race trail because it was, in fact, middling—a slight drop in altitude from Donner Lake with steep climbs but not so steep as the first section of trail that ran from the trailhead at Robie Park to Robinson Flat.

The sun was high and the heat direct. Owen, impatient from having to wait out the trip, already had lather forming between his hind legs when I allowed him to launch backward out of the trailer. I didn't let him pull any funny business, and he looked around at this new piece of territory with interest.

Isabel noticed the dark patches of sweat on his neck and the foam between his legs. "On race day, don't do anything to make him anticipate. Don't even bother to groom him before the start. He'll leave every last ounce of energy he has back at ride camp."

When the horses were tacked up, Frankie pulled out with the truck and trailer. "I'll check on you at Deadwood. That's about halfway, and it's the first place I can get to with the truck."

Although the trail ran generally uphill, to accomplish this

climb it bounced up and down from creeks at the bottom of the canyon to points along its walls. On the first descent I tried to stay out of Owen's way and let him choose his own speed, and he responded by jogging, then walking, in spurts. Darwin marched methodically behind us for a while, and this strategy brought him alongside Owen.

Isabel settled in the saddle. "You think there'll be a funeral?" she asked.

Because of the predicament James had left Stephen and Charlie in, I hadn't begun to look ahead to a ceremony for Grant-Worthington. "If I had to guess," I told her, "I'd say it probably won't happen right away. James had colleagues all over the world, and Celeste and Josh will have to give those folks time to get here. But don't worry—you certainly won't be required to go."

"Oh, I know that. Just thinking about all this," she said, explaining nothing.

The trail made a keen turn and briefly angled down the mountain. When it made the switchback and headed straight up, Isabel said, "I was raised a Catholic."

Coming from her, any personal revelation was a little startling. I tried to be noncommittal. "Oh, yeah?"

"It's simpler, isn't it?"

"Simpler than what, Isabel?"

"You either believe or you don't believe. You're on or you're off."

"Binary, Stephen would call that. But what does believing or not have to do with anything?"

"Just thinking," she said. "About Josh. He's some kind of Protestant, which makes this big gray area possible."

What the hell was she talking about?

"I'm supposed to know what this gray area is?"

She didn't answer for a mile or so. Then a hundred yards

from the top, where we could see the opening of the pass and the horses relaxed and just moseyed, Isabel replied. "You know, this idea that you can have God and evolution at the same time, that evolution happened because God directed the operation."

"I don't see any harm in that."

"You don't?" Her little voice cut through sharply, squeaking on the last word. It seemed that Josh Untermeyer had found the key to Isabel Rakow, intelligent design, and then wound her up like a talking doll.

I asked Owen for a little more speed and tried to get ahead of Isabel's horse. But she stayed with me. Except when they interrupted our riding, I didn't actually mind these impromptu lectures. They were Isabel's way of keeping company, and it was often easy to read into her comments about Darwin and evolution and see them as reflections on her own life. She wasn't easy to know, but over the miles, I was getting closer to the real person.

We were just northeast of Foresthill and heading toward Deadwood when she said, "Darwin himself understood that God and evolution are incompatible. And now, of course, evolution and atheism seem to go hand in hand. I mean, look how many scientists have renounced religion."

"Why did they have to do that?" I had trouble following her reasoning, and Owen was headed up a difficult piece of trail, a scary series of steep switchbacks.

Isabel didn't seem to notice these. "That's the question that made Grant-Worthington found his crazy little institute."

Little didn't apply, as far as I could tell. The place was exerting far too much force on Stephen and Charlie and me.

"Once he became aware of deep time—you know about that, right? Lyell?"

Clearly, I had wasted my years in college.

"Lyell was a geologist a little older than Darwin. He could look at layers of rock and read them like a history book. And this took him way, way back—and he figured no way could the world have been created in seven days. So Darwin read Lyell and put it all together—deep time, geology, sex, and variation—and he began to sense that God didn't order the world, God didn't make man, and men didn't run things. He saw it was possible that what made the world go round were random forces of nature."

The canyon wall ran up sharply ahead of us, and to finish her thoughts, Isabel kept Darwin on a stubborn march close behind. This was the longest, steepest path we'd climbed since we left the East Coast. I was standing in my stirrups to take weight off Owen's back, and breathing hard enough that only snatches of her continuing account reached me—"socially upright. . . . Held off publishing . . . Wallace forced"—and with enough distance, her voice faded out.

I suddenly thought I might fall asleep. I was tired. By this I mean something fairly specific. Since I had started riding for distance and thinking about endurance, I had had plenty of opportunities to parse the various words that described waning physical energy and wanting to sleep. *Fatigue. Weary. Tired.*

Seven months earlier, when I'd neared the end of my first fifty-mile ride, I suffered tremendous fatigue. My muscles went loose and flabby. They seemed unable to connect and lift and squeeze. As soon as Owen crossed the finish line, I looked around for a place hidden from view to dismount because I suspected that when I slid off the horse and my feet met the ground I would land in a heap. My eyes were dry, and in spite of the sports bottles I'd emptied, my throat was too. But I was also pleased and excited. That was *fatigue.*

Then there was *weary*, which is something I hadn't felt in a long time. Not since the last months of my third marriage, my second to Frank Elledge. Our fights had left me sleep-deprived and not looking forward to anything except seeing Stephen step down from the school bus. I dreaded the ringing of the phone and the throaty voice I might hear when I picked up the receiver. I went to the barn to look after the horses and maybe ride but only because those were my duties to the animals. I didn't have the psychic energy to start anything new except another fight. That was *weary*, but that was long gone now.

At the moment what I felt was *tired*. Several days of uncertainty, worry, and thought fractured by competing priorities—the race, the horse, and the limbo into which the AccuGen deal had slid—mixed now with the exertion of training under steadily increasing pressure to make my body and mind long for the opportunity to let my eyes close and breathe long and deep. Sleep wanted to overtake me as Isabel's Darwin talk went on. But I had to stay on the horse—and just ahead, where the trail crested and turned suddenly down again, there was some tricky footing.

We headed to the bottom of the canyon, where a narrow creek ran through. The horses would drink here, and to pull ahead of Isabel and evolution, I waited until her bay had dropped his head, then pushed Owen farther up the bank before inviting him into the water and slipping down into it beside him to wake myself up and sponge him off.

When the trail leveled off a little again, I said, "I wonder how Charlie and Stephen are making out," and she said, "His wife wrote him a letter."

I said, "Whose wife? These horses made pretty good time today, don't you think?"

But Isabel kept on. "She was his cousin, you know. She loved him very much, and the man-wife thing was much more formal then."

I had fallen out of Isabel's narrative several minutes before. "Said what?"

"She feared for his soul—and I think he did, too."

She had lots of material to use against Josh, and her sudden loquaciousness made me suspect that her conversation during our ride was a kind of war game, that she was girding up for the next real encounter.

"Isabel," I wondered, "do you fear for your soul?"

She smiled regretfully, seeing the humor in this but also the loss. "I think I do."

Maybe she thought Josh could help with that. I had the sense that in spite of Isabel's determined protestations about science and truth, it would take very little to draw her back to religion. For her, maybe, religion was an old friend from whom she had parted on bad terms but with whom she would love to kiss and make up. Her preoccupations, especially when they were amplified by Josh's presence, made me feel the kind of guilt I hadn't felt since I skipped Sunday school to go hunter pacing. I had kept my soul at arm's length for too many years by finding God through the power of one or horse or another.

The trail crossed a rutted double track that constituted the road. It was inches deep in dust, and the track wiggled around the boulders that jutted up into it.

"This must be Deadwood," Isabel decided.

The place now called Deadwood looked the same as any other point on the canyon wall, dry gray soil and huge conifers. A hundred and fifty years earlier the location had been the site of a boom-to-bust mining town. Some previously luckless prospectors found a few particles of gold and declared finding more of it, a real vein, "deadwood," a fact as unquestionable as a felled tree. "Deadwood" was their certainty they would make a fortune there. It was difficult to imagine a village of five hundred people in this place. I had read that there was an inn here to serve the men working the five claims nearby. Now, however, this remote place had no vestiges of human habitation, no abandoned buildings or even foundations, no wells or other sources of water, no suggestion of cross streets. It was too desolate to make anyone want to linger.

The dusty twin track was empty. There was no vehicle of any sort or tire imprints for as far as we could see. "So where is Frankie with the truck?" I wondered. "Maybe she didn't see the horse trail and drove farther down into the canyon."

"Let's go down and take a look. If she hasn't made it this far, we'll meet her on our way back." Isabel had a logical plan, and we turned the horses to follow it.

A half mile farther down into the canyon, the underbrush crept in to challenge the towering trees, and as the soil became heavier and damper, tire tracks begin to show intermittently. I pointed these out. "Frankie. She's gone past the trail."

We followed the tracks into a little clearing where there was some long grass. A noise off to the side, a light clanking, caused me to look back to the break in the trees.

Instead of Frankie with the truck and trailer, there were two people sitting on sections of log next to a freshly dug pit where they were trying to start a fire. A man and a woman. They were young but not kids. Their jeep was pulled off the road just behind them.

"Looking for something?" the man demanded. A pair of sunglasses perched on top of his crew cut, and his belly folded slightly at his belt. He was almost dark-skinned—probably a person of color, although not very much color—and he had a wedgelike head and wide-set cheekbones. Evidently neither he nor the woman had planned on camping. They were in street clothes. The thin branches in their pit smoked but didn't offer to flare into fire.

"We were waiting for our friend to meet us with these horses," Isabel said and asked innocently, "Did a truck and a horse trailer come through here?"

"Must've took a wrong turn," the woman said. She had a sharp, watchful face and henna in her hair, which had been tugged into short braids that stood off the back of her head like handles.

Since they had spoken to us first, I rode closer, and at this angle I noticed behind the pair a dark door in the side of the canyon. The man stiffened, and his jaw jutted up at me. "Looking for anything else?"

"Is that a mine back there?"

"You know a lot about mines?" He was answering every question with a question. I was close enough now that I could see that his eyes, set well into his tawny face, were light-colored and that lying in the dry dirt next to the log he sat on was a gun. It wasn't a rifle, it was a short, squat handgun.

"Not a lot," I answered the question looking back at him and then glanced quickly at the jeep and its license plate. A jeep, and even before I registered the numbers one and six I knew we had to leave somehow. I knew who these people were, and there were only a few inches between the man's hand and the gun. Over the past three days he had got so accustomed to using it that nothing could be easier. I looked away instantly and, pretending to be otherwise occupied, fiddled with the buckle on my stirrup leather. I didn't want to stare any more than I already had. Didn't want to alert these two to anything about us.

"Like to go in and take a look around?" he asked about the small dark door sunk into the side of the canyon.

"Yeah," the woman agreed, smiling down into the shallow fire pit.

That door would be the last one on earth I'd want to go through and, if I had taken it, the last one I ever would. No doubt it had already dawned on one of the pair that they shouldn't let us ride out of the canyon and report their whereabouts. Several yards behind me Isabel coughed. Her usual personal composure had turned into something quite rigid, and her face was determinedly expressionless. She said, "Tink—"

The man considered her now. His look was speculative, as if he were considering a purchase. Isabel's fists, clamped tight around the reins, were locked at her waist. She knew. She realized whose company we had wandered into, and she looked too scared to move. But if we were going to survive this happenstance, we would have to move. We would have to make just exactly the right moves. I needed to turn the horse toward the dirt road, but which way? To the right, I would have to circle with my back to the two fugitives. To the left, I would have to ride directly past them. Some people are frightened of horses, and because of his size and weight, Owen might threaten the man. A horse passing close to him might cause an instantaneous reaction. And the gun was within easy reach.

I said, "It's pretty clear we've missed our ride," and used my leg to push Owen slightly left. I am quite positive that Owen had never in his life been asked to make a sideways move like a dressage horse, but he slipped agreeably left for a few yards. Then I sent him straight toward the twin track. My back was still at an angle, and out of the corner of my eye I could just catch sight of the man and woman on their log seats. "We better head back up to the main road, Isabel. Maybe Frankie didn't want to risk the truck down in here."

"You know how far in the canyon you are?" Another of his questions.

"No. How far?" I'd reached the dirt road and and wanted to keep them talking. Darwin came promptly up behind us, more under his own direction than any from Isabel. He didn't want Owen to leave him behind. I hoped that now that our backs were turned to the two seated by their pit Darwin would spook if there was any sudden movement behind us. A horse's startle reaction is way faster than a human's, and Darwin's spook would give us a fraction of a second's advantage.

"Walk," I ordered Isabel under my breath. "Don't even trot until I say so."

"Could be a long way," the henna-haired woman lifted her voice to advise us. "A real long ride," she laughed.

Maybe she thought this was funny. It was a kind of threat. To keep her engaged I called back, "If our friend has gone farther down the canyon and you see her coming back up, could you tell her we're headed up to the road?"

My back felt very wide, very blank. It was a big target. In a minute, we would reach the trees at the edge of the clearing and begin to merge with their dark, massive trunks. Although striding forward in their normal walk, the horses seem to inch up the road toward our goal. I dropped my hand down between Isabel's saddle and mine to signal her to be ready. She let out a long, impatient breath. We passed into the trees. I counted the giant shaggy trunks of five sequoias, then said very gently, "Go!"

Darwin, taking me and Owen by surprise, leaped up and bolted forward. Usually, Darwin's engine ran at an idle, but Isabel had signaled him that something big was coming up and kept him in hand while at the same time she was revving him up. Owen took a longer moment to organize himself into a gallop, but once he struck into it, he was uncontrollable, essentially running away, struggling to catch Darwin. I held myself up in a half-seat position with enough air between me and the saddle to give an approximation of a race jockey. The twin track ran relentlessly uphill, rocks and even boulders jutting up through its dusty surface.

Then gunfire. So rapid I couldn't count the shots. I had fired skeet shot and allowed hunters with rifles on my farm during deer season, but I had never heard gunfire like this. Tree trunks must have taken the majority of the bullets, and a few buzzed listlessly past the horses. Then, mid-stride, Owen left the ground. I was crouched over the saddle, and he jumped straight up, like he was on a pogo stick, sending me into a standing position in the stirrups. I thought maybe he was hit, but since he landed scrambling and kept going, I didn't slow him or look back.

If I let my eyes drop, the stones and boulders and the road itself streaked past Owen's hoofs in a blur. I had no idea how long the horses could keep up this speed moving uphill. Isabel seemed to be allowing Darwin to slow up a little. I squalled, "Keep going!" And because Owen had closed in to within an arm's length of Darwin, I struck the bay's rump with the ends of my reins. Darwin startled. He struck out and back up to speed but not before Owen had pounced ahead of him. Now more content in the lead, Owen would've slackened his speed, but I kept after him with my legs and heels.

We were about a mile and a half up from the mine clearing when I felt certain that the couple couldn't catch us in their jeep. Sometimes a horse is the fastest all-terrain vehicle. I called an okay back to Isabel and let Owen drop back to a trot. When Isabel drew up beside me, her usually wandering hands had now flown out on either side, as if she were about to hug somebody. Her face was pinched and sweating. She didn't speak.

"That jeep can't catch us now—this road the way it is," I told her. "We've got to get to the top of the Divide and try to flag down a car."

She nodded and, in the moment before we moved the horses up to a trot, looked them over quickly for signs of damage.

"My God, Tink, look at that!"

The horses' flanks were pumping, and along the right side of Owen's pale gray rump was a thin, bloody mark. The horses kept moving, and Isabel leaned across to look more closely at Owen.

"Scratch," she declared. "Just broke the skin." We went on. After a few minutes of haphazard posting, Isabel said wonderingly, "That bullet went between you and the saddle. If you hadn't been off his back, you could have been hit"—this was the only time in my life when being up in the air, out of the tack, had promoted safety. "You could be dead. We could all be dead."

We still could, but I didn't say this to her. I kept up the pressure on Owen, thinking grimly that it was fun to be the one pushing him. As we moved up the canyon wall, the trees changed gradually from giant sequoias with a clear understory to smaller evergreens with shrubby undergrowth, and when these began to subside into more open scrubland surrounded by spruce trees, I knew we were near the top of the Divide and the main road. A hundred yards from the intersection, Frankie had pulled the truck and trailer under an overhanging edge of spruce boughs. I could see her in the truck—bare feet on the dashboard, reading a book, and munching on something. I began barking instructions to Isabel.

"I'm going up to the main road to wait for somebody to come by. You tell Frankie what happened—and have her turn the rig around. Tell her to back out to the main road if she has to, but whatever she does, do not go any farther down this track."

When I arrived at the paved road, it was empty, and for the first time since we had come across the couple at the mine, I had the leisure to become anxious. Very anxious. I didn't know how much time we had before the jeep would come up the road from Deadwood. How many minutes would it take Frankie to get our impossibly long rig up on the road again? How many minutes would it be before a car came along on the main road? How many minutes to load up the horses? And how many minutes would it take the jeep to come up the road and draw into range?

Frankie had turned the key. The engine started to turn over. Then she tried again. I closed my eyes and cursed. On Frankie's third try, the engine clattered into loud activity. A moment later, I heard another diesel engine, louder and heavier. I watched the narrow road until a big logging truck filled it from side to side. I sent Owen into the middle of the road and hoped he wouldn't dump me when the truck and its noise came close. I forgot about the air brakes on big trucks and, dropping my reins, stood in the stirrups and waved my arms.

The air brakes sent out a loud, violent hiss, and Owen leaped sideways, skittering. I stayed with him only because my legs on either side of him acted like an old-fashioned clothespin clinging to a clothesline. Then, because he was a horse competitive enough to march into war, Owen turned abruptly on his hindquarters to face the enemy truck. I rode up to the cab window. The driver was a small, very thin man with a cigarillo caught in his teeth. "The hell is this?" he demanded.

"Do you have a CB, a radio?"

He drew the cigarillo out of his mouth and rested it between his fingers on the steering wheel. "For what?"

"They're are down there." I was having trouble with words, finding them, making them strong enough to carry over the diesel racket. My voice trembled. My legs trembled. I threw my arm in the direction of the track that ran down into Deadwood. "We ran into the two of them. We—you—don't have much time."

He was having trouble letting go of his suspicion. "The two of who?"

The rear end of the horse trailer was edging up into the paved road. Frankie wouldn't have much room before the opposite side of the Divide dropped precipitously into the next canyon.

"You know what I mean." I was almost pleading. "That couple—that Bonnie and Clyde who've been shooting—LOOK!" I turned Owen to present his right haunch.

"Goddamn." The driver set his brake and leaned in toward his dashboard. "I'll get the cops." He had the CB's microphone in front of his mouth and began to call into it at the same time he was speaking to me. "Tell your folks to stop that trailer before they push it over the other side of the Divide—I'll get that turned around so you can load up the horses and get out of here."

"We might not have much time, and you need to get out of here too."

"I can't"—he set down the microphone—"until I get your rig out of my way."

He opened his door, dropped down to the pavement, and headed toward our truck and trailer, where Isabel and Darwin waited alongside. He waved them out of the way, and Frankie issued a startled yelp when he pushed her over and slipped into the driver's seat. I can't tell you how he brought the truck and trailer out into the road and facing in the direction of Foresthill so quickly—less than a minute—but Frankie told us later that it involved only the driver's eyes on the side mirrors, his hand at the bottom of the steering wheel, and a few small twists of his wrist.

We put the horses on the trailer without bothering to remove saddles and bridles. A half hour later we drove by the incorporation sign for Foresthill with the logging truck close behind. A small flock of troopers' cars came past silently from the opposite direction, heading back up the road toward Deadwood. At a place in the village where the road split into the two parts of Main Street, the logging truck came alongside, the window on the passenger side rolled down. "Don't screw around and waste time here, ladies. Get on home."

We did that. Both Isabel and I wanted to keep up the frantic getaway, maintain top speed. But in the two hours it took to haul up to Donner Lake, Frankie managed to soothe us enough to allow her to keep the truck and trailer at the legal rate of speed. Isabel kept saying, "We could be dead, murdered right on our horses," and I kept saying, "Isabel, will you shut up?" I was irritable, raw and shaken, and having difficulty reacting like someone who was now safe. I had come within a hairsbreadth of never seeing Stephen and Charlie again. Of never seeing anything again.

Evidently, Isabel's thoughts were running in parallel with mine. After repeating "We could be dead," blah, blah, yet once again, she paused. "You know what I was thinking when we started up the trail with our backs to those people? First I thought maybe I wouldn't live to make it to the top of the road. Then I thought I wouldn't see my mother again."

"You see your mother often?" Frankie, who had been too surprised at first to be frightened, had come around to that. Isabel's talk about imminent death was making her apprehensive, and she was trying to draw Isabel away from the topic.

"Not very."

"When was the last time you saw her?"

"Oh, maybe fifteen, sixteen years ago."

That silenced Frankie. But I knew a story when I heard the beginning of it.

"You don't see eye-to-eye?" I prompted.

"About some things we do, but certainly not about me. She and my dad didn't see any reason I should go to college. My dad did okay for himself. He was an electrician who built up a business as an electrical contractor with a fleet of trucks. But they said that if high school was good enough for them, it ought to be good enough for me. So I put myself through college, working and borrowing money. Right about the time I graduated, he died and left my mother some pretty good money. I mean, it wasn't money like the two of you have, but it was enough so that she could have helped me with veterinary school. She said no, there was no way she would consider it, not even a loan. Then I found out my father had paid for my brother to go to college. He had a savings account for that all along."

"That must have smarted," Frankie observed. "What did you do about it?"

Isabel sat up a little straighter and said quite clearly, clipping her syllables, "I told her to put her head in a place where the sun does not shine."

"And you've made it to where you wanted to be without her."

"I survived," she agreed. "My brother sells software and lives in her house, and I'm doing fine. So maybe I'm the mutation that will change how things go in the family."

"Only if you have children," Frankie said bluntly.

Isabel ignored the correction. "I try not to look back, so I don't know why she was the first thing that came to mind when the horses were charging up the hill this afternoon."

"Maybe you can fix things with her," I said.

"Maybe."

Eventually Isabel dropped into silence, but then, as we passed the turnoff to the private road leading to the Institute, she spoke up. "I can't wait to tell Josh about this."

Farrell must have been watching for us. Shortly after Frankie made the turn into the ranch lane, he emerged in the middle of it, and she hadn't shut down the engine before he was beside the truck, motioning for us to roll down the windows.

"Was that you, girls?" He was agitated. "You weren't the riders who ran into them, were you? Oh my God, that's what I was afraid of. It came over the scanner at the Institute—Josh called me—and I just saw it on TV."

"Calm," Frankie advised quietly. "Calm. We will tell all, but not until Tink has patched up this horse—and not without a martini."

It would be a while before that martini. We went immediately to get the horses off the trailer and then the tack off the horses. Farrell, bless his heart, had put fresh bedding in the stalls, and as soon as Owen dropped his head to work on the pressing of hay I set down in front of him, I began scrubbing the long, slim wound on his haunch. It was shallow, just deep enough to take the hide off, and once the blood was gone, a glob of antibiotic ointment almost obscured it. Then Isabel and I went over the horses carefully, checking legs, vitals, pressing the gums for hydration and hams for muscle tone, while Frankie put the trailer and gear back in order and ready for the next outing.

Farrell had the TV on in the sitting room, the volume way up, and he had set a tray of drinks near it. He was agitated, hovering, moving from side to side unconsciously in front of the screen. It was as if now, having watched so long for us to return, his eyes locked him to the broadcast. Speaking above the TV sound without looking at us, he said, "They only got one of them."

Frankie, approaching for her martini, tamped the air with the flat of her hand. "Down? Can we turn it down, Farrell? Hate to spoil this fabulous drink."

Farrell saw that he was far more riled up than any of us and went meekly to the remote.

"What do you mean, only one of them?" I asked. "Which one of them?"

"Her. The woman he had with him. They caught her trying to drive the jeep up to the main road. Nelson is still down in there somewhere. Must have taken off on foot."

"Running around like a rabid raccoon," Isabel commented.

"What about the woman? Was there anything more about her on the news?" I wondered.

Farrell looked at his watch. "Don't remember—it was Nelson Laidlaw I wanted to hear about—"

That was his name, the name of the guy with the light eyes by the mine opening.

"—but if we wait for five minutes, they will run the news on her again."

We gathered around the screen and found the woman friend was still the lead story. Filling the frame, pigtails sticking out, she was led into the police station in Auburn. Her name was Angelica Chenoweth. Her passage in front of the camera, with her guilt implied by her hobbled ankles and cuffed wrists, was just like others that Charlie liked to call the perp walk—except that she had something she wanted to say. Twisting to speak to the little assembly of press and onlookers by the door, she spat out, "Should have killed those"—BLEEP—"riders."

"Well!" said Frankie indignantly. "Too bad she missed her chance. Because she won't get another one."

"Don't be too sure about that," Farrell said glumly. "She's the one who sprung Nelson a while back before Celeste gave him a job. Both of them are really slippery—gawdamighty, he has turned evil."

"I'm not surprised those people at that crazy organization hired somebody like that." Now that Isabel had recovered from being shot at, she was furious about that and about Owen's wound, and she was, of course, finding the cause of it all in the Institute's mission.

Farrell looked bothered. He turned off the television and excused himself to tend to dinner. I followed him into the kitchen on the pretext of getting another drink. His reaction to the killings, to Nelson rather than to the woman he had teamed up with, seemed way out of proportion to me. "You're taking this pretty personally, and it wasn't you they tried to shoot."

"Yeah," he agreed. "And I bet it doesn't make sense to you. I knew he was trouble, knew that right away. And I told her that."

"Celeste."

He nodded. "But I never expected anything like this, anything this bloody."

"But what you told her doesn't make you responsible," I argued. Farrell looked glumly into the salad greens he had been spinning.

"Celeste isn't *the* friend, is she? The one who helped you buy this place?"

"Yeah," he said readily enough. "Thought I told you that."

"You didn't say her name." I wondered if he would be sorry to see Charlie and Stephen take over the source of the Institute's funding.

"Why did she fire the guy?"

"Guess she had to—"

At this point Frankie trailed into the kitchen, empty glass in hand. Farrell automatically moved to fill it. "Seems like he was working out pretty good, then he started bothering folks."

"I'll bet," Frankie breathed. "And now he's still out here wanting to bother folks."

6

It was a good thing I had suggested Kravitz attend the Tuesday meeting by phone, because Charlie was suspicious about the reasons the meeting had been postponed in the first place and thought the presence of a standard-issue corporate lawyer would normalize a meeting that might easily run off the rails.

"It'll be good to have Kravitz sitting in because there are already signs that this outfit at the Institute could have a pretty skewed agenda," he told Stephen on the way to the meeting. "I mean, why, for instance, are the four people who have something to offer traveling way out here to meet with someone who has nothing to offer because she is essentially an employee of James's? Halefellow—you and I—are bringing capital to this party, the real estate guy might have some kind of capital stake, and no doubt the lawyer is getting her percentage."

"You mean, the mountain to Mohammed?" Stephen interpolated, and Charlie realized he might be unnecessarily worrying his younger partner.

"Exactly. But—"

Stephen indicated the carefully maintained gravel road, and Charlie turned into it.

"—we are going to have to play this as it lays."

A half mile or so after they turned onto the gravel, the guardhouse came into view. The same security guard who had stopped their car the day before stepped out to halt them now. Charlie, too, repeated his procedure from the day before, handing his wallet, driver's license flopped out, through the window.

"We're here again for a meeting with Celeste Fuertes. Have the others arrived?"

"Just Savage and Untermeyer. Didn't say nothin' about another meeting."

Charlie thought, Savage. Then he returned his attention to the guard, a thick, barrel-chested man, who wasn't unfriendly, just careful. The man drew out a small handheld radio from a holster on his belt. After a bit of squawking he spoke into it. "Josh, you guys havin' a meetin'? I've got a Reidermann here and an Elledge. . . . Oh, a lawyer? Okay."

He waved the car on, and in a moment, having been turned back at the guardhouse the day before, they saw the building for the first time.

"Jeezus!" Stephen said under his breath.

"Exactly," Charlie quipped about the purpose of the place. But in fact his reaction to the building was almost the same. Although he had been surprised by the lawyer's revelation that such a place existed, he was somehow shocked by the sight of the Institute. It made a soaring spiritual statement he hadn't expected of Grant-Worthington, but knowing what he now knew, should have.

"Did all this come from AccuGen?"

"Hard to say." Charlie parked the car head-on to one of the boulders that outlined the parking lot. The front door was a winking, steeply trapezoidal panel of glass, and walking up to it with Stephen, he tried to recall his encounters with

Grant-Worthington, to remember whether the scientist had ever indicated any interest in spiritual matters. But he drew a blank. Maybe that was because Grant-Worthington would not have presumed to evangelize or to impose his beliefs in any way on new friends.

They stepped into an expansive and surprisingly bright foyer. The huge glass panels of the front wall that looked so dark, so mysteriously powerful from the outside, shed daylight through the enormous room. Charlie felt as if he were standing outside on the floor of the mountain valley. Stephen was looking up at the highest joints in the glass wall panels, as if he was trying to figure out how they were put together.

From a hallway that led from the reception foyer to other areas of the building a man hailed them. He was a young, blond guy, coming toward—actually *at*—them with a strong stride and an outstretched hand.

"Welcome!" he said even before he reached Stephen and announced, "Josh Untermeyer. I'm a friend of Isabel's—and Tink's, of course."

Charlie had already recognized him from Tink's description, but he said, "Very nice to hear that."

After this handshake ritual, Josh straightened a little, glanced back toward the hall as if checking for something, and said in a voice too low to be heard beyond the three of them, "Maybe a word with just the two of you?"

Charlie came alert. Stephen was staring.

"Kind of a wild day here," Josh reported in confidence. "You may already know this—it's been all over the news out here—the couple on the killing spree? A man and a woman."

Charlie had a fleeting, truncated memory of an image on Farrell's television. He wondered impatiently what the killers had to do with Stephen and him.

"Four victims," Josh continued. "The woman was captured on the other side of the Divide, near Foresthill, this afternoon."

Stephen was watching Josh cautiously, and worried by Josh's cautious delivery, Charlie prepared himself for some kind of emergency.

"When they nabbed the woman, she was alone. The man is still on the loose."

"I really don't understand." It was an anxious demand, and Charlie made it in a hushed voice.

"He is an ex-employee of the Institute. He was fired not too long ago."

"You're doing the PR?" Stephen was putting things together more rapidly and methodically than Charlie. "Must be crazy-making."

Josh shrugged. "Not really. How much time does it take to say 'No comment'? Okay, so the woman was caught near a mine on the Tevis trail. A couple of riders—"

"Ma?" Stephen interrupted anxiously. Charlie felt his chest tightening, trying to keep him from breathing.

Josh indicated *slow down* with a slightly raised hand. "We don't know who the riders were yet. And they seem to have left the scene under their own power. So I think it's most likely that nobody has been hurt. I've been listening to the scanner, and Farrell will phone me if he hears anything or if Isabel and Tink pull into his place before you get there."

The three of them stood for a few moments without speaking. Charlie was aware that in the past two days everything in his life that had seemed part of an ordered realm had shifted into unpredictability. If the riders had left with their horses, then Tink, if she was one of them, was all right. He realized he should think about the deal ahead. Nevertheless, standing in the unusual light in the foyer he felt scattered, dislocated. He could have lost her. Stephen could have lost her. Scored a deal, but lost her, his long-legged blond wife. Tink, who only pretended to look after what he thought was a delightful appearance. Her hair, usually straggling out of a stiff ponytail caught at the back of her neck, and her clean-featured face—she remembered only on the most formal occasions where it was she kept her lipstick and mascara. She liked to take off her boots and stretch out on the sofa in his study. This and lying side by side in bed were the situations in which they most easily shared ideas. Hers usually ran counter to his, and correspondence from the ACLU was always good for starters. He thought about her in bed—but now Charlie tried to corral his thoughts, and finally he said to Josh, "Good of you to let us know."

"Meeting still on?" Stephen prompted, and Charlie admired his presence of mind. At least one of them wasn't shaken.

"Absolutely." Josh stepped back into his official role. "There is only one of the others here right now. But let me introduce you."

He led them down the corridor and into a meeting room where another expanse of glass offered a close view of the parking lot behind the building and the spruce trees that mediated between the grassy valley and the mountains that rose up on either side. A long, irregular table of a bright burled wood occupied the room. There was only one person sitting at the table, a man Stephen would have called a suit. Josh's introductions revealed that this was Paul Savage, a man not much older than Charlie.

Paul Savage. A ping of memory, and Charlie realized there was something he should associate with this name.

"I've been expecting to meet you under different circumstances," Savage said. He gestured toward two of the chairs that stood empty at the table, and Charlie took one thoughtfully.

"I handle Grant-Worthington's real estate, including the building and lab that AccuGen occupies, which I leased to him."

Right. The association was with AccuGen via James.

"If James were still alive," Savage continued, "we would be restructuring the lease. But it's a sad time—"

No. It wasn't James and AccuGen. It was Tink. That's why he knew about Paul Savage. Or at least he thought he did.

"—and tragically, James won't be here to help out with that."

"It's a loss for everyone," Charlie said rather automatically because he had noticed Stephen giving Savage a cautious once-over. Then he asked, "What about this building?"

Savage smiled at this and said with a shade of pride, "I don't own this. But I arranged the sale of the land, the deal with the architect, and acted as contractor."

"Awesome," Stephen congratulated him on the building.

"Thanks." Savage was grinning. "It is a huge source of pride."

And income, Charlie silently amended. The guy was, as Tink would say, up to his capital ass in Grant-Worthington's assets. But whether he had identified this man accurately or not, real estate and Savage would be essential to any deal.

Silence fell all around the table, and after a minute or two Savage said, "We're still waiting for Carol Messmer—Grant-Worthington's lawyer—and Celeste, of course. She's the director here."

Charlie waited glumly. If Grant-Worthington had ever mentioned the Institute, Charlie didn't remember that. But he'd certainly never mentioned an executive director. Ever since Stephen and he had arrived in these mountains, Charlie had been feeling somehow betrayed by Grant-Worthington, and now Tink, riding through the same mountains just to give a horse training miles had put herself in danger.

A chime sounding in the meeting room announced another arrival in the reception area, and Josh went out to escort a woman, Grant-Worthington's lawyer, back to the meeting room. Charlie and Stephen had been in close communication with Carol Messmer, who had been representing Grant-Worthington in the Halefellow buyout, but until now they had not actually met her. She stepped forward with self-assurance, announcing "Carol Messmer" with a professional smile. She was an emphatic presence, trim and preppy except for her punk crew cut, which stood up aggressively. Stanford Law, Charlie guessed about her. Looking around the table, Messmer appeared ready to take charge of the meeting. "So now it's just Celeste."

"And the Halefellow counsel," Charlie put in, and making an effort at cheerfulness, indicated a black starfish-shaped speaker device in the center of the table.

They made small talk for a few minutes, and when that found its limit and faded out, Savage shifted uncomfortably. He said, "I better see about Celeste."

Why, Charlie wondered, did Savage appoint himself for this errand? After ten minutes or so, Savage returned to the room alone. "I can't find her," he admitted.

"You checked the office? Computer room? Her apartment?" Josh indicated the second floor of the building.

"Her car isn't in the drive," Savage made this point to halt Josh's inquiries, which for some reason seemed to be embarrassing him, and then resumed his seat at the table.

Another long silence ensued. Messmer gazed at the back of her hand and her ring, a tooled silver band gripping an irregular lump of turquoise. Josh grew subdued. He turned his chair so that he could look out the window.

All that Charlie knew about Josh—and this from Tink—was that he appeared to have fallen precipitously for Isabel, who in Charlie's estimation was too preoccupied with science and its performance requirements to be ripe for a fall herself.

Paul Savage doodled on the pad in front of him. It was not clear to Charlie who was holding what cards. Savage had a big financial stake in the Palo Alto lab building and perhaps still did in the Institute's site. Josh's income, at least, was in play. But it was not clear how those interests were dependent on Celeste. He wondered about the hands he and Steven might be dealt or perhaps had already been dealt. Charlie caught Stephen staring at Savage with open curiosity, and finally, when Savage noticed this himself, he looked at his watch and said, "Truly sorry. This is very unusual for Celeste"—he apparently knew her habits well—"but then she's had quite a shock."

Charlie wasn't sure whether this referred to Grant-Worthington's death or to the lethal ex-employee. He was finding it difficult to sit passively idle when he was so unsettled about Tink. His only worry about her coming out to these mountains had been the cockamamy horse race. She was back on the horse after more than a year of recovery, and he had suspected that there was a lot more to this endurance riding than what she had admitted. But the danger she—if she were one of those riders—had encountered had nothing to do with horses. And certainly nothing to do with Charlie's rationally ordered world. Right now, he too felt a long way from rational. It didn't look like the people gathered at the beautiful table would be able to accomplish anything, and he was anxious about getting back to Farrell's place. He hoped Tink would be there, but if not, he and Stephen would wait as long as necessary. He wished himself out of the meeting, back in Farrell's ranch house, and he started to calculate the opportunities for rescheduling the meeting yet again.

Then, in the window opposite him, the broad roof of a large car appeared. He rose to his feet. "Would this be Celeste?"

"Gold Hummer?" Savage craned his head to see out the window. "Yup."

Charlie was in for a meeting after all. He resumed his seat dutifully, and a minute later a tall, slim woman came through the door to the meeting room. She was poised, purposefully graceful, and taking attendance. After greeting the others with a nod and a smile, she turned to Charlie and Stephen, sizing them up, and then, evidently coming to a decision, extended her hand first to Charlie. It was a decision about their relative status that reminded Charlie of one that Tink's terriers might make. Tink often remarked that a dog couldn't meet up with another creature, dog or human, without calculating relative status. But there was nothing haughty in this calculation, just caution.

"Celeste Fuertes," Josh stumbled in with introductions. "Charlie Reidermann and Stephen Elledge."

"Oh dear, I'm sorry to keep you waiting. We've been having quite a time of it here today. So stressful." Evidently referring to the ex-employee running amok. Celeste's mellow voice carried the necessary sincerity, and she accepted a chair Josh pulled out for her next to Savage. Settling into the chair, she reinserted one of the combs that held back her straight brunette bob, and her tawny hazel eyes swept over the rest of them and lit on the starfish-shaped speaker in their midst. She raised her eyebrows inquiringly.

"Halefellow's counsel will phone in," Messmer explained, and Celeste nodded her compliance.

Messmer drew a sheaf of papers from a leather portfolio. "Okay. Good to have everybody together." She nodded meaningfully at Josh, who leaned across the table to prod the black speaker. As soon as there was an online connection, the voice of Henny Kravitz, Halefellow's counsel, came on cheerily. "All ears," and his voice was as clear a presence as if Kravitz himself were in the room.

Messmer launched into substance. "You won't be surprised that what I have here is Grant-Worthington's will. He had intended to revise it as soon as AccuGen was sold and restructured, but unfortunately he didn't live to do that. So we'll have to abide by this and work out how to carry out the takeover by Halefellow—which was his clear intention.

"The will names me and two others in my firm as executors," Messmer explained, "and we will be working with you—"

"I'm sorry," Celeste said in a tenuous advance, "but I really don't think that's the case." She hesitated, like someone who has lit a fuse and is waiting for the detonation. But no one else said anything. "As everyone here, except perhaps Charlie and Stephen, knows, I was very close to James and spent a good deal of time with him."

Charlie was beginning to feel sorry for Grant-Worthington. Foolish old man. He had been seduced by his employee, who was now timidly defending her place.

"I was with him when he died." Celeste seemed to take special pride in this and went on as if going on required effort. "And before then, he was having second thoughts about restructuring with Halefellow's capital."

The starfish-shaped thing in the center of the table coughed, but none of the others actually present made a sound.

"He wanted the company to go to the Community and be managed by a board of directors drawn from the Community."

She was revealing an entirely different Grant-Worthington than the elderly scientist with whom Stephen and Charlie had made an agreement.

Josh looked straight ahead, stone-faced. Perhaps in deep self-conflict. Was this news a surprise to Josh? Or did he already know about Grant-Worthington's change of heart? Savage, whom Charlie decided probably had the least to lose from this new direction in Grant-Worthington's thinking, listened with his head cocked at an angle and his pencil moving in circles on his pad.

Without being disrespectful, Stephen said, "The *Community?*"

"The Institute's Community," she explained. "Our friends, our donors, and supporters. There's a good deal of capital there, James told me, both financial and intellectual. He said there would be significant tax advantages to his estate when we put that in order."

Kravitz came forth from the speaker again. "That has already been structured into our buyout."

"Celeste," Messmer put in a little impatiently, "we can certainly appreciate the very personal relationship you had with the man himself, with Grant-Worthington. But we have to go by the will. A wish is not a will."

"I'm really sorry"—and Celeste, whose apology had the veneer, at least, of sincerity—"really sorry, but that will you have isn't the right one."

"What's that?" Kravitz demanded. "Is she saying there's another will?"

Charlie didn't answer this, and Messmer said, "Now Celeste, be careful. My firm has been representing Dr. Grant-Worthington and you—at his expense—and we know nothing about this."

"Of course you don't," Celeste responded as if her feelings had been hurt. "He was my *friend*."

The illogic of her account silenced Messmer.

Seeing Celeste's discomfort, Charlie tried to maintain a genial tone. "Celeste, how come you didn't tell Carol about this?"

But this friendly appeal was disrupted by Kravitz booming from the home office, addressing himself to Messmer. "Counsel? Halefellow will need to see this document, even if you don't."

"We'll all need to," Messmer snapped.

Celeste rose. "Oh dear, why don't you come with me? I was sure you would need to see the will."

Everyone in the room left their chairs obediently to follow her.

"Wait!" Kravitz squawked. "Tell her to bring it to you. Tell her she has to bring the document to you!"

But Celeste proceeded down the hall with downcast determination. Charlie leaned toward the speaker and said, "Sorry, Henny. We'll get back to you."

"But you're without counsel, Charlie. This isn't the way to do this. This just isn't the way to—"

"I know," Charlie said apologetically. He knew Kravitz was right, and because Halefellow would now be faced with the terms of a competing will, he was certain that Grant-Worthington had not died of any natural cause. This was no longer errant speculation—a conclusion that Tink had leapt to and he was inclined to support—but an almost secure fact that made keeping Kravitz happy absolutely necessary. It jolted Charlie into a state of apprehensive suspension, which now conditioned everything that happened. But he couldn't afford to be left behind and not witness what Celeste had to show them, and he punched off the speaker.

He was surprised when the procession behind Celeste trailed past what seem to be the Institute's main office, which was where he had assumed they all were heading. She led them up a flight of stairs at the back of the building. These brought them to an ornate door made of the same burled wood as the table in the conference room. The door was carved to follow the swirling patterns of the burl and make them stand out in bas-relief. It opened on an apartment, in which the outside wall was glass, the same kind of soaring glass panels that lit the building's reception area. These looked out on the edge of spruce forest that followed down the valley after the road left off, and they gave the apartment the same out-of-doors effect as the big cathedral-like room at the building's entrance.

Celeste ushered them through an interior of muted colors and fat square cushions, white on white, pale taupe on paler taupe. This austere scheme, which seemed to Charlie to come straight from a magazine on offer in a doctor's waiting room, carried through to the bedroom where they stopped. Stephen wandered in after the rest, gawking unabashedly at the furnishings, and Charlie recalled Grant-Worthington's office, where no surface was clear of stacks of paper.

A large, high bed with more fat, square cushions occupied a good deal of the room, and there was a long desk of a pale wood, a severe piece of furniture, against the far wall. The only disruption in this decor was an anachronism sitting on the desk, a desktop computer that had aged so that the white plastic housing of its monitor had yellowed. While Stephen was examining this, Celeste went into the desk's file drawer and drew out a stapled document of perhaps twenty pages.

"James typed this himself," she said, indicating the old computer, "and I witnessed it."

Messmer took the document and flipped through it to get a sense of its content. "We'll need copies of this—two for our office, one for Paul, and one for Stephen and Charlie. I'll fax this to Kravitz in New York."

"There's a good machine in the main office," Celeste offered, and Messmer took the lead, exiting the apartment. As Charlie turned to follow, he noticed Stephen examining something on the floor beside the bed, a black plastic box a little less than a foot square and, just behind the box, a small green tank connected to it by clear tubing. It made sense to Charlie, but evidently Stephen had never seen one.

"CPAP," he named the thing. "For old guys."

They caught up to Josh in the windowless workroom at the heart of the spiritualistic building. Charlie's anxiety about Tink had been intensifying, and although he wasn't sure of Josh's role in these derailed proceedings, he hoped that Josh, whatever the reasons for his apparent attachment to Isabel, had similar worries.

"Anything from Farrell?"

Josh shook his head. "But I think if he had any news, we would have heard. The landline is right here."

As they listened to the swish of the copy machine issuing reproductions of the will Celeste had produced, Messmer said to her, "You may not be aware of this, but you have put my firm in a conflict-of-interest position. We can't represent you to challenge the current Grant-Worthington estate and the buyout. You need to hire your own counsel."

"I was worried about that," Celeste said immediately. Charlie found this the least surprising exchange of the day. This woman couldn't have come up against James's lawyer without worrying about her own position.

"Glad to hear that's not a surprise." Messmer was being carefully polite. "We'll be in touch." Charlie noticed she didn't say when or how. Stephen and he trooped out along with the lawyers to the parking lot, where Savage was waiting, leafing through the will on the hood of his car.

"This is difficult to believe," he announced to them. "Very difficult. I worked with Grant-Worthington for six or seven years. I *knew* the man."

What, Charlie wondered, did this man have to lose from a substitute will? He owned the building in Palo Alto, the rent for which the Institute's community could easily take over, and hadn't he already been paid for his investment in and work on the Institute building? Why should Savage be distressed?

Messmer was nodding sympathetically. "This certainly doesn't align with what we knew of him," she said. "But let's not get too excited. I need to take a really close look at it. And as soon as I've had a chance to speak privately with Celeste, I'll be back in touch with all of you."

Charlie didn't think it should be that easy. "Carol, please allow some time before you schedule that next meeting. I think Halefellow should send counsel."

"I see." She was trying to think fast. Charlie saw that she was intent, now that Grant-Worthington was out of the picture, on securing Charlie and Stephen as clients and retaining the AccuGen business. She said, "Charlie, you realize that having been legal counsel for the preliminary agreement with Dr. Grant-Worthington, we could easily represent your interest in any proceedings here."

"I think it would be cleaner, safer, if Halefellow sent its lawyer. This morning made it clear to me that there are things about Grant-Worthington's circumstances that I was not aware of—and of course, my responsibility is to protect Halefellow in any transactions in which I involve the company."

Messmer pressed ahead. "Well, of course, we will need to preserve client confidentiality with regard to Dr. Grant-Worthington—"

Charlie shook his head. "Halefellow will need to give it some time. We can't meet without Kravitz actually present."

Unless you counted the unsettling recognition of the probability that Grant-Worthington had been murdered, they weren't coming away from the meeting with anything. Not what they had decided they needed, not a clue about another offer for AccuGen. Charlie drove out the private road behind the lawyer's car and passed the guardhouse with a casual wave. Stephen, who had been full-on and thinking on his feet throughout the meeting, now seemed to sag a little under his new sport jacket. Neither of them spoke until Charlie turned onto the main road and split off from the other car, at which point Stephen said, "Pretty weird."

"The lawyer? The Fuertes woman? The real estate man—Savage? Or all of the above?"

"So, Charlie, what do you think?"

"They're hiding something." Charlie made this rather neutral understatement to avoid alarming Stephen.

The ever-logical Stephen said, "At least some of them are hiding some things."

"But it's going to be very hard for anyone to hide what's eventually going to come to light," Charlie predicted ominously but didn't say more. He wanted to talk over his theories about James with Tink before burdening Stephen with them. As Charlie thought about this, he eased up on the accelerator and their rental car dawdled. A car pulled up behind theirs. It was a dark blue sedan, and it pulled out impatiently and passed. Charlie gradually began to increase his speed, not because he'd been overtaken but because he was eager to get to Farrell's. He said, "I'd like to see Tink."

"No kidding! But Charlie, you know she's all right, don't you?"

The rational Charlie knew that was most likely the case, and Stephen's confidence soothed the irrational one.

Stephen thoughtfully thumbed the document they had taken away. "You know how you always say that if something—anything—doesn't smell right about a deal, you should leave it alone? Maybe we should pull out of the deal, Charlie. It's starting to smell bad."

Definitely bad. James himself now seemed somehow implicated in his own death, maybe undone by his lack of candor. But did that mean that James hadn't put the best, most honorable intentions into his business dealings with Charlie and Stephen or in his nascent friendship with Tink? Charlie wasn't willing to discount these factors. He said, "Maybe the reason it smells bad is just this Fuertes woman. Maybe if we can get past *her*, the deal will go straight down, like real business."

"Maybe." Stephen held one page close to his face and pronounced suddenly, "She's already got a big hole in her story. This thing wasn't typed on that old computer."

"It *wasn't*?"

Stephen shook his head. "It's too old to have this font."

"Would you be able to figure out which computer did spit this out?"

"Me? Probably not. I could probably just tell you the age range. But there's guys who could figure out what kind of *printer* generated this."

Charlie took this in carefully. The information might become useful or even necessary. He glanced up in annoyance when the same dark blue Plymouth sped past from the other direction. "Idiots," he said mildly, without really dismissing the issue of the computer. "Stephen, is that the same car?"

The sedan was parked just ahead of them on the shoulder of the road. Stephen turned to look at it as they passed. "Yeah. They must be lost."

Because he was now certain that what had gone on at the Institute was a planned death and because this realization had unsettled him, a wild thought sprang into Charlie's mind. Maybe those guys *aren't* lost. Then he felt foolish and spoke sternly to himself. Get a grip. Get a grip, Charlie.

Good sense prevailed, and a few moments after he turned into the ranch lane, Charlie looked in the rearview mirror and saw the blue Plymouth tootling past the lane opening on its way to whatever the occupants had been trying to find.

7

I was just out of a long shower, in my bathrobe and standing in front of the bathroom mirror to try to do something with my wet hair. Usually I went through these routines without noticing them. But now I let them pass slowly and paid attention to their details. The adjustment of bra straps, the rush of hot air from the hair dryer—these activities were so mundane that I found them comforting. They were a corrective dose of everyday reality to balance out what now seemed the surreal encounter at the mine and the out-of-control chase up the canyon.

Because my hair is, in fact, real, it wasn't behaving. I had wet it down and gone after it again when Charlie poked his head in the door to our room. "Tink? Are you decent?"

"Fairly."

He opened the door, and Stephen followed him into the room. Charlie stood looking at me, his arms wide so they could go around me. I was on my way to him when he sat down abruptly on the bed in a kind of collapse and shook his head slowly.

Stephen peered into his face. "Charlie? Are you okay?" Then he looked to me. "He seemed fine at the meeting, Ma."

It was a little startling. Charlie was not given to emotional display. I sat down next to him on the bed and drew him close. "Something bad happened, Charlie?"

I had to wait for his response. He drew a long breath and said, "I almost lost you."

Stephen stood with some papers in his hand, watching Charlie with concern. "You seemed okay, Charlie, until right now."

"I almost lost you," Charlie repeated.

I tried to jolly him up. "No, you didn't. Didn't even come close. All that happened is we saw them and got out of there."

Charlie nodded miserably and worked to recover himself.

"I better talk to you later," Stephen suggested to excuse himself.

"What's that in your hand, Stephen?"

He looked at it as if he had just discovered it. "Oh. A new will."

"Grant-Worthington's?"

Charlie nodded. He was perking up enough to come into the conversation. "It seems he had something going with the executive director, Celeste."

"Of course. I thought I told you about that. May I, Stephen?" I took the document from him. "So basically what does this mean?"

"That AccuGen will go to the Institute and its supporters," Charlie summarized. James Grant-Worthington was becoming a serious disappointment.

"The Institute and its 'community'"—Charlie used both index fingers to frame the word in quotation marks—"will make up a board to govern the company."

"So you and Stephen are out. What about Celeste?" I was afraid she was going to turn into my next disappointment.

"Apparently she is included separately, just as she was in the original will. But she won't have an ownership role—which makes the new will a little more believable."

I began flipping through the pages, feeling betrayed by James. Was he really such an old fool? And what really had been the basis of Celeste's affection for him?

"But only a little more believable," Charlie cautioned, "because we don't believe Celeste's story about where the will came from."

I looked up. "You think she fabricated it?"

Stephen shrugged. "It's possible somebody did, because it wasn't produced by the old computer she said James typed it on."

As far as I was concerned, Stephen's word on anything to do with computers was indisputable. I came to the last page. "But look. This thing is notarized."

"Right," Charlie said slowly. He was reappraising the document and likely James's mental soundness. "What I cannot begin to understand is how James could endorse a scheme like this."

"But anything we've found out about him out here has been pretty hard to believe," Stephen pointed out.

"Maybe this is what Celeste meant by a competing offer," I suggested.

"I might believe that if James had died of natural causes."

"But who, Charlie? And why?"

"*Why* is the easier question," he said. "There was a good deal of money involved."

"Potentially," Stephen qualified this. "Potentially a huge amount of money, if the company was—or is—able to actually implement the pharmaceuticals it has in the pipeline."

The word *pipeline* had been coming up at our house with increasing frequency. Stephen and Charlie had understood it's potential all along, but until now, I hadn't given it any thought. James could have developed a recombinant technique with such fabulous potential that he had become its victim.

"*Who*," Charlie continued, "is a damn tough question."

"What I have trouble wrapping my mind around," Stephen said to lead us to a possible suspect, "is this thing James had with this woman. I mean, it makes him look kind of stupid."

"An old fool," I agreed. "But looking back on it now, I know he was lonely. In fact, he told me as much. Once when he came to the farm he was really down, and we talked about that."

James had arrived in the late afternoon, before Stephen left the office and Charlie's train arrived from New York. He came in the back door, as sooner or later everybody seems to do, left his suitcase just inside, and sat down heavily in the round-backed chair beside the telephone table in the hallway.

"So good to be here."

"And how nice to hear you say that. Long day?"

"Not too bad, Tink. Would you have a whiskey?"

I didn't bother to answer this, just went for a glass. This wasn't like him. I poured two inches of scotch and said, "Are you feeling all right?"

"I'm not ill," he said. "This is very nice, Tink. Can you sit down with me? Somewhere besides Charlie's study?"

The terriers followed us into a front parlor that Charlie and I seldom used unless we had invited a big crowd. A large wing-back chair seemed to suit James. He said, "I struggle from time to time with depression."

"You're not alone." I said this, although I would have been hard put to name a time when I could have described myself as depressed. Angry. Elated, frustrated, infatuated, determined, hopeful. Yes, any of those. But I didn't tend to sink into the sloughs between those states. Nevertheless I knew what depression was and found the thought of it frightening.

"Well, of course, I *am* alone," James said with candor. "That's just it. I had a beautiful wife, Tink. She's been gone four years, but still sometimes I can't get used to that—oh dear, I've made you cry."

"Which is not difficult," I assured him about the salt water dribbling over my cheeks.

"Actually, she wasn't beautiful," James corrected himself. "She was like you, Tink. Tall and blond and attractive—and very smart. Maybe that's why you are the one who is hearing this."

I took the handkerchief he offered. "Could you remarry?"

"I can't see how that would work for me." He didn't pause long enough to actually consider the idea but instead asked, "What can you do with love that stays after a person is gone?" He wasn't expecting me to answer. "After enough of these periods—they are brief—of depression, I began to realize that not everything about human existence can be reduced to scientific reality. Molecular biology can't drill down far enough into intercellular activity to explain love—or for that matter, hate. There is probably some biological precondition for these events of the spirit, and isn't it probable that these little dogs Spit and Polish experience something like our own love and hate and reverence?"

"I have always assumed they do." I was surprised he thought that was a new or somewhat remarkable idea and also a little nervous that I wouldn't be able to keep pace with his heady, intellectual conversation much longer.

"I think the usual thing to do with this leftover love is to put it to use in the family. But we had no children," he told me, "not even a wonderful add-on like Stephen. That's why I am trying to put my love to use in the larger context, you know?

I am putting considerable money into the study of the links between biology and the life of the emotions and spirit. Darwin himself recognized there must be such a connection. You know about Darwin, I assume?"

I said, "Evolution," and hoped that would suffice.

"Oh, my dear. Look at what I've done. Still crying, are you? Could I get you a glass of this?"

"I'm very sorry for your loss," I told him without bothering to answer his question about the scotch.

"I knew you would be. That's why I have valued my time here with you and Charlie and Stephen. I have hopes that now, when I won't have to worry about the infernal business, I will be able to focus on a higher mission." He smiled at this elevated term. "And get to spend more time in your barn—which is obviously where you need to be heading."

Walking down across the lawn, James did seem quite a bit cheerier. But I don't think it was because of the scotch or my clumsy conversation. I think it had raised his spirits to talk in simple terms about his wife and the emotions he could barely live with. I think he even felt somewhat optimistic.

I certainly did. But now, looking back on that walk down to my barn, I found a certain amount of irony in that optimism. And of course, I wished I had had the presence of mind to ask James if—in the process of putting his love in a larger context—he had been able to find even companionship with another woman.

"His life was pretty empty," I concluded my briefing.

"Right, Tink. Empty. He was in late life, when sex can be a comfort to a man."

Stephen looked vaguely disgusted. "But Charlie, I mean, is *that* worth giving away the store?"

Charlie laughed. "Maybe not at your age."

"I think you two are looking in the wrong direction," I told them. "First of all, I don't think Celeste has the starch to cause someone physical harm. And second, if Charlie's correct that James had already included her in the first will—and if he did, she was probably aware of that—what would be her motive?"

Charlie shrugged. "Valid point. And as I said, *who* is the really tough question.

Now that he seemed to have everyone collected in the kitchen, Farrell was putting the full force of his concentration on finishing dinner. He saw me rummaging through the recycling bin next to Baby's cushion. "What are you looking for?"

"Yesterday's paper."

"Want to see it all in black and white?"

"I thought I'd save it so people at home will believe me."

He grinned. "Better save tomorrow's papers then."

"What's not to believe?" Frankie demanded, and Isabel nodded. "I'll probably still have the dust from that road in my teeth when I get home."

Although I was interested in seeing the press's account of Nelson and Angelica's rampage, what I was looking for was a name—the name of their first victim. I could pretty much assume their motivation for killing two bank tellers and the officer who responded to the bank's call, but the motive for gunning down the Canadian man or the situation in which they did that had not been mentioned on television, and nothing other than his name—Charles McCarran—appeared in the newspaper report. I used a pair of Farrell's kitchen shears to trim the three full columns from the newspaper. Laidlaw had a strong connection to the Institute, and if I could find out more about his first victim, something about McCarran might help explain James's death.

"Is that the piece that mentions Celeste?" Farrell asked.

"Just a brief quotation saying she hired him and fired him."

Frankie, who had known about the deal that was hanging fire since the time I'd recruited her to play tennis with Grant-Worthington, gave me a significant look. "Charlie, did the old man ever say anything to you or Stephen about her?"

Charlie spun his glass very slowly on the counter, and before he could respond, Isabel turned to Stephen. "So the same old man owned this ridiculous institute *and* the company you and Charlie are trying to buy?"

Farrell shot a glance at the two of them. The potential purchase was news to him.

"The company funds the Institute." Stephen smiled and made another correction. "And maybe it's okay to call him an old man. But he was a brilliant old man and, I mean, very hip."

Farrell smacked a long-handled ladle against the counter. "You can say that again. Mind ran at the speed of light."

"Doing what?" Isabel wondered.

"Recombinant proteins," Stephen told her, and she understood that immediately.

"That anything like pheromones?" Farrell teased her.

"No," she said seriously. "It uses PCR—polymerase chain reaction—often on yeast—to generate hundreds of generations of artificial proteins."

Farrell raised the ladle. "I'm lost, I'm lost!" he protested, but he wasn't the only one. I was grateful when Stephen intervened.

"A few of these proteins turn out to be useful, especially in medicine."

"That's where the money comes in," Frankie explained.

"Right, and Dr. Grant-Worthington was the one who figured out how to pinpoint a protein that might be useful and then generate a whole lot of proteins just like it."

"It's like high-speed evolution," I commented.

"Actually," Isabel pointed out, "it's more like high-speed intelligent design, where God thinks up evolution and puts it into practice—except that the mind that's controlling this rapid-fire evolution is the mind of a human scientist."

Farrell, more excited to learn about the science behind Grant-Worthington's wealth than he had been to learn about pheromones, positively crowed. "Rapid-fire means more money!"

"*Possibly,*" Charlie said carefully. I saw that he wanted to put a damper on this open group conversation about his business with Stephen and to halt Farrell's speculations. The aging mechanical chime above the front door accomplished this, and without leaving his cooking, Farrell hollered out a general welcome. Josh Untermeyer arrived in the kitchen.

"Hi," he said apologetically and glanced uneasily at Isabel. It seemed clear he was worried about how the rest of us perceived the afternoon's meeting. "No thanks, Farrell. Maybe just some water."

"Have a beer," Isabel instructed magnanimously. She was in inexplicably high spirits.

"Okay with you, Farrell?" Josh said hesitantly.

Farrell's large refrigerator yielded a chilled bottle of the same local brew Stephen was drinking. "Door's always open to anyone who does God's work. Stay for dinner, kid?" Farrell invited, and Josh's relief at being included was puppylike.

At the table Stephen surreptitiously swapped his chair next to Isabel's for one beside Frankie. Josh accepted the empty chair, and Baby wound her way through all the legs under the table to collapse on Josh's feet. Charlie's nice, slow sit-down dinner got under way.

Farrell repelled all offers of help with the dishes, except Frankie's, and Charlie announced pointedly that he was tired and going to turn in. Although he had every reason to be tired—he and Stephen had started the day in Sacramento and driven out to Donner Lake to endure a meeting with at least one liar—I thought he was probably excusing himself to allow the younger people to gather without us and perhaps to allow some physical one-on-one. So I followed him meekly to our room. But it wasn't about sex. It was about history. I hadn't even taken off my boots when he said, "What do you know about Savage?"

It was a sucker punch. I was stunned. I had planned to make a moment to tell Charlie sometime after the Tevis. But he was too fast for me. He was always too fast but not usually so direct. "Savage?" I said stupidly.

"Paul Savage. Your first husband."

My voice caught in my throat. This was just what I had feared would happen. Why had I been so stupid as to think that I had a little time and could put off telling Charlie? He was too smart, too quick not to immediately catch on to who Paul was. Now what? Was he going to ask me about the sex? Lingering attachment? Money? I couldn't say anything that might hurt Charlie, this warm, gentle man who was taking such good care of Stephen and me. But I also could not lie to him.

Charlie waited.

"He does real estate in California," I said, ignoring the fact that the present bedroom was in that state.

Charlie said nothing.

"That's the latest thing his daughters told me."

I couldn't bear the silence that followed. We listened to the voices of Stephen and Isabel and Josh from the living room. I couldn't speak until Charlie said impatiently, "Tink, this is not about jealousy."

"Oh." I was somehow humiliated by this statement. "Okay, Charlie. Okay. So Savage is out here. I didn't *know* he would be out here. I think he has something to do with the Institute."

"Have you spoken with him?" This was something a jealous man might have asked, but it wasn't a jealous question.

"I've just seen him from a distance. Josh told me who he was."

"Too bad," Charlie observed, startling me a little. "I was hoping you had chatted. We might have learned something."

"I don't want to talk to him. I don't want him to know I'm out here. And I don't want to meet him."

"Why?" Charlie was nonplussed, and at the same time he was being impossible. "Why don't you want to have anything to do with him?"

He appeared willing to accept whatever I said as uncritically as usual. "Are you afraid of him? You're not afraid of anything else."

"Charlie, how can I explain this? It's shame, and it's very painful. When I saw him and then realized who he was, it gave me a jolt like hanging on to an electric fence with my teeth."

"Really," he said with a shade of astonishment but completely confident I would go on. I did.

"I was a terrible person." I had to work to keep from bawling, and when he put his hand on my knee to comfort me, I failed at that. "Terrible person," I sniffed. "I'm not making this up."

He kept quiet and patted my knee occasionally. When I stopped crying, he said, "Does Stephen know this?"

"He knows about his dad—the other women, the fights, the god-awful fights his dad and I had. That's enough. He doesn't need to know about Savage."

"As a matter of fact, Tink, he does." This was a friendly correction, and his hand hadn't left my knee. "Paul Savage came to the meeting today because he handles all of Grant-Worthington's real estate. He has a big stake in this deal. I know that much. But he may be more deeply involved than appears on the surface, and Stephen and I need to know everything we can about him. You'll need to talk to Stephen tomorrow."

"God, Charlie . . . I don't know." It was a rough assignment. "I suppose you're going to tell Savage that you're the fortunate son of a bitch who's sleeping where he used to."

"No. Not right away at least. Before he finds out anything about Stephen and me, I need to figure out where he fits in, what his dealings with the rest of them are—the lawyer, Josh, Celeste—*and* what his relationship with James was. For instance, was there any reason he might have wanted James out of his way?"

"Charlie, that is such a long shot it's impossible."

"Impossible?"

"He would not be capable of anything that underhanded and brutal."

"So far, though, starting with James, nobody has been what they seemed."

"No. I know him, Charlie. I was married to him."

This made him laugh. "Good of you to remind me, your current husband. First it's a secret and then it's your debating point."

"Charlie, you brought this up."

"Never mind, Tink. At some point it may work in our favor for him to know we are married. And at some point, it's possible he will have to meet up with you."

"Oh no. That's not—absolutely not going to happen." I skittered away from the idea.

Charlie ignored this and went into his suitcase for his pajamas. He wasn't going to let me off the hook.

"I can't, Charlie. I can talk to Stephen if you want me to, but you can't make me just walk up to Savage and announce my name."

Charlie considered me speculatively. He had one leg in the pajamas. "What did you do, Tink, that was so terrible?"

I listed the possibilities, denying them at the same time. "I didn't cheat. Didn't do anything to embarrass him in public. I tried to mother his girls."

"Then what was so terrible?"

"I didn't love him—without thinking about what I was doing, I used him." I couldn't look at Charlie while I told him this. "I slept with him and spent his money when I didn't really care about him. I was too young—I'm not trying to excuse myself—but Paul was what my parents wanted for me. He was my dad's business protégé."

"I see," said Charlie without judgment.

"Big fucking wedding—white tents, waiters with trays of hors d'oeuvres, champagne—the whole bit. But it didn't change much of anything for me. I kept riding, training, doing the events. He picked up the tab."

I looked critically at the nightgown I pulled from a bureau drawer. Why hadn't I brought something decent? Because I hadn't expected Charlie would be with me.

"I had his little girls, darling kids. But I wanted a baby of my own—mine, mine, mine. I lay down on my back for him, Charlie—but I was thinking about something else. Everything else but him."

Charlie was slipping under the covers, lifting the other side of them to make a place right next to him. "There's no need to tell Stephen all of *that*," he said. "You're pretty hard on yourself, Tink."

"Well? It could have worked if I hadn't been so goddamned selfish."

"Maybe." Charlie wrapped himself around me.

"It would be too humiliating if I had to see him again. Too much pain."

Charlie switched off the bedside lamp. "You may have to change your attitude. We don't know yet how James died."

He may have put the room into darkness, but Charlie's long day—and my harrowing one—wasn't going to end with the two of us drifting quietly off to sleep. The phone in our room rang. When Charlie picked it up, I could hear the barking of Henny Kravitz, whose excitement had kept him up way past his bedtime.

"This gambit is as old as dirt, Charlie! Messmer faxed this new thing to me, and let me tell you, I don't give a damn about this notary's seal. It's probably as phony as the rest of the will, and I'm going to track the number on it back to the so-called notary."

Charlie let Kravitz carry on without commenting. I lay beside him listening because there was no way to pretend the lawyer's blaring didn't reach beyond the receiver.

Before he hung up, Kravitz instructed, "Keep it under wraps, Charlie. And I want you to set up something with Messmer. Not out there in the boonies, where you are. In San Francisco. I'll fly out."

Charlie's answer was in the briefest form, and after he had hung up, I said, "You barely spoke to him, Charlie."

"Somebody picked up on another extension. So I just listened."

Who in Farrell's ranch house—Farrell, Isabel, Frankie, Josh—would have been interested in Kravitz's conversation with Charlie? Josh and Farrell were the only possibilities.

A few minutes later, there was a second interruption, a light tapping on the door to our room. When Charlie opened it, Josh Untermeyer stood there with Farrell's dog poking her rust-colored snout between his legs. Having regained his usual forward momentum, Josh had left the little group in the sitting room to pay this visit.

"Sorry, sorry. I know it's late. I was afraid you were asleep. Could I have a few minutes with you? I would have phoned before I got here, but I didn't want this going over Farrell's landline." Evidently, Josh was aware of Farrell's phone as a source of intelligence. But if he had learned anything from trying that source a few minutes earlier, it was only that Kravitz was furious about the new will.

Now with Josh right in the room with us was a good opportunity for us to do some fact finding about him and the people he worked with at the Institute. Josh said. "I'm in a tight spot, and it's possible I'll need you to back me—and I may need help keeping this straight with Isabel."

"I'm a terrible matchmaker." I tried to excuse myself and segue to the questions of who was steering the course at the Institute and what, exactly, the course was. But he ignored this.

"Charlie, here's the problem. I have no idea what is going on at the Institute anymore—maybe I never really did—and I am worried. Usually, a client will be up front with me if there's a weakness in the operation that they want to put offstage. But

Celeste never said anything about the trouble with the estate, and I've never seen her act the way she did today. I didn't know how you would react or what you would think of me, and I was suffering. Absolutely suffering. So I want you to know where I stand."

Charlie nodded. I kept my eyes on Josh. So far I might have believed what he was saying if it hadn't been for the fact that someone had eavesdropped on Henny Kravitz's call.

"And this is not just because of Isabel. It's because of Dr. Grant-Worthington. He was a fine old man, and he gave me my start just after he founded AccuGen. At first, business was really slow. There wasn't a lot going on. But he paid me, and he would invite me to the office anyway, and maybe we'd just talk. I learned a lot about genetics and evolution and even Darwin, who was very important to Dr. Grant-Worthington. I probably understand AccuGen's business as well as you and Stephen.

"Dr. Grant-Worthington was a Christian, and I am too. And he truly believed that our ideas about God could make room for ideas about evolution. So when he decided to create the Institute, it seemed kind of natural to just expand my work to include the mission there."

Stop, I thought. You're sounding too righteous to be real.

But Josh didn't stop. "Now, since he's been gone, Celeste hasn't been herself. I'm confused by some of the things she does, and today the new will was a real shock. I'm considering resigning, and if I didn't feel obligated to Dr. Grant-Worthington and his goals for the Institute, I would have already done that."

Charlie may have been moved by this, but he certainly didn't appear to be swayed. "I wonder why you're telling me this, Josh."

Me too, Charlie.

Josh gave a sheepish little laugh and scrubbed at his unruly hair. "Well, I knew you were making a bid to buy AccuGen, and I was hoping that if the takeover happened, I could just continue working for the company. And I don't know, maybe it's the same thing with Isabel, wanting to continue."

"At this point," Charlie told him without a hint of humor, "there's nothing I can do about either of those situations. So what else is it that you want me to do?"

At this Josh looked a little crestfallen. "Just to know, I guess, that I'm considering resigning."

"If you're looking for advice, I'd say don't do anything right away. Wait and see what happens. And of course Tink and I will keep what you've said in confidence."

After Josh had closed the door behind him and Baby, I said, "That was pretty mean, Charlie. But he may have deserved it."

"I can't be giving out information to any of their people. I mean, do we want this deal for Stephen or not?"

"Right, and I bet he knows more than he's telling us."

"Definitely. So you had that impression, too?"

"And I'm beginning to wonder if what he knows might prove that Grant-Worthington didn't die of natural causes."

As if sleep hadn't already been hard enough to achieve, a few hours before dawn the bedside lamp came on again. Charlie was laying out a crowded game of solitaire on the little bedside table. He usually carried a deck of cards with him because he liked to play against himself before going to sleep, sometimes in order to be able to sleep. This habit was directly connected to one of the great pleasures in his life, calculating the odds. He loved to think about probability, and he loved to bet. That was the facet of my life with horses and competition that made it endurable for him.

I raised myself on one elbow. "Something worrying you?"

"I feel stupid," he said. But *stupid* was a label no one would have slapped on him. "I feel stupid because I can't see how James died or why this deal is going so screwy."

He placed a card on a row of others. "I'm being chummed— you know, the way a fisherman throws out loose bait."

I didn't know anything about this.

"I'm following the boat because I don't see it's only chum and—this is the worst part—I'm drawing Stephen right along behind me."

I tried to make my way through this fisherman-in-the-boat metaphor. "Why is that worrying you?"

"Because the sharks have already smelled the chum." Charlie surveyed his brief rows of cards. "And because I can't figure out which fish is which—"

"And you're already out in the water."

"Exactly."

"Put your goggles on, Charlie, and keep your eyes open."

He gave a short laugh. Then he really laughed and gathered his cards together to put the game away. I waited until I heard the gentle beginnings of a snore and then reached across him to turn out the light. I'd never seen him in swim trunks, and the closest he ever got to even a swimming pool was a deck chair.

Farrell kept the coffeemaker on a timer, and we found Stephen standing worshipfully in front of it, mug in hand, waiting for it to finish gurgling. Farrell was nowhere around. Charlie nudged me, but I had already recognized this opportunity. When the mugs were full and I had located creamer for Stephen, I said, "Hon? Charlie says I have to tell you something."

Charlie disappeared from the kitchen, and I got on with the assignment he'd given me. "There's a real estate guy involved in this, right?"

"Right." Stephen was still waking up, listening without focus.

"Just so you know what's what, a long time ago, a very long time ago, I was married to him."

Stephen blinked. "That's him? That's the same Savage?"

"You know about Savage?" I was relieved but couldn't figure out how this had happened.

"Remember the silverware, Ma? I asked you about the initials on the handles and you said *S* was for Savage. And you said the same thing you did just now, 'It was a long, long time ago.'"

"Well, it was, and that's who he is."

Stephen thought this over. "I can believe that."

My stepson always surprised me and had ever since the night he chose me over his father.

"He's about your age," Stephen began, trying to make the facts fit his observations. "He's got some money. . . ."

I thought the toughest part of my day was over and began to give my coffee the attention it deserved. But he had a question.

"So Ma? Who did it?"

"Did it?"

"Which one of you broke it up?"

"I did." This probably had to come out. "It was me. I was too young and too self-centered to be married, Stephen."

He nodded. "Took you a long time, didn't it, to find Charlie?"

"Slow learner," I admitted and hoped this would be the end of it. It would have been, except that Stephen was now thinking of his own situation.

"You think I'm too young to know what I'm doing?" he asked about his plans to marry Alex Delgado, a girl he had come to know because of my life with horses.

"No, I don't, Stephen. For starters, you're older than I was. You've worked, made your own money, started a little company that turned into a bigger company. And you're making the choice for yourself—my father chose Savage because he was his protégé, almost like Charlie and you. You really love Alex, and you're not as selfish as I was."

"You've given me everything, Ma," he contradicted. "You've been doing that all along. Charlie's just part of that."

How sweet, too sweet to know how to respond to it. So I didn't. I said, "You know there's something you could do for me."

"Yeah?" he said cautiously.

"You have your laptop here, don't you? Could you do a little research for me?"

8

Down in Auburn rigs had been pulling into the fairgrounds for the past couple of days. Heavy-duty trucks pulling trailers long enough to carry six to eight horses but actually, like Isabel's trailer, occupied by space for only two horses and living quarters—*living* being a generous term for the way a bathroom, kitchen, table, and bed were crammed into an area that would otherwise have held four horses. Here was our competition, waiting for the Tevis, waiting to hear "The trail is open!"

Up at Farrell's place near Donner Lake, we were all waiting too. Isabel and I had finished our two remaining training days on some trails north of Donner Lake, a hundred miles from the danger around Foresthill. Now we were on hold with our horses resting for a week but still breathing thin air until the ride camp at Robie Park officially opened. Or, in the case of Charlie and Stephen, until Henny Kravitz arrived in San Francisco where a meeting, to which Celeste Fuertes would be delivered by her new lawyer, would convene. The temperature rose every day, and watching the Weather Channel became a regular morning and evening ritual. Riding a hundred miles is difficult enough, but riding a hundred miles on a hundred-degree day is an assault on a horse's body. Down in the canyons, where the air was trapped, it was even hotter.

During the lull, Nelson Laidlaw and his exploits faded from the news and the public eye. When I phoned the ride manager to ask if the possibility of a killer roaming the Foresthill Divide might cause the ride to be canceled, he laughed. "If he's still down in the canyon in this heat, ma'am, he's not going to be a danger to anybody. He's gonna be kitty food."

"What does that mean?" I asked Farrell after I hung up.

He smiled. "He means cougars hunt even in the heat."

Taking advantage of this moment with no one else present, I posed another question. "Farrell, did someone named Charles McCarran ever stay here?"

He tipped his head while he considered this. "McCarran. Sounds familiar. Seems like I should remember if he was my guest. Let me go back through my accounts and—oh, now Baby! What the hell?"

It was Josh. Again. Yet again. He was becoming a fixture, and Farrell's snappish red-and-white collie was developing a passionate attachment to him. Josh ate dinner at the ranch so often that I asked Farrell who was picking up the tab, and he grinned and put off my question. "It's not you, if that's what you're worried about."

Josh actually paid very little attention to Baby. When the dog saw him coming, she writhed ecstatically near his feet, pawing the air. At the same time, her antipathy toward Isabel intensified, and when Isabel ventured close to Josh, the dog expressed her displeasure by showing her teeth in a sneer and emitting a low, rattling growl.

"You know, Farrell," Josh pointed out, "Baby is not acting very nice."

"You're the one alienated her affections," Farrell laughed. "You can't expect me to fix that, can you?"

"Baby needs a job," I pointed out. "She's a working dog with nothing to do. Nobody who's unemployed acts their best. She needs some sheep."

Isabel, who had taken little notice of Baby's offenses, said, "That's right. All her work drive has been bottled up, and she's stir-crazy. And Farrell," she offered some professional advice, "I know you're crazy about this dog, but all your pampering probably just makes Baby miserable."

"I guess Baby's right about you vets," Farrell defended himself. "All she's trying to do is to protect Josh from you."

Isabel was starting to take some teasing, and Farrell was only one of her tormenters. One morning when Farrell arrived in the kitchen after Isabel and me, she perched a little too upright on a stool and stared down into her mug, apparently not in a mood to talk much.

Stephen wandered in looking for coffee and said, "How late did you two stay up last night?" witlessly releasing the information that he had left Isabel and Josh alone when he'd gone to bed. Isabel stood up, set her mug on the counter, and left the kitchen.

"Jeezus!" Stephen sent me a look of disbelief. "You're gonna have a sweet little time with the horses today, aren't you, Ma?"

Isabel returned to the kitchen with her purse strung over her shoulder and the keys to her truck in her hand. "Want to go check out Robie Park? I heard some of the riders have already come in."

"I thought I'd have breakfast with Charlie."

"Fine," she snapped and would have marched out of the kitchen but Farrell inserted himself.

"You know," Farrell informed her, "I have quite a few guests who like to have breakfast in their rooms. Not everybody's real good every morning. Get yourself a tray. Once you get to Robie Park, you'll be an hour from any food. You could get plenty hungry."

She was disarmed by Farrell's artless command over social tension. She allowed as how the sausage smelled really good, and then somehow not feeling the need for a tray in her room, settled herself with the rest of us at the table. Admiring Farrell's several talents, I found myself thinking he should be declared a national living treasure, like those people who sing Delta blues or weave Athabascan baskets. But I avoided actually trusting him, seconding Charlie, who had had asked me to avoid open discussion of the Grant-Worthington negotiations, especially with Farrell. "We don't know enough about these locals to know what they can do with a little information."

On our way to the barn I said nothing to Isabel about her snit in the kitchen, which was a good thing, because the cause of it was already feeding Darwin. Josh would spend as much time near Isabel as he was allowed, and he would push his luck. "What would you say," he asked her, "if I said I'd like to crew for you at the Tevis?"

"I'd say no," she said flatly. "That's Frankie's job. She's done her homework and paid her way out here."

"But she has two horses to look after, and some of the guys who win this ride have a crew person for every leg of the horse."

I thought this was a point worth considering, but Isabel said, "I won't need that. I have Frankie."

Isabel was right about Frankie. In any competition, she was an asset, although in some instances this friend of mine who adored prizefighting and couldn't resist an opportunity to smash the tennis ball just behind you on your left when she saw you start right, needed to be a managed asset. She enjoyed roaring along back roads in Isabel's truck, passing other crew trucks on the way to the next hold. At our first distance ride, held near the Chesapeake, Frankie missed her turn, which had been very clearly described in the crew directions. This was probably because she was driving too fast to notice the intersection, and of course she responded to the problem by backtracking at an even higher rate of speed. Even so, she was too late at the hold to help Isabel and me with the horses as we rode up to it. We looked around for her and for Isabel's truck in the crew area jammed with vehicles, and we were stripping the tack off the horses when Isabel's truck pulled in. Pitching back and forth behind the wheel, she suddenly slammed on the brakes. Another truck, carrying crew for one of the front-runners, was backing out of the precious space. As its front bumper began to emerge, Frankie shot in at a dangerous angle, Isabel's truck cutting off the departing truck's exit.

Isabel gasped, and when Frankie, all business and weighed down by buckets and hay nets, hustled over to the horses, she said, "You can't do that."

"Do what? And why not?" Frankie was already sponging Darwin, trying to keep the water from running down her arm.

"You cut those people off!"

"What people?"

"That was very rude," Isabel admonished her. "Very unsportsmanlike. We can't afford to alienate other competitors."

"I thought this was about getting the horses through as fast as we can. I was not aware," Frankie said stiffly, "that this was an exercise in diplomacy."

But she tempered her enthusiasm, and at a race up and down the Blue Ridge in Virginia, she meekly accepted the only remaining parking space in the crew area. She could afford to be meek because it was an extremely large space and it was next to a creek. The reason it had been left vacant immediately became obvious. There was a bear on the other side of the creek and a cub playing in the water. Frankie did not move the truck. She did not retreat. "Prime real estate," she crowed when we rode in, "even if the neighbors are a little weird."

Frankie would leave nothing to chance, and now the thought of other riders and horses and, especially, crews gathering had Frankie in a state of high excitement. She took Isabel's truck to a mechanic Farrell recommended for a going-over. "You've driven this vehicle nearly three thousand miles hauling a couple of tons," she pointed out to us. "What's not to go wrong?" Good point, and I knew she would get her way, even about new tires for the rear dual axle. I may have expected this from Frankie, but Isabel was caught off guard.

"I can't afford that!" she protested. "Those tires are worth more than either of the horses."

"Do you want water at Chicken Hawk or not?" Frankie made this a threat. "Okay, never mind. I'll pay for the tires myself."

"You will not!" I said, but I never did find out who actually took care of the bill.

When Frankie dropped off the truck at the garage, Farrell picked her up, and she coaxed him into driving his rattletrap down to the fairgrounds at Auburn so that she could check out the competition. She brought back two important findings: The other riders had crews with at least two people and at least two trucks. "We're going to be outmanned and underpowered."

"When Josh comes over today," I suggested to Isabel, "tell him you changed your mind."

"Right," Frankie chimed in. "We'll rent another truck."

Isabel shook her head.

"Why not?"

"He's doing crisis management at the Institute."

"Well, crewing is a more fun kind of crisis management," Frankie contended.

"Nope. Won't work."

"Think about it, Isabel." I encouraged her because if Josh went to the ride with us he could not be working under orders from anyone at the Institute. And because having him as crew, I would have some moments during the holds to tease out more information about Grant-Worthington from him. "What's Frankie going to do if you and I get separated on the trail?" This was an easily imagined scenario; in fact, it was almost predictable. As long as Owen could see a horse in front of him—any horse—he would pull out to pass and strive to make sure the next thing that horse saw was his own silvery tail. When riding with only Isabel and Darwin I had been able to persuade Owen to be more moderate, and while I expected him to be more easily rated than during his first endurance event, when he surged and lunged against me for the first twenty-five of its fifty miles, I would have advised even Charlie not to bet on it.

"You have him around you all the time anyway." Frankie pointed out. "Why not let him help and give yourself that advantage?"

"I have to be free to ride the ride." Isabel's tone was a little too imperious. "I can't be tied that tightly to Josh."

"Oh, I get it." Frankie heaved a fake sigh. "You are afraid the heat of competition will turn Isabel Rakow into a bitch."

Isabel didn't respond to this. She said, "Okay then, if you want him to help, give him to Tink. I'm not giving you up, Frankie."

I wasn't surprised by this. I had come to understand that Isabel, who had scrambled up from the fate of her working-class roots, had accepted Darwin's ideas about species and their persistence as an explanation for her own success. Like money, competition, and fitness talk—and the Tevis Cup was pretty important to her. Although her competitive streak usually ran well below the surface, it was rising up in plain view.

"Do you remember that race in New Jersey?" I teased her. "I think it was my first one. You and Darwin stayed behind me and Owen the whole time, even at the finish."

"I was on my good behavior," she admitted. "I wanted to give you a chance to top-ten. I thought that might encourage you to keep riding Owen because, you know, I need a backup horse. But don't expect me to be that nice next weekend."

I didn't. Truth to tell, I wasn't planning to be so terribly gracious myself, and this was one reason why I agreed with Frankie about the need for more crew. The other reason was that I wanted to keep an eye on Josh.

At dinner that evening, Josh accepted my invitation to crew with characteristic unstoppability. "We will win, Tink. We will win!" He was the only person at the table who seemed to think that.

"To finish is to win, right? So all I have to do is finish." I said.

"Okay, let's talk about finishing," Frankie proposed. "This is just a horse race, fastest horse over the distance. But it is not a *simple* horse race. Because there are mandatory rest periods— the holds—built in to protect the horse. So maybe the first way to have the fastest horse is to just go fast on the trail. But the second way to have the fastest horse is to get through the holds in the least time. The time in the hold is the same for every rider. *But* in order to get *into* the hold, the horses have to pass the vet check—you know, where they take pulse and respiration rates and watch the horses trot. Pulse rate is the key here. It has to fall at or below a certain rate—at the holds on the trail it's usually somewhere around sixty beats a minute, but at the finish it's even lower."

Frankie was warming up. Farrell passed the wine bottle in her direction and waited to clear the table until she had finished.

"The longer it takes for the horse's pulse to come down, the more time it takes to get the horse into the hold and the more minutes added to the horse's overall time. Our job will be to help the horses breeze through the vet check and get into the hold as efficiently as possible. Then we can look after Tink and Isabel and make sure the horse is comfortable and can really rest."

Josh nodded. "Doesn't sound all that difficult."

"Well, not when you're just talking about it," Farrell corrected him. "But let me tell you, it is hard work. For one thing, you've got to get yourself and a boatload of gear down into the holds—and in these mountains, with the canyons and crummy roads, that can get tricky—*and* to do the most for the horse, you have to beat the rest of the crews into the hold so you can get the best spot to rest the horse. You know, the most shade, the easiest footing. After all that, you're hauling water to cool down the horse. Mucho buckets. It's the great American horse wash."

"We will be the first crew into the holds," Frankie assured him. "But that doesn't mean we can win."

Exactly. That would be up to the horse and me. Although I wouldn't admit it, my competition nerves were tuning up. These nerves just gave off a mild tingling now, but as I waited for the announcement that the trail was open, they would get tighter and tighter until, by the time I mounted up to walk toward the starting line, I would hardly recognize the people around me, Josh included. As soon as I was out on the trail, he would have his work cut out for him. That would test his loyalty.

Charlie and Stephen didn't have long to wait now either. The next afternoon, Thursday, they would drive down to San Francisco to fetch Henny Kravitz at the airport for their Friday morning meeting. At the table I noticed that Stephen had again dropped into a deep quiet, and I assumed that sitting on his hands while the AccuGen deal hung fire was getting him down. I also assumed that because I'd found him talking to Alex on the phone in Farrell's hall several times over the last couple of days, he was finding some comfort in that— that and Farrell's drinks. Before dinner I noticed he left a bottle of beer on the counter and headed in to the scotch. Now I wondered how much of that he had put down and if he was in his cups.

Charlie rounded up people for poker. We played for pennies, and I gave the game my best. But after I had to fold for the fourth time, I made my excuses and went to the barn. When I flipped the switch to turn on the dim lights over the horses, I saw that Stephen was following me into the barn. He walked very carefully, as if he was afraid of stepping on something sharp, and arrived at the door of Darwin's stall. He said nothing but stood there as if he were waiting for something to happen. This was something he used to do all the time when he was just starting high school—follow me to some horse chore with apparently nothing on his mind. But this hadn't happened for years. I was on my way to the spigot to top off the water buckets.

"Looking for work?" I joked.

"Sure," he agreed. "Got some?" Then he fell silent again.

"Stephen? Are you drunk?"

"Undoubtedly."

I took hold of a hay bale by its wires and slid it next to him. "Sit down."

He followed orders, and I opened another bale, passed out packets of hay, and moved to the other night chores. I was baffled and worried. None of this—the drinking or the self-absorption—was like Stephen. Sure, he had always been a quiet person and prone to preoccupation. But his preoccupation was a cheerful contemplation of things like radio frequencies and natural numbers and ions. "I'm not absentminded," he always explained about himself. "I'm present-minded someplace else." Tonight, though, it seemed to me that someplace else was decidedly inward.

Much as I wanted, needed, to find out what the problem was, it didn't seem right to ask him when he was inebriated and might say more than he wanted to. So I didn't push. When I had finished with the horses, I tapped him on the shoulder and indicated the light switch. He stood and reached over to send the barn into darkness.

"Big glass of water," I suggested about his condition, "and a peanut butter and jelly sandwich."

"Yeah," he said carelessly, "peanut butter."

I said nothing to Charlie about Stephen. Ordinarily, I would have been only too happy to raise the alarm and stir everyone into activity. But the situation wouldn't yield to that. Stephen's trouble was something personal, and I had no idea what kind of action should be called for. Besides, it was possible that the situation would soon resolve itself. The next afternoon the two of them would drive down to San Francisco to be in place for Friday's meeting, where real crisis management would be called for.

In the morning, Stephen appeared for breakfast in much the same mood as the night before. He poked at Farrell's fluffies, the lightest scrambled eggs I've ever been offered, and endured the conversation—as close to mean as I'd ever seen my sweet-natured stepson. He trailed out to the barn after Frankie had started laying out gear to take to ride camp—buckets, hay nets, pitchforks, coolers—according to the lists she'd made, and I had almost finished the chores. He watched murderously as Josh pulled up and opened the car door for Isabel.

"Real date, maybe?"

"Who knows?" I said. "How do you feel, hon?"

"Big head—and I feel stupid." He glanced across the barnyard, maybe to verify that Frankie was still at a safe distance. "Ma?" This was the way he often started a conversation. "Alex is pregnant."

I couldn't believe my luck. After all the years I'd spent mourning my barrenness, grieving over my inability to conceive, this was exhilarating news. "How wonderful!"

"Is it?" he asked solemnly.

"Of course. It's fabulous! What? Do you think I should be worried about this for some reason?"

"I am," he told me.

My head was so filled with baby, small and warm and close, that I hardly registered his discomfort. "I hope you didn't tell her that."

"Well . . ."

Evidently in one way or another, he had told her that. "But you've probably hurt her. My God, Stephen, what were you— what are you—thinking?"

He was looking down through the inadequate barn light as if he was trying to find something on the dirt floor.

"I didn't expect this, Ma."

"The baby?"

"The way you would react."

"How can I react any other way?" He still had a lot to learn about me, about women in general. My mind was flitting off to plump little fists, onesies, a mobile to hang over the crib.

"I don't know how I can pull this off."

"You already have." I was vehement because I was a little shocked by his gloom. "You are blessed, Stephen. You and Alex."

"And trapped. I didn't want it to happen like this. I wanted things to be better. I mean, the best they could be. That's what I told her."

I couldn't understand his difficulty.

"I wanted to be really settled and happy."

"Happy? What does that mean?" I asked impatiently. "And how are you going to know when you are that?" Then I thought I saw the problem. "Oh. Because of me, the way I was?"

He shook his head and smiled a little.

"Elledge?" I guessed next. "Your father?"

He shrugged, acknowledging this might be the case. "He was so fucked-up—and every time he did something to try to make himself feel better, he got more fucked-up."

Suddenly after all the years that had passed since my marriage to Elledge, I realized that he had made Stephen as miserable as he had made me—all the time promising affection and a thousand laughs in the days ahead—and it was misery that had driven the little boy to me when he could have left the house with his father.

I don't think I would have repeated my mistake of marrying Elledge if it hadn't been for Stephen. He was three years old. Everything about him seemed bright; his green eyes, his fascination with light switches and fans, and his interest in putting back together things that had come apart. Another powerful incentive was that for all practical purposes, he was motherless. I was childless and desperate about that. He had the same knack as his father for convincing me that I had a special place in his world—except that he was honest about it.

As I reviewed my stepson's history with me, I could remember times when he had as much as told me about the hurt and I hadn't really registered it. High school wrestling, for instance. I had always given Stephen his head, let him try things to find out what he was good at and what he could leave to somebody else. He had the run of the farm, the machines on it, and the workshop that had been my father's. So when he was a sophomore in high school and wanted to try out for the wrestling team, I relied on my usual principle. "Sure, hon, go out for wrestling."

The matches, however, were torture for me. The boys lunged at each other, grappled, strangled, and twisted each other while parents in the stands were shouting, booing, egging the boys on to further violence. They may not have cared about their sons' necks or spines, but I cared about Stephen's. When his neck and spine had survived another match, I would leave the gym in a state of relief. Perspiration dripped down my back and into my bra. I was frightened for Stephen in a way I had never been frightened for myself. I wanted him to drop off the team, but I was determined not to say anything negative about his wrestling or wrestling in general.

What I said was, "You're doing so well in wrestling, Stephen, why don't you go out for basketball?"

"Because I like wrestling. I don't like basketball."

"You know," I pointed out, "girls really go for basketball players."

"I like wrestling."

"Oh, okay. What is it about the sport that you like?"

"You can learn how to get the other guy down and hold him down. You get to control him so he can't hurt you."

Evidently Stephen was still wrestling his father to the ground, still trying to get the old man in a headlock.

"I guess we worked it out," I suggested now about the ways I had tried to raise him and the ways he'd tried to grow up without Elledge.

"He's still fucked-up."

"But you are not," I argued.

"I could get there," he said speculatively.

I was irritated by his self-pity. "Don't wallow."

"No, Ma. I'm not." But he was quite sorry for himself.

"Pony up, Stephen!"

He started. I believe this was the harshest thing I had ever said to him. I said it because I was thinking about a baby on the way and the place he could make for a child. And, of course, the place I would make for his baby. "Pony up and make things better for this baby than they were for you—and better for Alex. When you and Charlie get to San Francisco I want you to buy something very pretty for her. And I want you to call her and tell her you're bringing something—I mean, she could be vomiting her guts up right now—do you hear me?"

"I already called her."

"Last night? When you were drunk? What did you say?"

"I'm not telling you that," he said, and he was quite right to say it.

Stephen would have to learn how to get his father's monkey off his back. I knew that wouldn't be easy, because in some low moments, Elledge came back to me with the full delirium—the promises, delights, and betrayals of our time together. That must have done some real damage to a very young boy. I know I shared some blame for my part in keeping the roller coaster running, but it wasn't likely Stephen would admit that.

Not an hour later, when I was helping Frankie pull equipment out of Isabel's truck and trailer, Stephen came out of the ranch house carrying his laptop. There was now a second truck in the drive, which Frankie had rented for Josh. We would inventory the equipment and restow it in the two trucks and the trailer. Stephen appraised the rented truck.

"Wow, very nice. I wonder what the daily rate on that thing is."

"We're not talking loudly about that," Frankie admitted. "But it's only for a few days, just for the race."

Stephen nodded. "Did you get a second set of keys? I mean anything where Ma is involved—"

"Done," Frankie assured him. "Both trucks."

I wasn't offended by his concern. He had been looking after me about car keys since he was seven. "Where are you headed, Stephen?"

"Do you have time to take a ride into Truckee? Farrell's signal is too crappy."

"Farrell's signal?"

"My assignment." He patted the laptop bag to remind me. "Like to get it done before Charlie and I leave for San Francisco."

Charles McCarran, Laidlaw's first victim. I had asked Stephen to help me find out more about him. Now I was torn. Of course I wanted to go with him. I might find out what, if anything, connected McCarran to Laidlaw and the Institute. Furthermore, his invitation was a gesture of solidarity, an indication that things between us would stay the same in spite of my criticism. But Frankie had at least a full day's work ahead of her getting ready for us to ship the horses out the next day.

"Oh, boy, Stephen. I probably better—"

"Go," Frankie commanded. "Right now you're just getting in my way. Josh will be here before long. Let us sort out all this stuff. Then when we figure out what goes where, you can be the gofer."

I sat in the passenger's seat. This arrangement had been customary since the time when Stephen was a teenager learning to drive. In those days, I wanted to allow him to gain confidence on his own, and I had to discipline myself not to grab the armrest or draw a sharp breath or even brace my feet in front of me. Now my passenger status was a luxury. I watched the mountainsides and the vacation homes glide past and, out of the corner of my eye, observed my stepson. He didn't usually talk much, but this morning his quiet was a sunken mood. Even more telling was the fact that he hadn't bothered to wash his hair. It occurred to me that he might feel happier if Alex were out here with him. But I didn't ask about this.

Stephen had in mind a coffee shop in Truckee where he had seen a sign in the window announcing Wi-Fi. The place wasn't crowded, and Stephen looked around to determine the best place to light. I headed for the service counter. "I'll buy. Cream?"

"You always buy—yup, cream. Doesn't this seem crazy?"

The barista delivered the coffee in mugs, real ceramic mugs, for which I was grateful. All the way across the country I had tasted paper or Styrofoam along with my coffee, and now Farrell's coffee in real cups had thoroughly spoiled me. By the time I set the mugs on the table, the screen on Steven's laptop was brightly lit.

"What seems crazy, hon?"

"I developed one of the fastest modems available to consumers, and then I have to drive ten miles and get coffee in order to get online with a decent bandwidth." He wasn't actually smiling when he made this point, but it seemed to me that its irony was a crack in the door to better humor. I didn't bring up Alex or the baby on the way and neither did he. I sat with my mug between my hands while Stephen's thumb and forefinger tapped and slid on the trackpad.

"Okay, starting with the newspaper," he said, and I looked on.

There is nothing more stultifying and somehow agitating then watching someone else direct the activity of a computer. I knew Stephen didn't actually need me to be there, but maybe this detached form of togetherness was somehow comforting him. I waited to see what he would find.

"Nothing much new here. Wasn't McCarran from Vancouver? Let's drill down a little bit on that. . . . Okay, businessman. . . . Philanthropist. . . . Supports Christian causes."

"The Institute, Stephen," I said, connecting the dots. He had already figured that out and nodded, still clicking the trackpad.

"Laidlaw worked there, so he must have known him."

"It wasn't a random shooting," Stephen agreed.

"Can you find out where Laidlaw is from?"

"Wait a minute."—still clicking and watching the screen— "One thing at a time, Ma. I'm still on McCarran."

I sat back, devoting myself to the coffee and listening to the music piped in from the ceiling. Stephen poked at the computer for perhaps a quarter of an hour, then looked away from the screen to report his findings.

"McCarran started out in shipping. Now primarily an investor. Diversified holdings."

"Like Halefellow."

"Including," Stephen continued, "*pharmaceuticals*." He laid stress on the word, as if he were afraid I might not take note of this. It seemed important, but I certainly couldn't have said what it meant.

"Worth several billion. But low taxes because he supports a large church or religious organization. That group owns a big chunk of Vancouver real estate. Doesn't pay land taxes, of course. . . ." Stephen droned, and I tried to lock these facts into memory so that I could return to them later and perhaps make sense of them.

". . . Okay. You want to see what he looks like?" Stephen clicked into a file of images. McCarran was an elderly man, stooped but with a taste for good suits, hair evidently dyed to match its original dark shade and its few remaining strands combed over a bare pate. Given Stephen's summary bio, this was about what I would have expected.

"Who's the guy with him?"

"What guy?" Stephen was clicking through photographic images. "Oh yeah. Him. Here he is again. Fashionista, straight out of the magazines. Wouldn't you say?"

Exactly. The man who was shown alongside McCarran in so many of the photos was tall and slim and light-haired. He wore horn-rimmed glasses with a modish antique aspect and, in each photo, a tawny sport coat over a crewneck sweater in a paler shade.

"I wonder if he ever changes the outfit," I speculated. "What's his name?"

To pursue this, Stephen began clicking into the images in search of identification text. Finally he said, "Spokesman. That's the only identification. So much for news items. Now on to the obituaries. . . ."

These were both more detailed and less revealing than I had expected. McCarran was born in Alberta and graduated from McGill University. Brief list of affiliations, including mention of McCarran as founder of the megachurch, and a slightly longer list of corporate directorships. First wife died. Second marriage, to a woman named Laidlaw, ended in divorce. One child, a daughter, with first wife and with the second, a daughter and a son.

"Laidlaw. Stephen, he shot his father? Any mention of Nelson Laidlaw?"

"Not yet—" Stephen leaned more intently toward the screen.

"Oh, this is interesting. One of his obits mentions a government investigation of the church's finances. Apparently they were looking to challenge its nonprofit status."

"Hon, what about Laidlaw?"

"Hold on, Ma. Looking at the church now . . . three thousand plus members—I'm having to read lots of holy copy—looks kind of fundamentalist."

"In other words, anti-Darwin."

I was anxious to see what he could find out about Laidlaw and Celeste. The computer's path to Laidlaw led to a dead end. Its path to Celeste stopped after only a few facts. "Married to a distant Vancouver relative of Louis Agassiz Fuertes, authority on birds and natural history. Divorced eight years ago."

"She's only been at the Institute about a year."

"Too long." Stephen actually smiled at his reference to the roadblock Celeste had become. But he didn't seem to emerge from his somber mood.

When we walked out onto the sidewalk, I was awash with caffeine and a little jittery from watching the laptop screen jump hither and yon. I was anxious to get back to the horses and preparations to leave the ranch, but the ride home allowed me to try to piece together the fragments of fact that Stephen had turned up. Stephen had gone quiet, and now I was the one offering up.

"You know," I proposed, "the person who might know a little more about all this is Josh."

"He's on the Institute's payroll," Stephen warned me.

"I realize that, hon, and Charlie thinks he might be involved somehow in James's death. I'm not sure that's the case, but I certainly can't afford to trust him. I am just pointing out that he probably has more information."

"Don't go there, Ma—and why do you need to know all this?"

"Because Laidlaw shot at Isabel and me. Because someone is pulling a fast one that may prevent you and Charlie and Halefellow from buying AccuGen."

"I wouldn't go there, Ma." Stephen was standing in for Charlie in warning me away from Josh. "If you're going to work this down logically, what are the next questions you need to ask?

"Why did Celeste fire Laidlaw?" I proposed.

"Or for that matter," Stephen added, "why did she hire him in the first place?"

"Better yet," I agreed.

"Maybe it's a simultaneous equation," he suggested.

"You've lost me."

"I just mean that maybe everything that's been going on is interrelated in more than one way. You know, Grant-Worthington dies. McCarran gets shot. Laidlaw runs amok. The new will."

"Okay"—his simple definition certainly fit the situation—"it would be nice if you could solve this equation and get your deal done."

"And it would be nice if you could win your race, wouldn't it?"

"Finish, Stephen. All I need to do is finish."

When we returned to the ranch, I went immediately to brief Charlie on our findings. "I don't think we discovered much that will give you an advantage in your meeting tomorrow," I said when I found him. He was in our room packing his suitcase. "But the information on McCarran could be helpful. Turns out he wasn't an 'elderly tourist,' he was an elderly billionaire who gave lots of money to his megachurch. Also, turns out that maybe—maybe—some of that money was profit, not charity. The Canadian government was—maybe still is—looking into that. And—now this could come into play tomorrow—it seems that McCarran was probably Laidlaw's father."

Charlie turned that warm gaze of his on me a little absently. "Hate to go off and leave you to all of this. In fact, I just plain hate to go off and leave you."

"Charlie, you could charm a snake out of its skin," I accused him happily. "But I bet I am more fun than Henny Kravitz." I was trying to put my arms around him, but my mention of Halefellow's lawyer sent him to check something in his briefcase. Grant-Worthington's new will lay on top of the other papers, and he moved it to the side to dig further into his thick sheaf of notes and financial analyses. I edged in beside him to have another look at the will Celeste had furnished. When I came to the last page of it, I said, "You have that letter with you, don't you?"

"The letter of agreement?"

"Right. Could I see it?"

He located it in the middle of the sheath. I flipped immediately to the last page and the signature at the bottom of it. "We know James signed this because we watched him do it. Now"—I held the two signature pages side by side—"let's see if their notarized one matches up."

Charlie tipped his head up to focus on the handwriting in the two signatures. "Pretty close," he decided.

"Maybe not. Look at the hyphen, Charlie, and the *W*. James connected them, ran the hyphen right up into the first stroke of the *W*."

"Right," he drawled, slowing the word as he reevaluated this detail. "You're right. But I think a man wrote it."

"Why?"

"Well, because women are neater. They try to kind of package a word within the space."

I gave him an evil little smile. "That's just too sexist for words, Charlie. The only thing anyone can say about this signature is that whoever wrote it knew James very well, very well—and practiced a hell of a lot."

"So okay," Charlie accepted my thought and pushed ahead to his next conclusion, "A man who knew James very well. A man like Savage."

"Wrong," I challenged. "I'm not saying the person is not a man. I'm saying it isn't Savage."

"For a person who couldn't bear the thought of meeting this guy again," Charlie teased, "you're awfully quick to defend him."

"Well, find out for yourself then. When you go to your meeting tomorrow, show Paul the two signatures and see what his reaction is."

"I don't think so," Charlie said. "I think I'll show them to Kravitz once we get to San Francisco. He can advise us on how and when to state our doubts. But right now, let's show this to Stephen."

We gave Stephen a few moments with the two signature pages before we asked for his assessment. Something—our trip to town or maybe another conversation with Alex—seemed to have restored some of his customary brightness, and he inspected each page with wary humor. "This is like those what's-wrong-with-this-picture quiz questions. Yup, they're different, but I'll bet we'll have to find a handwriting expert to back us up."

By the time he stowed the suitcases in the car that afternoon Stephen seemed to have recovered his balance. When he came over to hug me good-bye, he said very quietly, "Charlie doesn't know about Alex, and I don't want him to right now."

"Oh?"

"Too much pressure," he explained in all seriousness. "You saw how he was when he thought something might have happened to you. He's not good with pressure."

But I had to laugh. Charlie could take that kind of pressure and come out with exactly what he had expected to receive in the first place. Maybe more than that. Although he might not admit it, Charlie enjoyed—at least in hindsight—having to think on his feet. He could negotiate, weigh and balance, propose and retract, with grace and fluidity. I watched their car pull away, wishing I could go with them and watch the deal go down. My hopes for that and now for the new Elledge-Delgado person in very small form soared.

Quite late in the afternoon, when Frankie and Josh and I had nearly finished the elaborate ritual of organizing and stowing the gear for two horses and two riders, the farrier arrived to take care of the only remaining preparation Isabel and I had left; shoeing the horses.

"Sorry to be running so late. There's a lot of them were waiting until today to get the shoes squared away."

"No problem. You're probably late enough that Farrell will offer you a drink before you go home." I was being polite about his timing when what was really on my mind was "a lot of them," the riders I would meet up with the next day at Robie Park. At home in my own sport, I would've known many of my competitors, and they would have known me. I had a reputation. In this sport, I had just two friends, Isabel and Frankie, and I had no idea who the other riders were or what they could do. In part I was curious, and in part I dreaded being surprised and humiliated. I knew I wasn't a candidate for the cup or even top ten, but I didn't want to have to pull Owen. All I had to do was finish. It was that simple, I said to the farrier.

"That's okay for a goal," he said, "but you'd be surprised the ones who come out, the ones with big names and good horses, who get pulled even before Foresthill."

What the farrier brought out of his van was not what a very traditional farrier would've kept in his—a small forge, bellows, tongs for manipulating hot iron bars—it was a couple of boxes of synthetic booties in various sizes. They were plastic shells shaped to conform to the outside walls as well as the bottom of the hoof. I had been relieved when Isabel, who had a righteous—I won't say religious—adherence to natural hoof care, had summoned this man and his high-tech horse socks. As I had complained more times than she wanted to listen to me, it is one thing to ask a horse to travel a hundred miles in a single day. But it's another to ask him to go that distance without shoes. It didn't seem fair—"For want of a nail!" I carped. Now this man with his plastic booties and his heat gun was here to mediate our differences.

He outfitted Owen all the way around, and I brought out Darwin to have his feet covered. The farrier brought out four blue plastic shells. Blue.

"You've got to be kidding! Little pictures on them the way they do in nail salons?"

He shrugged. "It's what she wants."

This was true, Isabel agreed when she and Josh returned, and she took over for me with Darwin. "Makes it easier for the timers and vets to spot him. Okay?"

Of course she had not suggested that I avail myself of this advantage.

Josh watched intently as the heat gun melted the plastic to Darwin's foot. "Tink, you're not going to expect me to put one of those back on, are you?" He was joking, but he did seem to be making an inventory of the tasks involved in crewing. "I didn't see *heat gun* on any of Frankie's lists." Later when he caught up with me in Owen's stall, he said, "Is this really okay with you, Tink? Me coming along? I don't have any experience, you know."

"How much experience does it take to throw water on a horse?" Then I realized I needed to make him feel somewhat essential. "Of course, I'm happy for whatever help you can give. But what about your time? Haven't you been neglecting the company and that Institute?"

He leaned across Owen's back to speak directly to me, his eyes a little wider in this effort. "You know what, Tink? I wasn't lying to you and Charlie the other night."

"I never thought you were, except"—now I lied and smiled to make the next part easier to take—"for maybe a lie or two of omission."

"I wasn't omitting," he said emphatically. "At least not anything I know for a fact. In PR, you don't deal with non-facts, you deal with facts—and if it's a fact that could make somebody look bad, you give it a positive spin.

"So what were you spinning, Josh?"

"Nothing. I told you and Charlie the one fact I had. Some strange things were—"

"Such as?"

"Celeste. Mainly Celeste. People I've never seen at the Institute before getting together up in the apartment. This new will—how am I going to deal with that if there's a lawsuit over it? Celeste is making things very difficult."

"What's she doing, Josh?"

He glanced quickly back over his shoulder to verify that Isabel was still at the head of her horse. "She's . . . Well, she is—" A prim Christian thought seemed to interrupt him. "Oh, come on, Tink. You know. . . ."

I made it easy for him and said, "She got you in bed with her."

"No. No, she didn't." He was flustered.

"She tried then."

"Put that in the present tense, Tink. All the time. I finally told her I had a rush-rush job with another client."

"How did that go over?" I could see why Celeste would want Josh. She was newly bereaved, and he was strapping, friendly—and—young. As I tried to imagine her attempts with Josh, I could not help but reflect that seduction is a very passive form of assertion. From my few encounters with Celeste, the seduction mode, which was meant to stir action by a man, seemed perfectly attuned to her proper, polished personality. But her personality must have made her attempts comic. Maybe pathetic.

"She said there was never any need to rush with her."

"Right," I hooted. "She's said that before!" Beyond sex, though, she must have had another goal. Was she worried about Josh's sudden and ardent attachment to Isabel, a member of the opposite camp that had competing interests in Grant-Worthington's estate? Or did he know something Celeste wanted to know—or didn't want anyone else to know?

He shook his head. "I feel bad for him, for Dr. Grant-Worthington."

"Josh, what do you have that she wants?"

9

On the way to ride camp on Friday there was a place on the state road where it dropped down so sharply that for a brief moment we could see Lake Tahoe at the foot of the mountains. The lake was stark and glittering, a cooling presence in the early heat. At this north end of the lake, the body of water was all about health and healthy recreation. At its south end, separated from us by two hours of road along the shoreline, the lake was about neon, lavish buffets, nightlife, and—overwhelmingly—gambling.

Our trucks turned onto a dirt road that led out to a long, flat ledge that stretched between Mount Pluto and Mount Watson. The road was narrow and difficult but not steep. Although it made orderly turns in its path to Robie Park, it was still very slow. I rode with Josh in the truck Frankie had rented as a second crew vehicle, sticking close to him because of Charlie's and my shared suspicions about his involvement with the Institute. It wouldn't be hard to keep an eye on him, but I was finding it a little difficult to distrust this person. He was brash but sincere, a good-looking but unselfconscious person, and he was flat out infatuated with Isabel, who probably needed something like that to warm her up. Nevertheless, against my native impulses, I kept my mouth shut—not a word about AccuGen or Celeste Fuertes, Paul Savage, or the problematic will.

We lurched in slow motion over the twin track just behind the horse trailer drawn by Isabel's truck. In front of us, the trailer pitched and wallowed slowly, and I fretted about Owen and Darwin, imagining them bracing their legs like commuters on the subway—except they had no straps to catch themselves. "I hope those two horses still have all their teeth when we get them off the trailer."

"Never heard of horses losing teeth getting to the Tevis," Josh said quite cheerfully. He was happy about everything that morning and excited, like a kid bursting out into the playground at recess. "This is like a vacation, isn't it?"

"You're not riding," I pointed out, although in truth I was looking forward to that challenge. He just laughed. He was off duty and for the time being free of obligation to the Institute.

It took us a half hour to travel the three miles to Robie Park, and when we arrived, I was surprised to see how many other trucks and trailers had managed to get over the impossible road and how many tents crowded the trade fair. This remote site was a place that came alive just once a year, a kind of stomping grounds for the horses and riders, their crews, and the squads of volunteers. It was named after Wendell T. Robie, who pioneered the trail that the Tevis ride used and who rode the first Lake Tahoe to Auburn trail ride in 1955. It was called the Western States Trail Ride, which is still the official name of the Tevis. Robie and four friends finished the ride in twenty-two hours and forty-five minutes, just an hour and fifteen minutes inside today's twenty-four-hour maximum limit for the ride. It was a gust of postwar bravado, a campaign in which there was nothing to be fought except the terrain. Robie was a wealthy man who had started in the lumber business in Auburn, become president of a savings and loan, and invested early and successfully in ski resorts. He was a figment of Old West imagination, an autocrat cut from John Wayne cloth. He kept two guns in his office at the bank and his secretary happy on the side. I probably couldn't have stayed in the same room with Wendell T. Robie for more than five minutes, but all of what would have rubbed me the wrong way went hand in hand with his attachment to the Sierra's high country. He left the trail association the money to buy the land for the ride camp, which was a grove of big sequoias with truck paths worn through in loops and squiggles around bare patches of forest floor. Horse trailers were tucked snugly into these openings and set at angles to maximize shade. It was only about ten in the morning. But the sun shone intensely through the branches of the conifers, and even in their shadow cover, the heat was strong.

At the first intersection of truck paths, Isabel stopped the truck and trailer and walked into the encampment to scout a good space to set up camp. Josh turned off our engine, set the emergency brake, and trotted off in pursuit. I wouldn't have tolerated Charlie behaving like such a puppy dog, but Isabel didn't seem to either notice or mind. They returned together to restart the trucks, and our brief caravan advanced at a crawl to the site they had chosen.

We had a couple of hours to settle in before a big squad of veterinarians would open the process known as vetting in, the individual examination of the horses entered in the race. That would be when we would get a good look at the riders and horses who would race the trail with us. We brought the horses out of the trailer and set up a portable electric corral on one side of it and an awning and camp chairs on the other side.

Owen looked out from the little corral at the village of trucks and trailers in apparent satisfaction and turned to his flakes of hay. Darwin had zeroed in on the hay immediately and wasn't interested in looking up from that—for him this was just another day at the office. The four of us humans were behaving much like him, hunkering in our camp chairs over a cooler Frankie and Farrell had stocked with breakfast.

The canvas wing of Josh's camp chair was snug against the wing of Isabel's. With a mention of *competition*, he had drawn her into a quietly intense conversation, barely audible to us, about natural selection.

Isabel took the bait and said, her voice low to avoid our attention, "Well, even though it's about competition at the individual level, because we now know about genes, we know that *survival of the fittest* also refers to breeding fitness. You know, the ability to reproduce and have your offspring reproduce successfully." But even at that volume, her voice had the penetrating edge of a child's, and we were listening.

Finishing a bite of yogurt and drawing the spoon extravagantly out of her mouth, Frankie said, "Okay, Isabel, so what are you doing to forward that cause?"

Isabel's face colored, but she said lightly, "The cause of reproductive fitness? That's where female choice comes in. Even Darwin knew that animals pairing off as mates isn't all determined by males sparring over females."

"He recognized that females have a lot of influence," Josh put in. "Look at any woman you know. Or look at just the three women right here."

I found this disarming and laughed. "I've made plenty of choices, and I'm still not reproductively fit."

"Right," Frankie concurred. "Plenty of choices but never entered the competition. Neither has Isabel."

"But Isabel still has time," I pointed out.

"*If* I choose." She was teasing, but it wasn't clear who she was teasing.

"Talking about sexual selection and competition"—Josh waved a hand at all the horses in camp now grinding hay between their teeth and soon to be in a grueling competition against each other—"why are there so many geldings, so many eunuchs, in this race?"

"Because," Isabel explained in her thin, childish voice, "pair formation is very distracting."

"And"—I had been thinking off and on all day of Charlie—"the longer you're paired, the more distracting it gets."

The day was getting under way in no great hurry, and this was reflected in the way people in camp moved among the trailers and in and out of the vendors' tents off to one side of the encampment. It was an anything goes crowd—full cowboy silver-buckle regalia, running shorts and tank tops, fatigues and sombreros, breeches paired with sneakers, T-shirts that announced CAN'T REMEMBER EVERYTHING WOMAN and YOU CAN REST WHEN YOU DIE. Whatever it took to make your statement and keep you comfortable. Isabel, who had studied up on the race entries, made a number of forays out along the truck paths to take attendance, identify the horses and riders she had read about. I never attempted to judge a horse until it was in motion. I didn't see how you could tell much about a horse standing idly beside a trailer and figured I would see them all soon enough.

It was warm and peaceful. The only sounds were those of the occasional rig passing slowly on the truck path and every so often the whinny of a horse seeking a friend. I found it hard to believe that in less than twenty-four hours I would be undertaking the longest, toughest ride I had ever contested. The competition nerves I had come to expect were strangely quiet, as if someone had disconnected them from their source. Maybe this was because I didn't know enough about what to expect in the race the next day to worry about it. And maybe it was because my thoughts were so divided between Charlie and Stephen and this race I had entered that the two preoccupations neutralized each other.

The run-up would be slow. The veterinary examinations, the afternoon briefings for riders and crews, then dinner and early to bed. Josh wouldn't stay the night at the ride camp. He would head down to a chain hotel on the outskirts of Auburn to be within easy distance of Robinson Flat, the first hold where the crews had access to the horses and riders. He said he would wait to leave camp that day until the vetting was over, the horses had their numbers, and he had sat in on the briefing for crew members. That was his plan, but the day wouldn't go exactly according to it.

Shortly before noon, people in Day-Glo orange began to move toward the biggest open area at the campgrounds. These were the veterinarians and their scribes, and they gathered in a small spot of shade under a single tall tree. Eventually there would be more than thirty-five orange-vested people in the middle of the enclosure, seventeen or eighteen vets and as many assistants. It would be an honor to present a horse to this highly skilled audience, and with Josh's help, I brushed and sponged Owen until all the travel smudges had vanished from his gray coat, his mane and tail had returned to silver, and he looked ready for the show ring. Isabel scoffed, "Owen is going to stand out like a sore thumb in this crowd."

I knew she was right because I'd seen the turnout of the other horses at my qualifying rides. In this sport presentation of the horse is about heart rate, respiration, muscle tone, and hydration—the horse was a machine that needed to be primed, oiled, and fueled to cover the distance. But I enjoyed the rituals of grooming and would have felt I was neglecting Owen if I hadn't turned him out the way I would one of my event horses at home. Josh waited with Owen and me alongside Darwin and Isabel in the queue outside the vetting area. The veterinarians spaced themselves across the clearing, each one becoming a station, and the process of vetting in proceeded like the security lines at an airport. Each rider and horse that entered the area approached any vet who was available.

At this point the horses trotting out and being handled by the vets turned into competitors I could assess. One of the first riders to present a horse was a tall, gangly kid, about fifteen, with curly red hair, and the horse he led in was also a redhead, a bright red chestnut. Because of the kid's age I discounted his chances and took up a more serious appraisal of the gray mare the woman coming along behind him had in hand. This turned out to be a misjudgment, because Isabel advised me later that the woman was the kid's mother and, as the required chaperone of a young rider, was just along for the ride. The two of them would finish, or maybe not finish, together.

At the other end of the vetting area the vets were evaluating a mule. The man at his head was a tall, white-haired guy with drooping mustaches that somehow hooked up with his bushy sideburns. He wore an enormous beat-up sombrero, and the angle of the brim tipped in old-fashioned courtesy to the vet and her assistant. I was feeling a little sorry for this old man and his sorry, long-eared mount, when Isabel leaned toward me and said, "Keep an eye on that guy. Skinner Flemington—he's finished this race more often than anyone here."

"On *that*?"

"Not on this particular mule. She's new this year." Isabel had had a not-too-brief interview with him on one of her forays through the camp. "Give him a chance, and he'll tell you all about it."

Three skinny, hard-muscled guys in running shorts brought out three Arabians in red, copper, and chocolate shades of chestnut and the same highly tuned physical condition. "Semipros," Isabel informed me as if that term were pejorative. But they were to endurance what I had always been to eventing, and I didn't see any need to be condescending about that. Anyone who wants to excel in a horse sport needs to expend enormous amounts of time to be able to do that, and unless you have some independent income like I do, it's hard to train and make a living too. The three geldings displayed the benefits of rigorous training, and their riders, standing in direct sunshine, were hardly perspiring. I, standing in conifer shade, could not make the same claim.

I was fairly confident Isabel would finish in the top ten with Darwin, and I was trying to pick out nine other horses that looked likely for those positions. This was an apples and oranges proposition, not because the two hundred horses entered were so difficult to compare, but because the riders were. There were flyweight young women and burly men with beer bellies—the load the horse had to carry certainly ought to make a difference. Although Isabel had pointed out to me heavy riders who had finished well in previous years, I would still have given the best chances to the flyweights and the three guys in running shorts.

The three chestnut horses these men presented had caught my eye, and for purposes of my race strategy, I made a note to chat with the men when an opportunity presented itself. It was clear to see that they themselves could go the hundred miles, and I wanted to find out more about their horses.

I was totally absorbed in my odds making until Josh startled me with a question. "Is it too soon to be hearing from Charlie and Stephen?"

"Probably. And we'd need a landline." His question indicated that he hadn't been completely on vacation and free of cares about Grant-Worthington's enterprises. That was on both of our minds, and I wondered why it was on his.

Isabel presented Darwin to one of the vets, and I led Owen to the next one available. Both exams proceeded without much comment from the vets, and the horses trotted out fresh, happy, and sound. Darwin and Owen emerged from the vetting area with the numbers 106 and 107 declared in waxy orange livestock marker on their hindquarters.

Isabel and I moseyed with Josh and Frankie past the vendors' tents on our way to the pavilion where the briefings were scheduled. Frankie had insisted that for ideal rider-crew synchronization the next day, we should all attend the briefings for crews and riders. The merchants' tents were offering shade, along with riding tights, lightweight saddles, magnetic therapy systems for horse muscles, electrolytes, and stacks of T-shirts and fleece pullovers. At a concession offering very expensive bras for riding, the three of us women lingered. Josh was eyeing something two tents beyond us and abruptly turned and departed—but in quite the opposite direction of what he had been watching.

"What's with him?" I wondered, and Isabel said, "Maybe all these bras made him uncomfortable. We should move along."

We didn't see Josh again until a little crowd gathered for the first briefing and he set up his camp chair between Isabel's and mine.

"Where did you go? Did our shopping embarrass you?"

"No, oh no," he objected. But he looked a little distracted, and as the rest of the crew people gathered, he occasionally looked around, glancing behind him.

The three superfit men who would ride the chestnuts joined the group and took seats at a picnic table. I wandered over to introduce myself. The men were Ben, Donald, and Tor, and they trained their horses and themselves in the Colorado high country. They answered my questions about the horses matter-of-factly, without boasting, and Donald joked, "Taking the measure of the good ones, I see. I don't imagine you would have trucked that gray horse across the continent if he weren't pretty good."

"You know, I'm pretty green at endurance," I told him, "and I honestly don't know how good he is."

"Tomorrow will tell, won't it?"

A ride official began issuing crew instructions involving holds, vehicle access, water and refreshments for riders, and it gradually became clear to me that there were only a few places along the Tevis trail where Frankie and Josh could meet Isabel and me. That, combined with Owen's determination to pass every horse in the field and stay in the lead, meant that for most of the next day I would be out of contact. I would be alone and out of reach of not only Frankie and Josh but also of Charlie and Stephen, who would have returned with news, good or bad, from San Francisco.

"Josh, is there any way—"

He was staring at someone a few camp chairs behind us. He let his breath escape in a kind of sigh.

"Something wrong?" I whispered.

He shook his head. "No. It's okay. I thought that woman back there was her."

"Who?"

"Celeste. But it's not. Just someone who looks a little like her."

When we stood up to stretch our legs between briefings, I said, "Could you point her out?"

She was a tall woman whose dark hair was streaked with shades of blond and auburn, and she had tough-looking, heavily tanned skin and hazel eyes. She wore jeans and had a small notebook open on her knee. She could possibly have been a rider or a crew member. But somehow her clothes and her attention to her hair, face, and nails made her stand out a little from the rest of this crowd. It was hard to imagine her hauling a bucket of water—but then it was also hard to imagine Celeste, whom she did resemble, doing that.

"What's her name, Josh?"

Maybe he didn't know, because he didn't respond.

During the question-and-answer period the woman stood to be recognized and said, "Do you have any news about the fugitive, the gunman? And is there any concern that he may be somewhere near the ride trail?"

As is customary, the official briefing us was an old hand who had finished the race a number of times and knew the trail conditions. He was forthright.

"No more news than what's on the TV. Our assessment of the situation is that it's been too long, too many days, since he ran down into the Divide, and assuming he's had no outside help, he's not likely to be in any condition to hurt someone."

She looked around at the gathering and asked, "Has anyone here seen him or heard anything?"

When her question brought silence, the official closed the topic. "You know, ma'am, if you're still concerned about this tomorrow, I'd suggest you just ride a little faster."

Josh turned away from the questioner and resettled himself in the chair. His mood had gone way downhill. Something was working on him, and on the way back to our horse camp, I tried to draw him out.

"Are you on leave from the Institute, Josh?"

"No," he said and folded his ride map and starting instructions together so that they fit in his shirt pocket. "I'm a consultant. I work on my own time. It's true that the biggest chunk of my time goes to AccuGen and the Institute, but I do have other clients. And like I said, Celeste thinks one of them has a project on a crash schedule."

"So it wouldn't be good if she knew you were taking time off to hang out with us."

He shrugged, but I could see that possibility was worrisome.

"Does Celeste know about Isabel?"

He didn't answer this, and I said, "Are you afraid of Celeste, Josh?"

"Tink," he was clearly annoyed. "It's already clear that you and Charlie don't trust me. Why are you giving me the third degree when you're not going to take anything I say for what it is?"

He had figured Charlie and me correctly. But his irritation didn't stop me. I said, "Because I'm a friend of Isabel's."

How could he argue with that? He looked ahead to our horse camp, where Isabel was tending to Darwin and Frankie was toting a folding cot to the trailer's horse compartment— that was where I would bunk. Josh and I stood on the edge of the dusty truck path a while longer. He seemed to want to join the others but also to stay.

"Okay, Tink," he said reluctantly. "I'm not afraid of her, but she is worrying me. I know a lot more about AccuGen and the work that is going on there than she does, and I knew Dr. Grant-Worthington a lot longer than she did. Maybe she's jealous. Maybe now that she's gone out on a limb with this new will, she's afraid I'll come up with something to call it into question."

"Do you think the will is the real thing?"

He made a face like he had tasted something bad. "How could it be? Dr. Grant-Worthington was too savvy—I mean too wise—to be involved in something like that. When she pulled that document out of the drawer, you could have knocked me down with a feather."

We moved a little farther along the truck path toward our trailer. "So, Josh. What is the work at AccuGen? I mean right now, what is going on in the lab?"

"It's a protein, a new protein."

"Right," I came back impatiently. "What does it *do*?"

He looked at me cautiously. "Charlie hasn't told you?"

"Look,"—I had to explain this—"Charlie is my closest friend, my big squeeze, my darling. But he doesn't tell me every little thing about his business—and there are probably good reasons for that." I wouldn't burden Josh with a history of Charlie's and my struggles over this issue. To put a positive spin on it, I'm not the best person with money or business, except horse business, and this has given Charlie more than one scare. If Josh had pressed me, I would have admitted that before Charlie's time, there were instances when I was irresponsible and maybe downright dangerous with money. But seeing as how Josh wasn't pressing me, I would press him instead. "Is there anything special about this protein?"

"It's the way it is folded." He was stalling. I knew because Stephen had explained that the way a protein is folded characterizes how it works in a living organism, its therapeutic capabilities.

"They're *all* folded, Josh."

He deliberated, probably hesitant to compromise his position with Charlie, Stephen, and the buyout, then said, "This one could be a cure for addicts. We're not certain of that yet, but it's got as far as second-stage drug trials. It's for cocaine addicts, and the way it works is to block the effects of cocaine. So a guy could take all the coke he wanted and not get high."

"So it's for the public good?"

"Not just that, Tink. Think about all the residential rehab places across the country, all the beds filled by addicts trying to get clean. This protein could make a lot of those beds go empty."

I marveled at Grant-Worthington's ingenuity. "Sounds fabulous, Josh. Massive income."

He started purposefully into our horse camp, toward the chair next to the one Isabel had taken. "It's still a big *if*, Tink."

I was grateful for the information. The fact that Josh had offered it made me come close to trusting him. And then also, it raised the delightful possibility that my husband and stepson could make what Charlie called serious money and what the press called vast wealth. I found a beer in the cooler and sat on the step that folded down from the trailer's living quarters, thinking hazily about this prospect. I am a horse person, and there is no limit on the amount of money a horse person considers essential. That is, until a horse person's husband draws her close and says, "Is this really necessary?"

The horses, and we ourselves, were now at rest. The sun dropped lower and sent a more diffuse light through the big sequoias. We talked quietly about the trail we now knew better and about the competition, the horses we thought might be fitter than Darwin and Owen, and the riders who might push faster through the tougher, tighter sections, the passages with scary drop-offs—the three stringy fitness types in their running shorts, the kid with the curly red hair, the tiny woman with the big-boned bay mare, and the white-haired old guy with the sombrero. And there were probably sleepers we hadn't noticed. Any one of those many nondescript grays could slip up suddenly behind us out on the trail and any of their riders could ask to overtake.

"Overtaking is what Owen and I intend to do," I pointed out.

Josh was still there beside Isabel and showed no inclination to leave for Auburn. Frankie said, "Don't you want to get back to the state road before it gets dark?"

"That truck has headlights." He would be two hours getting down to Auburn, but that didn't seem to worry him. For some reason, he had his eye on the traffic through the park. "I thought I might stay for the barbecue."

Which was something, along with its cash bar, Frankie was looking forward to. "Suit yourself," she said.

"I think he should," Isabel declared in a sharp little whine, and I noticed that as we migrated toward the caterer's tables, she was letting Josh hold her hand. Isabel, I decided, was losing it. Maybe that was a good thing—if Josh turned out to be who he pretended to be.

Not far behind us in the line for dinner was the woman Josh had thought was Celeste. She seemed to be on her own in the camp, something nobody else was. If Josh was aware of her presence he didn't show it, and after the barbecue he lingered, helping with the horses.

"Josh, you should head out," Frankie ordered. "We really don't need you here." She was slipping into role as crew captain.

"I suppose." He had a couple of buckets in hand, and I followed him to the water truck with a couple of my own. I was less giddy now, thinking about the prospects for AccuGen and about the Institute's ex-employee still at large. Water from the huge tank on the truck bed spilled lazily into our buckets.

I noticed Josh was keeping a close eye on the people and vehicles moving slowly about the camp. I had to vie for his attention.

"Josh, does the name Charles McCarran mean anything to you?"

He started to shake his head, then came alert. "Yes. He was one of the people Laidlaw shot."

I hoped Josh's reaction was genuine, because if it was, it would begin to exonerate him. "A wealthy businessman from Vancouver."

"Maybe," he agreed. "I only met him once."

"Where? Where did you meet him?"

"The Institute, just recently. He was one of those people Celeste was meeting with up in her apartment. But I never really talked to him much."

That was too bad. "Was he a donor?"

"I don't know," Josh said thoughtfully, "because Celeste kept that list. Maybe Dr. Grant-Worthington introduced me to a couple of those people on that list. But that's all."

I set my buckets down for a moment, and Josh paused with me. Although his attention continued to be divided between our conversation and something at large in the camp, I continued trying to draw him out because I needed to connect Laidlaw's firing with the murder of McCarran, who evidently had influence with Celeste. "Do you know why Celeste fired Laidlaw?"

"He was inept, hopeless. Then he began getting aggressive with anyone who tried to correct him. I don't think Celeste had any other option."

"Don't you wonder why she hired him in the first place?"

"That was obvious," Josh declared. "He's her brother."

This information was electric. Brother. Sister. It came over me like a shower of sparks. But I didn't let on. I said, "Interesting. I wonder why Farrell didn't tell me."

"He and Celeste are friends, and he probably knew Celeste didn't want that information to get around. She was ashamed of the guy."

"Okay." I accepted Josh's explanation and kept pressing my luck with him. "How did Grant-Worthington die?"

After some consideration he said, "Dr. Grant-Worthington died in his sleep, but he didn't die naturally."

I waited for more.

"You're not surprised, are you, Tink?"

I shook my head. I was, in fact, relieved, because it was now clear that Josh hadn't been involved in the killing.

"I can't prove it beyond a doubt right now. But it won't take me long."

I had to wrench my thoughts from the horse and the long, long race the next day to try to piece together what it might mean for Charlie and Stephen and me and for Josh and Isabel if Josh were able to prove how James had died. "So you think it was—"

"Of course it was. She needed Dr. Grant-Worthington out of the way."

Why? I wondered. Both wills included her. So if not her, who else would benefit from the new will?

"And she had the means," Josh pointed out.

The means? "Josh, have you notified the authorities?"

"Not yet. I don't want to do that until I can prove what I say."

Josh hung the water buckets on the side of the trailer, low enough to be within the horses' reach but not so low that they could get entangled in them.

"You're invaluable," I told him.

"Already?" He seemed pleased. "That's what I was hoping to hear *after* the ride."

A Land Rover passed slowly on the truck path. Josh watched it labor out of the park on its way to the state road. As if its disappearance were some kind of signal, he said, "Okay. Got to go."

Because of the dark, I could only guess at the Land Rover's color, probably a military green or gray, but I felt more certain about the identity of the driver whose departure Josh had been waiting for. I knew who she must be. McCarran had had three children, and if I was right, she was the third one I had encountered. Whatever her name was now, Josh knew it.

10

Midday on Friday, about the time Isabel and I were waiting with the horses in the queue for vetting in, Charlie and Stephen were crossing the Bay Bridge, riding above the thick blanket of fog between them and the bay. Having dropped a well-satisfied Henny Kravitz at the San Francisco airport for an early flight, they were heading up toward Sacramento and then on to Donner Lake and the Farrell ranch. Stephen had shed his sport coat and pulled his tie loose.

"What do you think, Charlie?"

"We may be in a somewhat better position." Charlie kept the rental car resolutely in the right lane because the California drivers were flying in swarms past them and he didn't want to miss the turn after the bridge. He wasn't as sanguine as Kravitz about the outlook for the buyout. "Celeste's lawyer hadn't spotted the problem with the signatures—we took them by surprise with that."

"So we're back to the old will and Carol Messmer calling the shots. Right?"

"It might not be that simple. Celeste and whoever forged James's signature—assuming these are two different people—could get criminal charges. In which case, we'll have to wait out the trial."

"Why wouldn't Celeste have wanted the first will to stay in place? That's what I don't get." Stephen was applying his usual clean logic. "She stood to gain more."

This was new information. Charlie navigated the exit ramp onto I-80, then shot a glance at his younger companion. "You sure?"

"Read them, Charlie. Read the two of them."

"I'll have to do that." Charlie had compared only the signatures. "In the meantime, the first will looks better and better, and Savage—who was worrying me because I couldn't figure out where he fit in—now has no question marks after his name."

"I never really thought he was working against us, Charlie. But it sure surprised me how he stood up to Celeste and her lawyer. That was pretty risky. I mean, she has to be one of his primary customers."

"Right," said Charlie. "But he didn't like throwing his lot in with people who are crooked, and he knew he held a lot of cards. Even though he's already been paid for his work on the Institute and the estate owns it, he is still the owner of the AccuGen building."

"He figured out the lease thing, didn't he?" Stephen applauded Savage's gambit at the meeting. "If he actually did cancel their lease, think about the expense of moving that entire lab—and they could lose some biological materials in the process."

"Just getting behind in their development schedule could be very expensive," Charlie pointed out. "It could run afoul of their grant contracts and even cause them to have to restart FDA protocols."

"I think he's with us, Charlie."

"Oh, I agree. Otherwise I wouldn't have told him about Tink and you."

As the meeting was disbanding, Paul Savage had invited the two of them to lunch, a gesture of solidarity. Charlie took that gesture at face value and decided to reveal that he was married to Tink and that he knew Paul had held that position before him. Savage had responded with a blank gaze at Charlie. It wasn't just that he was surprised. It was that he was mentally scrambling to make the connections necessary to figure out what this might mean for him. He put down his fork and said bravely, "How long have you been together, Charlie?"

"Married? A little over five years but together quite a while. Stephen has been in the family a lot longer. He's Tink's stepson."

"And Tink, is she—"

Charlie smiled. "Still riding and quite well, in that order."

Savage nodded and dropped the subject until the waiter brought the check, when he said, "Thank you, Charlie, for leveling with me before we actually had to begin doing business together. I hope you and Stephen know that I am not going to let my history with Tink interfere with our dealings. Thirty years is a very long time, and it allows me some perspective on that experience."

"I can imagine." Now Charlie's curiosity was rising.

"Tink was very young."

"That's what she says," Stephen reported, and this made Savage smile.

"And I was too easily pushed around."

"By her father," Charlie suggested. He and Savage reached for the check in its leather-bound folder at the same time.

"I can see that Tink's story and mine match up—why don't we split this?—and we've both moved on to happier marriages. In fact, Grant-Worthington introduced me to my wife twelve years ago. We had a very close friendship with him, and that's one reason why I cannot go along with Celeste. That, and the Institute's lack of basic integrity recently."

"There is that," Charlie responded, "and of course, Stephen and I can be completely comfortable working with you."

"Tink?" Savage put this question forward a little timidly.

Charlie shrugged. "She'll be fine. Maybe a little nervous about meeting you after all this time."

"And that will go away," Stephen predicted, "after the first five minutes."

It would be an alliance, no matter what Celeste's next move was. Thinking about that move now as he drove I-80, Charlie muttered, "Community effect."

"What?"

"I don't think Celeste is in charge."

Stephen nodded. "If what Ma and I found out about McCarran is any indication, we may be trying to deal with an organization."

"Stephen"—Charlie's foot moved inadvertently against the accelerator to accompany his speeding thought—"the competing bid. That's the competing bid Celeste mentioned to Tink."

"You sure, Charlie? Why should we assume there *was* a competing bid when the only thing Celeste can be counted on for is a lie?"

Acknowledging this was the case, Charlie said, "Still, I'd like to run this by Tink."

Charlie was looking forward to seeing Tink and reporting this. Mostly, he would just be glad to see Tink. Their time in California had been crowded with other people and the urgencies of the AccuGen deal and the Tevis. Their friends and associates had left little time or privacy, and he was looking forward to returning home where there was lots of both.

"Do you realize," he observed, "that the finish line for the Tevis is just a half mile from where we are now? We could drive down here to meet Tink and Isabel when they finish."

Stephen smiled. "If we can stay up that late." Being what he called a quant, he had done the time-distance-plus-hold-times math.

"I won't have any trouble," Charlie assured him. "I'm more than ready to see your ma."

They drove up I-80 from the foot of the Foresthill Divide at Auburn, climbing steadily up its north wall until they reached Donner Lake and seven thousand feet. Charlie's ears were popping the way they had when Stephen and he had made their first trip to the ranch ten days earlier. The off-ramp to the state road now seemed familiar. They weren't far from Farrell's place and maybe some news of Tink, but they weren't in any hurry. That's why Charlie was surprised to see flashing red lights in the rearview mirror. An unmarked patrol car was following them closely.

"Damn. How can I have been speeding?"

They were on a curve in the state road and had to travel a quarter of a mile before they found a place wide enough to pull over.

"Maybe it's not speeding," Stephen suggested, "or maybe it's not us they're looking for."

Two officers, local sheriff's staff, Charlie decided, came forward from the dark blue car.

"Can you try to dig out the registration, Stephen?"

The plastic folder holding the rental car's registration certificate was the only thing in the glove compartment. When the first officer's dark shirt and belt appeared in the car window, Charlie rolled down the window and when instructed to do so, relinquished his driver's license and then the registration.

"Okay, sir, we'll need both of you to step out of the car."

Wondering why this was necessary, Charlie scooted out obediently, and Stephen followed suit, coming around from the other side of the car.

"Hands above your heads." The nearest officer rested a hand on the butt of his holstered pistol. Charlie was experiencing something entirely foreign to him, the humiliation of being frisked. Stephen was enduring the same with an expression of contempt. But when a pair of handcuffs was unclipped from the officer's belt and presented to them, Charlie balked.

"Officer, why have we been stopped?"

His hands were pulled away from him, and the cuffs went on. "What is this?" Stephen demanded as his own pair locked on.

"You'll need to come with us, Charlie." One of the dark-uniformed men was now at Charlie's back. The hard nose of his pistol prodded rudely under Charlie's suit jacket. He and Stephen were marched to the dark blue sedan and ushered into it, Charlie in the front seat, Stephen in the back. As Charlie slid into the seat, a vagrant thought about the color and make of the car came into focus. Dark blue Plymouth. But that was his only coherent thought. He was baffled and shaken. Adrenaline was causing his hands to tremble in the handcuffs. In the brief moment he had to view his surroundings, he saw that the vehicle wasn't a squad car. It was an ordinary passenger sedan with no special equipment of any kind. Then a blindfold slid down to close his eyelids.

Stephen was silent as the car pulled out into the road. Too silent.

"Stephen? How are you doing?"

"So far," Stephen said, "so good."

"Don't worry, Steve." The man beside him in the backseat

spoke familiarly. "That's how you're going to be doing. We're not gonna hurt you."

That seemed unbelievable to Charlie, given the gun that had poked him in the back and his now extravagant pulse. But then the entire circumstance seemed unbelievable. He knew the reason he and Stephen had been taken captive had something to do with the AccuGen buyout. Celeste hadn't been happy when she left the meeting with her lawyer. Was this retribution? Did Celeste think it would forward her cause? And was it only her cause? Was someone else, Josh or maybe someone else in the organization that Tink and Stephen had discovered, calling the shots? He regretted getting involved and getting Stephen involved in the AccuGen deal. He regretted even more persisting, continuing to pursue a buyout after Stephen had suggested backing out. Who was supposed to have the more mature judgment? And why had he fostered this situation in which Stephen was a victim? Given the volatility of this situation and his own powerlessness, it seemed unlikely to Charlie that he would live to make things right with either Stephen or Tink.

He listened for indications of where they were. For a half hour, the car was on paved road, first the slow and therefore narrow paved road, then a brief stretch of fast open road, most likely I-80. More slow, winding paved road, and then a turn on rough twin track that tossed all the occupants of the vehicle slowly around in their seats. Charlie lost track of how long this dirt road went on, but finally the car pulled to a stop. He heard the driver setting the emergency brake. The door beside him opened, a hand gripped his elbow, and he was led over rough ground then through a door. There was a floor underfoot. With the gun in his back again, he began to anticipate his execution.

But the blindfold was removed, and he could see the place where he and Stephen had arrived.

It was a cabin but not a crude one. They were in the main room. The walls were brightly finished logs, and the wood floor was sealed with something hard and glossy. There were chairs, fairly new, with cushions, and a futon with a Navajo-print cover. At the outlet of this room was a small hallway kitchen, fully equipped with appliances—so there must've been a source of electricity—and this evidently led to other rooms. It wasn't clear to Charlie how many rooms or how large the cabin was.

"Have a seat," Charlie's minder in the bogus uniform invited. He was Celeste's security guard, a thick-bodied but trim man who had an air of military fitness about him. His face and hair were ruddy, and his cheeks rose up in little pillows under his eyes. Charlie noted this by way of preparing for a debriefing by an authentic officer. The other man, Stephen's keeper at the moment, had a narrower, wedge-shaped torso—he had spent time in the gym—pale brown hair, and glasses with narrow rectangular lenses outlined in black.

"Have a seat." This was repeated at several intervals in an unthreatening tone until Stephen, wrists still trussed together, headed for one of the chairs, a wooden seat with wide arms and thick cushions tied to its frame. Charlie was more hesitant to turn his back. He might be shot. Stephen might be shot. But if he watched everything and if he lived, he would be a witness. For the moment, their captors seemed to be ignoring their guns, and eventually Charlie sidled cautiously to the futon and settled stiffly there. The cuffs made it impossible to sit normally. He certainly couldn't think normally.

Their keepers took places at a small table where the main room met the kitchen. The ruddy-faced guy laid his gun on the table and stepped into the kitchen to inventory the refrigerator.

"No beer," he reported with some disappointment.

"No," his partner laughed. "What didya think, Kurt?"

There was one name, anyway, and Charlie predicted the other name would be forthcoming before long. Kurt brought a consolation prize from the refrigerator, a plastic container of salsa, and he opened cupboard doors until one door revealed a bag of chips. He passed the open bag in front of Charlie, who shook his head, and Stephen, who excused himself with "Just had lunch." The bag of chips and the noisy mouthfuls lasted a half hour. When the bag was empty, Kurt and his as-yet-unnamed partner sat back in their kitchen chairs to take stock. On this initial exposure, the two of them struck Charlie as rather ordinary, with rather ordinary appetites and ordinary capacities for work and duty and violence. They were working for someone, he decided. They weren't designers of the scheme or the tasks they had drawn. But once the products of idleness set in—boredom and resentment about having to be confined with their charges— one of these very ordinary men might start twitching.

The two keepers gazed dutifully at their captives. Time moved slowly. It was still early in the day. Outside the cabin windows, sunlight struck full force through the spruce and sequoias. Once dark fell, it would be much harder for him and Stephen to find their way up the long dirt track to the road. He was afraid of these two men but also bored. His thoughts moved restlessly. Kurt, the ruddy-faced man, stirred. "We got any cards, Dale?"

There was the second name. The man who owned it shook his head. "No idea."

Kurt rose then and went out through the kitchen to the other rooms. For a number of minutes Charlie could hear the muffled sounds of drawers sliding, then doors closing. When Kurt returned, he had a deck of cards. Dale said, "Good. You saved my life."

"You deal."

Dale began to shuffle the cards. The men emptied their pockets of change and laid their coins in two piles on the table. Dale's black-rimmed glasses made him look more intelligent than Kurt. He watched his cards intently, as if he were reading great literature.

Charlie spoke up. "So what's the plan? What happens now?"

"Nothing," Kurt responded. "Nothing happens."

Dale looked up briefly from his cards. "You're being detained," he said, as if that weren't already clear enough.

"For how long?" Charlie persisted.

Kurt shrugged and, watching the cards out of the corner of his eye, said, "However long it is before we get the word."

"The word?" Charlie pressed on. "To do what?"

Dale smiled down at cards. "To put you two back in the car."

Charlie was surprised at how easily his Q&A was going, but he expected his next question would shut it right down. "And what's the next destination?"

"Make things easy for you?" Dale suggested. "Kurt and me are going to Vancouver."

The word *Vancouver* resonated alarmingly with what little Charlie knew from Stephen about McCarran and his Canadian organization. Who, in fact, was responsible for their abduction? Celeste? Someone who had replaced McCarran?

"You two are going as far as the Canadian border. We'll drop you off someplace where you'll have a good hike out."

Drop you off was a euphemism, Charlie decided. "Why aren't you going to kill us?"

"It's too dirty," Kurt told him, "and they decided it wasn't necessary."

This was another lie in what appeared on the surface to be a bizarrely benign kidnapping. He tried to figure out the purpose of Stephen's and his detention. Was it simply to allow Celeste and her Community to completely derail the buyout? Maybe these two were just transfer agents. Maybe they would hand off him and Stephen to other connections—people who might more actively disappear them. If their two strangely complacent captors were actually planning to escape to Canada, did they know about reciprocity? Charlie wondered how much it would take to break up their languor, and he realized that almost anything might cause them to snap. A noise in the big trees outside the cabin. Inside, the ringing of a cell phone. A word.

Now Stephen took a turn with questions. "What's in Vancouver? Do you guys have family there?"

"Money," Kurt said. "It's money."

McCarran's money. Not a direct payment, Charlie reasoned based on Stephen's report of his research trip to town with Tink, but a payment through the organization that was McCarran's legacy. The nonprofit status of that organization had been investigated, and if the so-called religious organization was actually a profit-making corporation in disguise, perhaps the real goal of the new will was to merge the Canadian church-corporation with a new hybrid organization, the Institute combined with AccuGen. The new hybrid would have huge income-producing capacity—and two goons on its staff. A dangerous cash cow.

Maybe the pair would stay in Vancouver only long enough to be paid. But Charlie tried not to think too far ahead of where he and Stephen found themselves now, a cabin in the Sierra

Nevada within striking distance of Donner Lake. He inventoried the guns. One remained out of sight in Dale's pocket, and one lay on the table between their kidnappers while play commenced.

Blackjack, for pocket change. Charlie watched, at first from the distance of the futon. He tried to imagine how and when Stephen's and his absence would become known to Tink, and he experienced a flash of something like pain when he realized how distraught she would be. But it might be as long as thirty-six or forty-eight hours before she rode with Isabel out of the mountains and looked around for her husband and stepson. His frustration and resentment grew.

"Mind if I watch?" he asked the cardplayers.

"Pull up a chair."

Using his knee and his cuffed hands as a single tool, Charlie situated another kitchen chair a few feet from the table. As the host of a regular weekly poker game, he would be interested to watch the play. Stephen, who had been roped in to being an alternate at these poker nights, pushed his own chair closer. Charlie sensed this wasn't so much because he was interested in the game as it was because he would feel exposed, more helpless as the distance between him and Charlie increased.

The pair began to play a few bumbling hands. Neither Kurt nor Dale appeared to grasp the necessity for strategy. Charlie kept his eye on the cards and silently coached Kurt on how to strengthen his position against Dale's dealing.

"You play?" Dale pantomimed dealing a card to Charlie.

He nodded, then stood up and indicated his pockets. "I have some change."

Kurt removed the coins and moved Charlie's chair into a position from which to play. Charlie was surprised by his anger at his captors. Now that he was beyond his initial bewilderment and terror, he was nearly beside himself with anger. But then Tink always said anger was a response to helplessness. "Nothing makes people and horses more angry than taking away their power and leaving them helpless. That's what revolutions are about and that's what rearing is about." He anted. The cuffs didn't interfere with the movement of his fingers and wrists, and he accepted the card from the top of the deck. He wished his concentration in the earlier plays had been more absolute. But it was good enough to take the first hand. Dale invited Stephen into the next hand.

"I'm going to make you a little richer," Stephen promised but pulled up to the corner of the table anyway. "Charlie won't."

Over the next few rounds, Dale swept all the coins on the table toward Charlie. Their keepers and Stephen were broke.

"Damn," Kurt complained. "You are lucky!"

Charlie gave a tight little smile.

"You cheating?" Dale accused.

Charlie gave an emphatic shake of his head and suggested, "Stake you guys?" He began to divvy up the coins, and the four of them fell back into play. The pile of coins in front of Charlie grew. At this point he was playing to win because playing staved off fear and boredom and winning staved off helplessness.

Dale, evidently feeling his position as dealer threatened, demanded, "How are you *doing* that?"

"He practices a lot," Stephen said a little too quickly.

"It's almost like he's got another deck and he's just wishing those cards into my deck," Dale said suspiciously.

Charlie was taking a somber satisfaction from his small-change victories. Dale held the deck of cards without offering to deal again.

"Charlie," he proposed, "why don't *you* deal them?"

"Be happy to. But you may not like the results." Charlie's hands went up to remind Dale that the cuffs prevented this.

Kurt interceded by unlocking the cuffs, then said, "Let me shuffle them before he deals." He fanned the cards, and they snapped together to make a new deck. He repeated this twice more and passed the deck to Charlie.

Charlie began to deal. It was about four o'clock, too soon for anyone to have missed him and Stephen. He calculated that Tink and the rest of the entourage had settled in at Robie Park and had finished the vetting in.

It was probably as murderously hot there as it was outside the cabin. He thought of Josh being with the women and regretted allowing that arrangement. Nothing short of a misjudgment. Although it was not entirely clear that Josh was tied to Celeste and her cause in the same way as Kurt and Dale—Charlie couldn't estimate if or how Josh's attraction to Isabel had altered those ties—it didn't seem safe for Josh, an instant link for the Institute, to be traveling with the women. But the fact that Josh Untermeyer had managed to penetrate Stephen and Charlie's realm joined forces with the other regrets Charlie had about his latest business venture. He laid down single cards glumly, and his keepers, watching him closely with narrowed eyes, responded with various, almost immediately frustrated strategies. He pondered letting them win a hand or two but, now that he had their attention, decided to keep up the pressure.

"Shit!" Kurt exploded. "How many times can I lose the same fucking dimes?"

Dale leaned in quite close to Charlie's face. "What is it that you are *doing*?" There was an ugly edge to his politeness. Stephen glanced worriedly at Charlie. But Charlie knew they weren't likely to shoot him before they figured out why they were consistently losing.

"The same thing you are doing," Charlie said innocently, "playing blackjack. Is there going to be a ransom?"

This question startled them. They looked at each other and drew the same kind of blank they been drawing in their game. Kurt shrugged. "If there is, nobody told me about it."

This answer seemed more dangerous but also more advantageous than one indicating these two knew the plan. They weren't in command of the situation, and they would have very little influence on what happened. But also, they didn't seem concerned about their lack of authority, and Charlie thought this might nominate them as weak links. He would exploit that weakness by keeping the two of them engaged.

"Go again?" he asked with as much good humor as he could muster.

Dale eyed him resentfully. "Now why would I want to lose my money all over again?"

Stephen, alert to their dangerously changing mood, sat quite still with a pleasant expression plastered on his face.

"It's just a game. And we all have time to kill," Charlie pointed out. "Why does it matter whose nickels we're pushing around?"

Dale leaned in quite close again, tight with anger, and said, "I want to know what you are"—the heel of his hand struck the table so hard that the gun bounced off its surface—"*doing*!"

"Can we be friendly?" Charlie asked calmly. All at once he could see that he might be able to make himself useful to these opponents. "I'm playing by the rules, right?"

They nodded.

"And I'm winning a lot, right?"

"You're winning the whole goddamn thing!" Kurt raised his voice.

"There's no need to get mad about it," Charlie went on in a

genial tone. "So I'm playing by the rules, and I'm winning a lot. What does that tell you?"

"You're cheating." Dale came back to his first conclusion.

"Well, the folks who own the casinos might say that. But if I'm playing by the rules, I can't be cheating, can I?"

Kurt ventured his guess. "You're a fucking genius."

"Much as I'd like to think so," Charlie never dropped his friendly elementary school teacher's voice, "I'm not. I'm just a good player."

When neither of them answered, Stephen, who saw that Charlie meant to tell his secret for some reason, said, "He has a system."

"You know it, too?"

Stephen said quite seriously, "Well, I know what the system is, and I know how it works. I'm just not very good at it."

Dale eyed the deck in Charlie's hand glumly. "You're a professional?"

Charlie shook his head. "Not even close. It's just something I do for fun."

Kurt fixed on him avidly. "Could you beat the house?"

"It depends on the house—casinos don't take kindly to card counting. But yes, I probably could—for a while, until the managers kicked me out."

"That's what you're doing, card counting?" Dale settled tentatively on this piece of information.

"That's it. Not much to it," Charlie said reassuringly. "Anybody could learn."

"Why don't you show me?" Dale proposed, and Charlie guessed that he had taken to heart his earlier comment about beating the house.

He said, "Sure. Have some paper and a pencil?" He drew a chart and wrote in the card values. "Just one, zero, and twos.

Doesn't matter what the number on the face of the card is, just add and subtract the values for each kind of card. Keep a running tally. That way, with every card you draw you know whether you have the advantage or the dealer does."

Dale and Kurt followed all this earnestly, counting out loud as Charlie dealt exposed cards to Stephen. But a few minutes after he started dealing to the two of them, their frustration began to build.

"Take your time," Charlie coached soothingly. "You're going to have to give yourselves time to work on this. You know the old joke, 'How do you get to Carnegie Hall? . . . Practice, practice, practice!' That's all you need."

"How long you been doing this?" Kurt wanted to know. Charlie had to think. If he admitted it had taken him several years, the two of them might get discouraged and drop the project that was allowing him some control.

"Well, I've been doing it quite a while. But it only took me about a week to get pretty good with it." He dealt a few more hands, and his captors muttered their counts. Outside the afternoon light was aging, softening. Kurt folded. He scratched behind his ear and said, "A week, huh?"

The two exchanged glances, evidently weighing their opportunities. It was Dale who made the proposal.

"You know, we could take Charlie here down to South Tahoe, play some, and be back here in time to get a message when they send one."

Whoever *they* were. That was a frightening unknown. But he might have just counted Stephen and himself out of the cabin and into territory that offered more room to maneuver.

There was no way that his captors could sequester themselves to discuss Dale's proposal, so they debated it right there, as if Charlie and Stephen had vaporized. It would be a long night, they finally reasoned, but it would be a long night in the cabin anyway. They could collect in South Tahoe, then collect again when they got to Vancouver.

"Win-win!" Kurt declared, redder in the face from brightness and hope, and he left the room. Within minutes he reappeared in street clothes—khakis, a polo shirt, and a sport coat. After Dale changed clothes, the minders returned the guns to their persons and reapplied the handcuffs to Stephen and Charlie. The blindfolds slipped down over Charlie's and Steven's faces, and Kurt and Dale led them out to the parked car.

The blue sedan labored slowly up the dirt track, on its way to a night in South Tahoe, where Charlie would perform like a dancing bear.

11

On Saturday, I woke at 3:00 A.M. on a cot in the horse compartment of Isabel's trailer. Two hours before the start. I knew I was not the only person in camp who was awake, but the quiet was deep and interrupted only by the occasional stomp of Owen or Darwin. Maybe the other riders who had wakened long before their alarms were doing exactly what I was doing, lying still, staring at the ceiling, trying not to steal sleep from anyone else until a first brave person ventured out to feed horses and set off a dawn chorus of whinnying and trumpeting.

Night hadn't done much to cool off the camp, which meant the heat on the trail would climb rapidly and gather in suffocating stillness in the canyons. My competition nerves were finally making themselves known. My pulse bounded along, reverberating inside my head, and my mouth felt dry.

At the briefing the day before I'd discovered something Isabel had known all along. Darwin and Owen would start the ride without each other. Like runners in a big-city marathon, the horses would be gathered in groups to go to the start. The sixty top-seeded horses—including Darwin—would begin walking toward the starting line five minutes before the second group of horses, with Owen among them. With un-identified rivals surrounding him, Owen would be an aggressive, insistent, psychological train wreck.

My challenge would be to help save him from leaving every last drop of giddyup-go in the gathering pen. There was no way to keep him from getting riled up, so my plan was to keep the duration of this state as short as possible. I would ride into the gathering pen at the last legally permitted moment, briefly join the horses gathered there, and then walk out with them. As soon as Owen began to move, he would begin by infinitesimal degrees to calm. As soon as he caught up to Darwin he would become somewhat manageable. The trick would be to stay on until then.

That was the start, just the first couple of miles in the day. I had qualified Owen on the basis of fifty-mile races and a single hundred-mile ride over level terrain. I needed a strategy that would allow Owen to continue on steep terrain past the fifty-mile mark and down through the river crossings before the finish at the fairgrounds. Maybe I had overlooked something. I realized I had been thinking of endurance as a branch of horsemanship unto its own with no relation to the other riding disciplines. But a horse is just a horse. A rider is just a rider. What goes on between them to make things work doesn't necessarily need to change because the job is a little different. What about some of the tools common to all the different jobs riding horses do? Say, something like rhythm?

I reviewed my plans for water—water to cool Owen, water for me to drink, sports bottles clipped to every possible hook on the saddle and my belt pack—and spare equipment. In my saddlebag were two strap-on boots for Owen in case the synthetic coverings we had annealed to his hoofs tore away, a collection of spare straps and snaps, electrolytes to help balance

Owen's metabolism, a big dosing syringe to squirt them into his mouth, and clean socks for me. I began to review the more challenging sections of the trail—Cougar Rock, Elephant Trunk, Pucker Point, the Swinging Bridge, Last Chance, and the No-Hands Bridge the horses would cross in the dark.

I thought of all these things, these practical imperatives, but steadily interrupting this list rehearsal were thoughts of Charlie and Stephen in that order and the reverse order. They would be sound asleep in rooms at Farrell's and in a few hours would wander out in search of one of Farrell's mighty breakfasts. They would already know the outcome of their meeting, whether they had won the deal or not or whether there would be more meetings and more delays. I couldn't begin to guess what news they would bring because there were so many uncertainties, and each of these was compounded by internal uncertainties. The uncertainties had names. Celeste. Paul Savage. Josh. Laidlaw. If I thought about each of them in isolation, I could see fairly well what that person had done to bring about or help bring about the mess with AccuGen. But when I tried to link them, string them together the way kids cut out a strip of paper dolls holding hands, none of the hands touched. Their stories fell apart. As Stephen said, "It's pretty much like solving a simultaneous—"

The dark morning quiet was blasted apart by one of the loudest, most alarming sounds I had ever heard, the braying of Skinner Flemington's mule.

"Jesus!" I heard Frankie protest from inside the living quarters. "It must be prehistoric."

"Jurassic, at least." Isabel stumbled out of the living quarters to look in on me. "You awake, Tink?"

How could anyone in the entire campground have slept through that? Riders and crew tumbled out of bed, emerged from sleeping bags. On to water. Hay. Grain. Frankie rattling around the little kitchenette to make coffee. Owen had a bad case of bed head, but I took Isabel's advice and didn't groom him, didn't make any preparations to ride. Owen, however, wasn't so easily fooled. He stood, tulip ears straight up, watching the pace of activity in the park pick up. The saddles coming out to rest on other horses' backs, protective boots clapped on other horses' legs. Red ribbon braided into tails of horses that were kickers. He knew, but he kept his composure. I knew he would lose that as soon as Darwin was ridden away from the campsite, so when the top-seeded riders began to head for the first gathering pen, I took Owen for a walk around Robie Park. Then I led him back to the trailer, where Frankie was waiting with the tack and saddlebags we had laid out. Almost on the fly, Owen still moving, she saddled him. Frankie was the most valuable player in this game. I adjusted the bridle, swung up, and walked Owen in a circle around her as she ran through her checklist and finally said, "Good to go."

It was a strategy that quelled anticipation, but still, Owen knew. His stride and his breathing quickened. The timers released the top-seeded horses from their gathering pen, and the riders in my group reported one by one to the timing crew. Owen tensed, dropping his nose almost to his chest. He was coiled, imagining himself galloping. I pretended I didn't notice and rode him in big lazy circles through the campsite near the gathering pen. He thought I was an idiot and blew angrily. I was wearing my big-face event watch, and I rode him as slowly as I could—this now involved mincing on tiptoe and side passes— until a minute before the release time for the second gathering pen. Owen had no time to scope out the other horses in the pen before we fell into line at the gate and walked through. This caused Owen to be reincarnated as a warhorse, cantering almost in place. Gunfire wouldn't have slowed him, so the irritated call from the timer's scribe wasn't going to. "*Number?*"

"One oh seven," I called over my shoulder. It is decidedly uncool to lose control of a horse at a competition. The other riders have a right to assume you can stop and start and turn your horse without interfering with them. Owen was a barely contained explosion that could ignite any one of the other horses. Nothing new, but that didn't make it any less embarrassing. So we were off, overtaking at a cantering sidepass the horses that had started ahead of us and were trotting conservatively down the twin track that opens the trail. I figured nothing would ease Owen's mind until he spotted Darwin, when he could be satisfied with overtaking his primary rival and obsession. At that point he might be more receptive to a new way of doing things. I tried to be patient and not haul on the reins. What this required was a strong, upright seat and intermittent incantations under my breath of *asshole*. There was only one narrow passage where horse traffic had slowed through a bottleneck, and Owen was blocked. But he was smart enough to recognize this as an impasse and waited until the trail opened out and he could pass. Up ahead were Isabel and Darwin, and soon they were looking at Owen's tail.

"So what's new?" She teased as soon as Owen began to settle and I could relax and look around a little.

"What's new is a little music," and I started in on it, singing "Yankee Doodle" sotto voce and posting in march rhythm on beat two and beat four. Owen's left ear flicked back.

"Don't like my voice, Owen?"

Behind me Isabel was laughing.

"Better get used to it, Owen, because you're going to hear it until you figure out how to restrict yourself to taking life in stride, the strides I think you should take."

"That tune is going to get very old, very fast," Isabel predicted. "And Owen is right, Tink. Your voice isn't the greatest." Apparently she was oblivious to the quality of her own, her thin, plaintive call coming forth with a New Jersey accent.

There was a line of horses moving downhill ahead of us, and I was surprised to see that the rider at the head of the line was the lanky red-haired teenager. I was even more surprised that Owen, now that he had passed Darwin, didn't seem much bothered by the horses still ahead of him. I couldn't be sure, but I thought he might be settling to the rhythm I was imposing. In consideration of my fellow riders, I was gradually lowering my voice. I became aware of a horse coming up from behind, and the voice of its rider asking for room to pass. Thinking this would be Owen's first real test in the race, I gave way. A chestnut horse drew alongside, and I looked into the impish face of the superfit Tor, no helmet, just a baseball cap, sunglasses, and a big grin. He nudged his horse up into a perfect three-beat canter.

"Know any waltzes?"

The other horse's canter was too much for Owen to ignore. He struggled, hopping and bobbing, to stay with the other horse. But I kept up insistently with the one-two-one-two, posting emphatically and intoning the syllables of "Yankee Doodle." For a while this produced a gait with four scrambled beats, but when his cantering rival turned a corner and went out of sight, Owen ever so gradually backed off and, for the time being, seemed to be convinced that trotting was the way to go.

Except for Owen's occasional kerfuffles when other horses overtook us, the first twenty miles passed very much like our training rides. The tentative pinkish light that lingered after sunrise gave way to bolder sunshine, and riding on a path that carved into the sides of the mountains, we were sometimes treated on a switchback to the spectacle of the Divide, its sharply descending walls promising to converge in the distance. We rode through the backside of Squaw Valley, and at High Camp, a few miles east of Cougar Rock, the horses drank all the water they wanted.

Cougar Rock is probably the best-known landmark on the Tevis trail, but because the incident with Laidlaw and his girl-friend at the mine at Deadwood had stopped our progress north that day, Isabel and I, as well as the horses, had not yet laid eyes on it. The rock crouches like a big cat—a cougar, a mountain lion, painter, catamount, whatever you name this big cat—over a place where the trail drops down, and there have been many jaw-dropping photos of horses bounding up the rock with nothing but thin air visible beyond it. In reality, the mountain from which the rock juts up provides solid ground behind it.

On the trail that led up to the rock there was a line of horses stalled, waiting for the horses ahead of them to bound one at a time over the back of the crouching cat. As soon as I saw the horses standing still, I began slowing Owen. It was better for him to keep moving, even at a caterpillar's pace, then to stop and have his body—muscles, heart, and lungs—adjust to the lack of motion. And easier on him to give him room to pick up speed before catapulting up the rock. Isabel and I dawdled on the horses as long as we could. Then just as I was about to let Owen increases his speed and move toward the base of the big rock, Isabel passed me on the outside.

"What are you doing?" I demanded.

"Going around."

"Why?" I had been thinking of Cougar Rock like an obstacle on a cross-country course, mandatory. "The rock is there. Why not just go over?"

"I want Darwin to finish tonight."

"Isabel!"

"You ride your ride. I'll ride my ride."

So be it. I sent the gray horse up the back of the cougar as if it were the approach to a big drop fence, trying to guide him with my legs, seat, and hands. This was a mistake. Owen faltered, lost momentum, and began to falter again, to slip back down the rock. I nailed him with both heels, let him have his head, and grabbed his mane. He scrambled until his hind legs were well under him, dug in, and then drove forward. We cleared the head of the big cat, but that was his doing and certainly not mine. I had nearly brought him down. I looked back at Cougar Rock and noticed far below it, a man perched on the back of an all-terrain vehicle with a tripod holding a camera as serious-looking as artillery. I wondered which instant he might have captured and winced at the possibilities. But the rock had taught me something.

We went on without Isabel and Darwin, back to the old one-two. Owen had bought into rhythm and seemed not to mind that he was alone and that for the moment there were no horses ahead of him. It was only a minute or two before we saw other riders ahead of us. Their horses were walking carefully, painstakingly, along a very narrow trail that cut up along the edge of a canyon, then bent around a bulge in the canyon wall. This was Elephant Trunk. Navigating this passage was to be endured with patience, a test that verified the name of this sport. It was a long ten minutes before Owen could pick up speed again. With other riders coming up faster behind Owen, we reached the next group of horses, and passed one. Immediately in front of us was a sharply angled hind end, a tail like a whisk broom, and an enormous, battered sombrero. I called out to pass, and Skinner Flemington edged his mule to one side.

"You *have* to do that?" he asked.

"What?"

"That grunting."

He meant my humming.

I said, "I guess not," and likely the background music wasn't necessary any longer. Owen had become as calmly coordinated as I'd ever seen him, and besides, my mouth was getting dry.

"You're only about two miles from Robinson Flat," he advised me. "Vets will be waiting for you."

I didn't miss this veiled hint to slow down so that Owen's pulse rate could meet the parameter the moment he walked into the hold, but slowing this horse would only raise his heart rate. Instead I asked about the mule, "What's her name?"

"Her? This here is Abby. Pretty little thing, ain't she?"

Beauty in the eye of the beholder.

Robinson Flat was thirty miles into the ride. It was a small, level meadow enclosed by towering sequoias. Owen and I had passed a number of riders who had slowed their horses to a plodding pace, and after passing a rider leading her horse in hand, I decided to proceed more slowly with Owen. The trail opened out to a twin track under the conifers, and on either side of this boulevard, the crews were lined up waiting to help cool down their horses. I didn't have to search for Josh. He bounded up to Owen, drew the reins over the horse's head, and tugged at my foot to signal *Get down*—all of this with his customary energy and sociability. Josh had suited up correctly for his job, field trousers that converted into shorts, a bill cap with a flap in the back to cover his neck—like the ones advertised for fly-fishing—and wraparound, bug-eye sunglasses. We walked between the two lines of crew people toward the vet check area a half mile away. Josh's safari-flap sun hat and enormous bug-eye sunglasses couldn't conceal his excitement. It was not, as it turned out, about my arrival at the first hold.

"They got him," he said quietly. "Just heard it on the radio."

"Who?" I wasn't focusing on what he was telling me.

Josh was walking briskly and at the same time stripping off Owen's saddle exactly the way Frankie had showed him. Alongside Owen and me, he waded through the horses milling about the station where pulse and respiration—P&R—readings were taken. Owen's pulse and breathing were slow and regular, and we were sent on to trot in front of the vets. As soon as the horse checked out fine and Owen was deemed fit to continue, the clock started on his hold time. This was forty-five minutes of compulsory rest. Josh threw some hay in the direction of Owen and asked, "How far back is Isabel?"

"Maybe ten minutes." I said hurriedly because now I realized what he had told me a few minutes earlier.

"Josh, they got Laidlaw?"

"Yup. Crazy Clyde died. In South Tahoe. He came out of the woods, robbed a gun shop for ammo, and then went into one of the casinos to grab some cash. Cops were there with a SWAT team. They got him. One other guy did get shot, but I think he's going to be okay."

So Laidlaw had made it out of the canyons. The thought of him on the loose in a casino was horrifying, but it also belied what I thought I had observed about him.

"He wasn't very smart then, was he?"

Josh contemplated Owen working at the hay. "Not smart enough to be humble," he said. "And neither is his sister."

Which sister? But Josh didn't give me time to ask. He was on his way out to the track through the sequoias to meet Isabel and Darwin.

He reappeared with her and the bay horse. He had taken Darwin's reins from her, and the two of them moved quickly into the P&R area, conferring so closely they were practically head-to-head. Of course, I reflected, Charlie and I had been wrong about Josh, wrong to suspect him. If nothing else came our way on this trip west—if the AccuGen deal went up in smoke and I ended up having to pull Owen—the two of them, Isabel and Josh, would be one good thing that made the journey worthwhile.

When Owen had waited out the hold period, I swung up on him again and called out, "See you next at Foresthill." As I left the two of them standing side by side, it didn't cross my mind that maybe we wouldn't meet up again. Owen and I had a ten-minute lead on Isabel and her bay. Barring any mishap or misstep, stone bruise or stumbling, we were likely to keep it. Owen, I thought rather smugly without taking into account the fact that the most difficult section of trail was still ahead, was doing fine. The trail started out of Robinson Flat as a wagon trail but became a narrow ridge-topping path that gradually ran down to rocks jutting high over a wayward branch of the North Fork of the American River—Pucker Point. When Owen drew up there, I found it difficult to look down into the beautiful chasm. Somehow I would have to get the horse down to that river.

What this involved turned out to be a long series of steep switchbacks. Looking down from the top, I could see far below my hyperfit know-any-waltzes rival. I debated dismounting and leading Owen down into the chasm. But I didn't want the horse to get in a hurry, run me over on his way down, get loose, become frightened by that, and fall. Also, I could hear the voices of riders coming up behind me, and I didn't want to give way. So I stayed on his back, sitting as straight and still as I could to avoid interfering with his coordination. The heat increased with every yard farther into the canyon.

Bonnie and Clyde, Angelica and Nelson, were no longer a threat down in the Divide. But Angelica was only too available to the police. Celeste would be aware of that. By now she would have faced Charlie and Stephen's challenge of the signature on the new will, and of course she would have the news about Laidlaw. Pressure on her was intensifying. But wasn't she too passive to act on any of this information? Would the older sister arrive with an expensive lawyer to try to get Angelica out of jail? I regretted my failure to get her name from Josh. At Robinson Flat he had been too attentive to Isabel to draw him away, but surely with my ten-minute lead on Isabel and a longer hold at Foresthill, there would be lots of time to talk about Laidlaw's family.

For the first time that day, my gray horse was showing signs of wear and tear. Sweat streamed down his flanks and neck, and his breath came faster than I could ever remember. The rapid breathing, I decided, was due to anxiety rather than exertion. Whatever the cause, he needed to be cooled off. To get him into the river here at the canyon bottom, I would have to take a detour of about a hundred yards off the trail. There was a wooden bridge strung over the river just ahead, and I had heard that not far beyond it was a spring with a reliable year-round flow. I decided on that plan, but Owen decided against the bridge.

This horse had never balked with me, never said "No, I won't." More often than I liked he had said "Yes, I will. I'm going to and I don't give a damn what you think." But as soon as he put a foot on the suspended bridge and felt it swinging slightly, he scrambled backward frantically. This bridge could cost us a good bit of time.

I dismounted and flipped the reins over his head to try to lead him across. Even by the river the heat was intense, enough to poach the two of us. The only way out was along the trail—in other words, across the bridge. Owen was eyeing the bridge, rolling his eyes suspiciously. I put my hand on his neck and smoothed his sticky, sweaty coat.

"Darling," I said. "Sweetie pie. Work with me, darling. Don't be a shithead. We need to get to that spring and cool you off."

He said no a couple more times, and I pleaded, cajoled. Eventually he dropped his head and walked tentatively behind me, bracing with every step, over the first few planks in the bridge. Then as we were approaching the middle of it and the movement of the bridge was more sweeping, he panicked and bolted. He jerked the reins out of my hand and, ears flattened back, pounded over the bridge and leaped off the end of it. He disappeared around a bend in the trail. This could cost me the race.

This horse was capable of running through these canyons for a long time or until he found grass or other horses. As it happened, it was other horses that stopped him. Three of them were standing about fifty yards away by the spring I had been told about, the riders sponging them and letting the water drip over their own bodies. Owen stood off to one side, trembling. When he saw me, he gave me the most accusatory look I've ever suffered from a horse. But he allowed me to approach and get him back in hand.

"Darling. Sweetie pie," I told him. "You *were* a shithead."

I led him to the spring and dipped in my sponge.

"Back in the race?" one of the other riders concluded. It was the big-boned woman with the bay. "This mare did that to me out here once—all I did was get off to pee."

Owen and I left the spring with the three riders, the woman with the bay mare, a tall blond girl on one of the many narrow-bodied grays, and Ben, one of the superfits, a slight man with a heavy five-day beard and remarkably long feet. I was in good company, which was a fortunate because Owen had attached himself passionately to the three horses, as if they had rescued him from the attack bridge. With the descent from Pucker Point and the Swinging Bridge, some of the trickiest passages along the trail and the biggest drops in altitude were behind me and the horse. Now it was just a matter of miles.

With my new companions, I rode into a ghosted site named Last Chance. The camp had been established by prospectors who had arrived underprovisioned and overoptimistic. Almost immediately they found several deposits of gold, and this tempted them to linger until starvation hovered. The one rifle in camp had one bullet left, and announcing this was their last chance, one of the miners disappeared with the gun. He came back with a big buck. There was nothing left of the miners' enterprise now. The site was temporarily occupied by a few volunteers and a water tank hauled in by all-terrain vehicle.

We had come fifty miles, exactly halfway. Another five miles brought us to a vet check and hold at the intersection of the trail with the rough excuse for a road up from the Dead-wood mine. No crews were allowed to drive down the road, so we dismounted, loosened girths, and looked after the horses ourselves. During the hold, the horses drank and we ate the watermelons on offer and listened to the vets joke about Laid-law bumbling into a casino. The woman with the bay said, "I feel sorry for those riders who bumped into him down here."

I said, "I do, too."

"I bet they're laughing now."

I smiled weakly and waited for the subject to change.

Isabel came into the hold on Darwin, and just behind them, Skinner Flemington and his mule, both now roughly fifteen minutes behind me. She had looked a little tired but mostly contented. She pulled off the saddle and stroked Darwin's spine. "I am so happy with him." It wasn't clear that she was talking about the horse. But Darwin, conservative soul that he was, was still in primary bloom.

I was back on the horse and riding out in tandem with the big-footed superfit, when one of the vets, an older man with a pronounced stoop, swept his hand toward the pile of stones and rubble we would pass on our way out of the hold. "Back in the day, there was an inn here called the Half Way House. Had a platform to unload your wagons, a bar—"

The woman on the bay mare sighed. "I could really use a beer right now."

"And if you wanted to go on to Michigan Bluff," he informed us, "on the same trail you are just about to take, you had to pay the innkeeper a toll."

The man riding alongside me said, "This trail has already taken its toll." He certainly didn't look it, but I was beginning to feel it. My legs were beginning to tire, and I had a thirst that wouldn't quit. Now that the terrifying bridge was behind him, Owen was cheerful and game to go.

As we headed out of Last Chance, past the remnants of its cemetery, the trail abruptly narrowed and plunged down the side of the mountain in a sequence of switchbacks, which provided a reassuring way to negotiate the the alarming grade. This was the west wall of the El Dorado Canyon. At the bottom was the wide El Dorado Creek, which flowed into the North Fork of the American River, and on the other side of the creek the east wall of the canyon, which looked almost vertical, would be a daunting climb. As we proceeded cautiously down the switchbacks, the massive sequoias gave way to smaller, more spindly spruce that gave way to bare rock. Heat bounced off the rocks and collected more and more intensity as the horses moved down to the lowest passage of the canyon.

We put the horses into the creek and stood in the water beside them, bathing them with our sponges. I led Owen up the other side of the canyon—a hard climb that caused my thighs and calves to protest with pain and me to regret I hadn't devoted more attention to my own fitness. There are times when having four legs is a big advantage over having two. About halfway up the steep wall, I gave up doing the leading and, like the three riders I was traveling with, grabbed Owen's tail and let him pull me the rest of the way. It was humbling. I was glad Charlie and Stephen wouldn't witness this.

We emerged at Michigan Bluff, a hamlet of five or six houses perched on a narrow ridge between the El Dorado Canyon on one side and the Middle Fork of the American River on the other. A few yards behind me was Skinner Flemington and his mule. She had carried him straight up the canyon wall. In the side yard of one of the little houses were water tanks. The mule took a nip from the tank and walked past, easy does it, on her way again.

Owen thrust his muzzle into the water and blew, apparently quite satisfied with himself for having worked through the roller-coaster canyon and hauled me up its side. My respect for this horse was growing. He wasn't as daunted by what he'd seen along the trail as I was. And he seemed to be learning about conservation and self-preservation.

Frankie noticed this when she met us with horse food at the fly-by vet check at Chicken Hawk. "Wising up, isn't he? How did you make that happen?"

I hadn't. "Where's Josh?"

"I bet he's playing it safe." She laughed. She had walked the mile or so into the hold and was now on her way out of it with an almost empty hay net. We were only four miles from the actual hold at Foresthill, and it was possible that by riding as the crow flies I could make it there before Frankie did. "He's probably waiting on the road into Foresthill to be sure he doesn't miss you—or even more important, Isabel—coming into the hold."

The people of Foresthill had turned out to watch the horses come through. There were camp chairs lined up along the streets, and barbecues were in progress. On one side of town several acres were devoted to the checkpoint, and behind the vetting area, trucks and trailers parked according to the logic of shade, and vendors' tents and food concessions had sprung up. Frankie was waiting with the other crews along the road that led into the hold. We walked Owen toward the vetting area, stripping off his tack.

"You must have flown." I observed.

"Got a speeding ticket," she confessed and fit the stethoscope tips into her ears. "This little town could make its whole annual budget on ride day—hold up, let me check him." She listened to his pulse then nodded. "Okay, go on in."

The veterinarian who checked out Owen was young enough to be my daughter. "He's holding up really well. And you have only—what?—thirty-two miles to go."

With that remark, my hold time started, and Frankie and I tied Owen to her truck and waited for Isabel to come up the road.

"Still no Josh?" she observed. "I thought we would see him on the road coming in here. But I was wrong about that. Maybe he tried to do all the stops—Michigan Bluff, Chicken Hawk—anyplace he could look after Isabel. Maybe he's rushing over here now—on his way to a ticket."

When Darwin sauntered up the road carrying Isabel, walking to let his pulse settle, he was the picture of fitness. Eyes alert and luminous. Long, rhythmic, easy strides and clear sweat drying on him without leaving any residue. He was a horse who would finish the race, pass the others as they dropped back or dropped out, and walk into the last vet check in much the same condition he was in now. Isabel was saving him for those last miles in the dark. Having dropped the reins and leaving navigation of the road to Darwin, she sat on him pertly. Her slight weight was helping the horse, I realized enviously. She was looking around, spotting us but still searching the holding area.

"Where's Josh?" She dropped from the saddle to the ground.

"He's not with you?" Frankie looked irritated. Her command of our crew was slipping. She worked hurriedly with Isabel and me to get the tack off and the horse wet down.

"I haven't seen him since I left the hold at Robinson Flat." Concern slipped into Isabel's face, and a chilling possibility crossed my mind. Had he been intercepted somehow?

"Come on," Frankie scolded. "Let's get him to the vets, let's get the horse in there." With Isabel glancing around distractedly, they moved off toward the P&R squad.

I toured the parking lot, hoping to catch sight of Josh or his truck. Making my way through the maze of rigs, I saw it. The rental truck. There was no one in it, but it was unlocked. Inside, the cab was like an oven, as if the truck had been standing out in the sun with the doors closed for a while. Josh had left his fly-fishing cap and sunglasses on the seat, along with his trail maps and crew instructions. The glove compartment was also unlocked, and in it I found the rental papers, the truck's registration, and the duplicate set of keys Frankie had insisted on. Apparently he had left with the intention of coming right back. Thinking he might be using one of the Porta Potties, I waited. Somehow we had missed him.

I caught up with Frankie and Isabel as they were returning from the vet check to wait out Darwin's hold. Isabel came along slowly behind the horse, sunk in thought.

"He's good to go," Frankie announced.

I said, "The truck is here."

"Mine? Of course."

"The rental truck."

"He's here then?" For a moment Isabel was relieved—but only for a moment.

"He's not with the truck, and I haven't located him."

"Oh my God! Where is it?" Isabel turned her back on Darwin. "Where's the truck?"

The truck was still unoccupied. Isabel pawed through it more desperately than I had. Hysteria seemed to be taking hold of her. "Oh my God," she kept saying. In her mind she must have arrived at some terrible eventuality more specific than the possible encounter with the unnamed sister I had worried about. She took Darwin's reins from Frankie and put them insistently in my hand.

"Pull Darwin, Tink. I have to leave. Take him to the timer and have him pulled."

"What?" Frankie cried indignantly. "Are you out of your mind?" She was completely in the dark, I realized, about Josh and events at the Institute. I was merely in deep shade. I knew Josh had been worried and more than likely somewhat intimidated by Celeste's sister. But I didn't know the reason for his concern.

Isabel retrieved the duplicate keys from the truck's glove compartment and slid behind the wheel. Frankie was furious and sputtering.

"How can you do this to me? How can you do this to the horse? You are at mile sixty-eight—almost seventy miles—and you decide to *drop out*?"

Isabel started the truck, and I said, "There are reasons, Frankie. I'm not sure exactly what they are, but I have some notion of what this is all about."

"Well, good for you! I happen to think this is a terrible way to treat a friend who has paid her own way to come all the way out here just to help her ride—just to help schlep water, pick up horse piles, and get hay down my shirt—and now she decides to quit because she can't stand to be separated from her new little romance!"

Then we were in Isabel's rearview mirror. She spun the truck to follow the exit arrows, and the tailgate disappeared.

"Where is her pride?" Frankie's frustration and outrage at being blocked from a win—or at least a top-ten award she could see clearly—were growing. "I should just hop on this wonderful horse and ride him down to Auburn myself."

"You'd disqualify him. Probably better spare him the miles."

"I wish I'd never gotten involved with her. Little ice queen. Wish I'd never got you involved. This is the worst fucking deal—"

"Frankie, could you help me?" My request was serious. "There is a bar on the main street."

"You need a drink? I could use about five!"

"Please," I said, "go to the bar and use their landline to call Farrell's line. "Get Charlie on the phone and tell him Josh has gone AWOL. Maybe it's just that he and Isabel had a fight, but maybe it's because something's going on at the Institute. Then come back here and wait with Darwin for the pull crew. It won't be long. I saw a couple of pull trailers parked near the vets."

"Call Charlie?" Frankie seemed about ready to bawl. "This is so goddamned humiliating. We have a horse ready to top-ten and now we have to ask for help to haul off a perfectly sound horse—so what are you going to do?"

I said, "Get tacked up—I still have eighteen minutes on the hold, and when you get back here, Owen and I are going to start for Francisco's and Auburn—and Frankie, when you talk to Farrell and Charlie, tell them what time we expect to make it to Auburn where the cell phone will work. Tell them to call us there."

She was still muttering about Isabel when she left me with Darwin. I reported to the timer that Darwin was leaving the race.

"Reason?" He had to record something on his form.

I had to think a moment before I said what was true. "The rider is indisposed."

"Too bad," he said. "Real nice horse. You want him trucked down to Auburn?"

The redheaded kid on the chestnut was the first rider out of the Foresthill hold, and his mother rode her gray at the chestnut's flank. Only a moment later Skinner Flemington and his mule trailed after them. How did they get eight minutes on me?

When Frankie returned, she was cranky and frustrated. Her news was enough to put me in the same state. "Farrell hasn't seen Charlie and Stephen since they left for San Francisco and there has been no sighting of Josh."

"Good Christ!" I was now more than a little anxious about Josh and also irritated that Charlie wasn't where he was supposed to be. But I tried to put this aside by reminding myself that lawyers and legal transactions always take more time than seems reasonable.

"What are you going to do?"

"Ride. Isabel has gone to see about Josh, so there's not much we can do to help, except hope that he's okay. I haven't lost much time, and it won't be too hard to make up ten minutes or so."

"You could pull," Frankie pointed out. She had clearly lost heart. "Put both horses on the trailer for Auburn."

I shook my head. "That doesn't seem like the right thing to do."

But the idea of quitting and finding dinner in Auburn was still attractive to Frankie. "What's the point of getting back on the horse, Tink? You're not going to win. You're not even going to top-ten."

"You have that on good information?" I said lightly, but I was miffed about her assumptions.

"He just wasted so much energy in that first thirty miles—and in fact, there's a very good possibility that he won't even finish."

"If you don't want to stay on as crew, Frankie, I will be the last one to waste your time."

A real fight between us was rare, but we were coming close. I was wrangling with her because I was in conflict with myself. I was frightened for Josh and worried about Charlie and Stephen. At the same time, I wanted to ride. The finish line and grandstand waited down in Auburn. To Finish Is To Win. I had worked for months to bring the horse out to these mountains. I had made a commitment to him and to Isabel. How could I turn my back on the opportunity to finish when I had no hard information that could justify pulling, when it was possible that Josh and Isabel were just quarreling and Stephen and Charlie had encountered inevitable legal delays?

I tested the girth, then swung up. Owen lifted his head and looked around for an opening to the trail. Frankie glanced up unhappily. "Sorry, Tink."

"I know. I am too." I patted her head. How bizarre the day had become.

She and Darwin were on their way to the pull trailer. "See you at Francisco's."

12

Dark was beginning to move down over Lake Tahoe Friday evening, and inside the car their four faces were partly obscured. Charlie's regrets were piling up. The lights of the vacation homes scattered along the lake's shore pricked through the dark, and these tiny illuminations prompted a sad thought: He could have bought a vacation place for Tink and him. They were living in what had always been her home, and he had no housing expense of his own. Why had he been so cheap? Maybe he was sunk in negativity, but when he thought back on events of the past few days, he was very angry with himself. He should have pulled out of the deal when Stephen suggested that. He had intuited there was something illicit going on at the Institute. He had sensed he was being strung along. He should have at least tried to anticipate that what started out as underhanded maneuvering could instantaneously escalate to raw coercion. But he was too much of a Boy Scout to recognize evil when it came close, and as a result, he'd put Stephen in the same danger he had blundered into. He sorely regretted that, and he regretted his stupidity. He liked to think he was smart, and he liked to have other people—especially Tink—tell him he was smart. The past twenty-four hours had been hu-miliating. So far the only smart thing he'd done was to offer to play cards with these guys.

Charlie looked down at the cuffs on his wrists then at the forested shoreline flowing past the window, and he regretted his body. His hands were trembling again. Nerves. He felt stretched as taut as a piano wire. And tired. His fatigue was brought on by being whipsawed between terror and boredom. Even in ordinary circumstances he had only a respectable mod-icum of physical strength. He should have been able to grapple with these two dull creeps and incapacitate them in a few swift moves. But that was too far beyond the realm of possibility, and the only thing he could do was regret his lack of prowess and savagery. There was no way for him to talk with Stephen. He wondered if Stephen was riding up and down on the same emotional teeter-totter. He wondered if Stephen was as afraid as he was, as bored by their captors as he was.

The man named Dale was driving. He had the radio tuned to some of the noise Charlie hated the most, country-western with its self-indulgent whine and sticky nostalgia. Dale's hand was quick to the dial, though, and every time Stephen or Charlie shifted even slightly in their seats, Dale snapped off the music. The man was as hypervigilant as one of Tink's terriers, and his on-off between country-western bawling and silence was stretching Charlie's own nerves. Kurt, who rode beside him on the backseat, was less reactive and seemed to be watching Dale for cues.

Balancing his regrets and the frustrating, nerve-searing or-deal with Dale and Kurt was the opportunity of escape—if opportunity is what it was—that Charlie had glimpsed. He hadn't expected it, but if the trip to South Tahoe was an op-portunity, he had to take some comfort in the fact that he had created it. Now he had to figure out how to—what was the word that always came up in board meetings?—*optimize* it. It had been a long time since he had been in a casino—since before his first marriage, in fact—and he only hoped things worked in generally the same way as they had then.

Once he and Stephen made it as far as the casino door, it would be difficult for Dale or Kurt to enforce much of anything on them, much less shoot them. As long as they stayed inside the casino they would be relatively safe. They should prolong their time at the gaming tables, and they should not leave the casino the way they went in, as hostages. As he played, he would need to call attention to himself. When a manager fingered him, he would make a scene, demand to hold on to his winnings and to see the higher-ups. Do something to cause him and Stephen to be drawn away from the tables. That was the script, but he didn't know how that would sync with the script Dale and Kurt were reading from. He didn't know how far the two would go to assure they returned to the cabin with their captives.

Ahead of them an aura of artificial light shone against the deepening dusk, and as they drew closer to South Tahoe, the intensity of this light grew. By the time the car passed the city limits sign, the view was a fun house of neon, streetlights, fluorescents, and headlights. They were headed toward giant neon balloon letters that occupied one side of a high-rise hotel and entertainment complex to announce Harrah's. A bar in every corner, Charlie expected. Dale cut the engine.

Charlie looked down at the handcuffs. "Could I make a few suggestions," he proposed, "about what to expect when we go inside?"

"Sure." Dale sat back for moment, resigned to listening but impatient to begin.

"Sooner or later we are going to be asked to leave. The people who run casinos can recognize card counting, and believe me, they don't like it. The trick is to play and stay under the radar—try not to let the floor people notice you for as long as possible and take home what you can get."

"We'll split up," Dale announced as if he had already thought of it.

Charlie nodded. "And whoever stays with me—"

"That's me," Dale said.

"Hey, man!" Kurt protested.

"You're with me," Dale intoned a line the two of them had evidently rehearsed often. "I'm with you. Right?"

"Whoever goes with me," Charlie resumed his instruction, "plays in the game. Plays as if he's on his own and just happened to end up next to me. Stephen and the other one of you give us plenty of space—go to the bar or play something else. Just try not to lose too much money while you're hanging around. Then when it seems like the pit boss isn't watching, we'll switch, and I'll go to another table with the other one of you." Charlie didn't mention the security cameras, which he hoped would help protect Stephen and him.

Before he and Stephen slid out of the car and stood next to their keepers, the handcuffs were removed and their hands were free. The handguns Dale and Kurt carried would be evident only if someone knew where to look for them or accidentally bumped up against one of the men.

Charlie nodded at Kurt and Stephen. "You two go on in. Make yourselves comfortable." He watched their progress past the statue of the galloping Pony Express rider—"flapping and kicking," Tink would say—and up the steps to the door. Then he turned to Dale. "Are you going to stake me?" Behind the intellectual effect of his dark-rimmed glasses, Dale's gaze was momentarily blank. Then he dug into the pocket of his chinos and brought out a few bills. Charlie counted seventeen dollars. He stared resentfully at the money. Was he supposed to ante up for his kidnappers? Dale looked uncertainly at the bills in his hand, and Charlie waited to see if he could produce more of them. At length Dale said, "You got any?"

Charlie did. He always did. Tink never failed to express surprise at the thickness of the roll and the denominations in it. But he wouldn't show the roll to this creep. Without taking his hand out of his pocket, he separated a couple of bills from the roll. He gave these to Dale and said, "Don't ask me for cash while we're still at the tables, okay? Let's go."

Inside the casino, each area was lit with a different artificial glow. On the second floor, the bar was blue, the slots room a deep forest green, and the gaming rooms an orange-shaded yellow cut by cool track lights. Somewhere in the building, there was a show going on, live music, the same god-awful stuff Dale had played on the radio, and the noises of audience response.

The crowd here was younger and happier than the people in the casinos Charlie remembered. Nobody looked old or hard-bitten. Maybe this was because these were affluent people, playing because they could afford to lose. They were also louder than the casino customers Charlie remembered. He longed for the quiet of his study, where he and Stephen had spent so much time preparing for this California venture that had turned so disastrous.

Stephen and Kurt sat next to a faceted blue wall in the bar. Dale spotted the two beers on the little round table between them and because he seemed to understand that Stephen was buying, he ducked into their alcove to say, "No drinking. Get smart and cut yourselves off." But this didn't appear to frighten Kurt much.

The blackjack tables were conveniently corralled from the other gaming tables by half walls of gleaming wood lattice. There were three tables at play in the pit, and Charlie chose the one with the most vacant seats. The dealer nodded at Charlie's ante and without taking much notice of him, dealt. Just as Charlie had expected—after all, who would have found anything remarkable about a vaguely paunchy guy in a very rumpled suit, deep into middle age and losing the hair on the top of his head? Dale slid into the seat beside him, and Charlie concentrated on the cards.

"I'm in," Charlie said, and he watched the hand play out. Twice he raised a forefinger to beckon another card. Then he waved the dealer off. It was like bidding at an auction, and he was the bidder.

For the dealer this was business as usual. He swept the kitty in Charley's direction and dealt again. Apparently riding a wave of expectation, Dale countermanded his own orders and found a glass of whiskey. Charlie's next cards were low. He waited out the other players, and the kitty came in his direction again, chips to cash out before they left.

The pit boss was a stout woman in a green dress that seemed to squeeze her excess flesh up through the dress's neckline. Chips in hand, Charlie kept his eye on her and the floor manager lurking at a distance behind her and migrated to another table, another dealer. After a couple of minutes, Dale joined him. During the pause in the action, he had refilled his drink. Kurt, with Stephen in tow, emerged from the bar and, not moving in Charlie's direction, began to nonchalantly scout the room. Kurt was trying to figure out if it was time for Charlie to change minders. He was holding a glass of beer, which, evidently from the frost on the glass, was newly drawn. Seeing Dale, he remembered to put the glass behind his back. But then he noticed Dale's whiskey and brought his glass back into view. Charlie noticed all this and wondered whether the alcohol would improve Stephen's and his chances of escaping or their chances of getting roughed up. He was able to sweep up two more kitties. To look as if he were authentic, he forfeited the next hand and said to the woman who was dealing, "Maybe time to find another table, huh?"

Before he could start in the direction of a new table, house phones started ringing at the supervisor's station and at each of the blackjack tables. Charlie thought that the woman dealer had alerted the managers. But then a PA system came on overhead. "Ladies and gentlemen, we have an emergency. Leave your game and get under the tables."

This had nothing to do with counting cards.

Everyone in the room appeared stunned into immobility, but in what was possibly the most rapid series of actions Charlie had ever witnessed, the floor manager collected the house cash from each of the tables, waved an arm at the dealers, and bawled out, "The man said *Get Down*—under a *table*!" He immediately demonstrated how this was to be done, ducking under the nearest table and covering the house money with his body.

Faster than most of the others, Charlie got to his hands and knees and then went prone on the floor. It was dumb luck that had brought him agility in an unlikely body like his with such a long, thick torso—the same luck that had made him a good dancer. At least Tink always said he was good. Charlie lay on his belly beside Dale under the blackjack table and looked around for Stephen, whom he located a couple of yards away under the next blackjack table. At floor level the room smelled of spilled beer and booze. He was trying to take stock, wondering if this fire drill or whatever it was could be an escape opportunity.

Nobody was moving. Nothing suggested motion. There was quiet, an intense quiet. For what could have been an hour but was probably only ten minutes, the room and the building were sunk in soundlessness. Then there was gunfire, not close by but definitely on the same floor. At first, it was an intense round of firing. Then isolated shots. These were followed by a few more at longer intervals and the sound of glass shattering against something hard. After that, except for slight sounds of clothing brushing against carpet, silence.

The fear Charlie felt now was unfocused, uncomprehending. He didn't know what to be afraid of. That magnified the physical sensation of this fear into blind panic. He tried to quell it, to keep his wits.

Next to him, Dale shifted, reaching for the glass he had carried down to the floor with him. The back of his sport jacket flapped out beside him. Under the jacket hem there was a glint, barely visible, of metal. Charlie eyed it, hoping it was the gun Dale had been carrying. But it didn't seem big enough. When Dale reached for his glass again, Charlie recognized the metal glint as the keys to the car.

People were running. There were more gunshots, four or five in a rhythmic series of explosions. Between two of these shots, something fell, making a soft impact. Silence followed. After a minute or so, the stillness was shattered by sharp commands in male voices accompanied by brisk footfalls, enough feet tramping to suggest a small crowd.

Everyone in the room still held to the floor. Perhaps ten minutes passed. Occasionally, a voice, always male, filtered into the big room from the hall outside. Then heavy steps entering the room, moving somewhere behind the blackjack tables. Charlie could see four khaki pant legs and four black, thick-soled shoes. Then the people wearing the shoes announced themselves.

"Police."

Dale lifted up, his head jerking in the direction of the shoes. His sport coat lifted away from the car keys. Everyone on the floor except Charlie was trying to get a look at the officers. He stayed facing Dale's back, wrapped his fingers tightly around the keys to silence them, and drew them toward him across the carpet.

"What's going on?" This question came from under one of the other tables.

"We're going to clear the room," an officer announced, "as soon as we have collected any weapons that are here. We'll move table by table and we'll ask if anyone under it is carrying a gun, a knife, or anything else that might do bodily damage. If this is you, push your weapon away from you between the tables."

One officer changed position to retrieve any weapons that appeared on the carpet. He approached but didn't get very close to the table beside the one Charlie lay under.

"Weapons?"

Charlie was astonished to see Stephen getting up on all fours, then walking toward the state trooper. There was a quiet exchange between them, and Charlie recognized what was going on. He backed out from under the table and, pointing to indicate there was something under that table, moved toward the trooper. This officer was tall and looked reassuringly fit.

"Charles Reidermann," he informed the officer. "Stephen and I were brought here under force. You'll find a gun on the guy with the glasses under that table." The trooper took this in with no change of expression.

"Okay. I'd like the two of you to wait for a few minutes." He beckoned one of the other troopers and assigned Charlie and Stephen to him. "Back wall. They're still working out in the hall."

Kurt's and Dale's guns were rapidly losing their utility. If the two men under the tables fired at anyone in the room, they would instantaneously soak up return fire. But the tall trooper was taking no chances.

"Stay exactly as you are," he instructed Kurt and Dale in turn. "And slide the guns out on the floor where you can't reach them. Anybody else here carrying a weapon?"

Nothing happened. No guns were offered from under the tables. Charlie tried to figure out how the troopers were going to extricate the weapons from Dale and Kurt without getting fired at. For the moment, the troopers didn't appear to doubt Charlie's or Stephen's word on the presence of guns. They repeated their order. Charlie drew a slow breath.

Silence ensued. But only for a moment. The tall trooper nodded, and his partner went to the table sheltering Dale. He kicked it over. It fell on the carpet with a brief racket. This left Dale lying in full view on his side, his empty glass just in reach. The trooper had drawn his gun.

"Put that gun out here."

Dale slid the gun away from him.

"Get up."

Dale eased himself upright to find that he was still monitored by the tall trooper's sidearm. He watched sourly as the trooper who had exposed him repeated his order to Kurt, and when the officer got no response, he put his foot on the edge of the table Kurt cowered under. At that moment Kurt coiled and thrust himself at the trooper, sinking his teeth into the officer's ankle. The trooper spun out of Kurt's jaws, reversed the gun in his hand, and struck Kurt in the head with its butt. He swiftly retrieved the gun from Kurt's hand. He waited until Kurt seemed to recover from the blow, then said, "Get up."

But that hardly seemed necessary. Kurt had begun to lumber to his feet, woozy as a carsick kid.

"Cuff them," the tall trooper instructed. "And call in for another squad car."

After that, perhaps fifteen other people struggled to their feet and looked around in bewilderment, wondering why they had been ordered to the ground. A third trooper stepped up to usher the customers out of the building, and their questions began immediately.

The tall trooper interposed. "We had a robbery in the casino. The guy was armed." There was a lull in the questioning and exclamations. "He's no longer in the building."

That, Charlie would learn when they came out into the early Saturday dark, was something of a metaphor. He stood by watchfully until Dale and Kurt were led out of the casino. He and Stephen, also with an escort, followed them outside, where police were taping off the area immediately around the casino. There were three ambulances parked along the curb near the casino entrance. One of them pulled away. There were lights on inside the two remaining ambulances. In one the lights were switched off, and in the other they were dimmed.

"Somebody died," Charlie told Stephen. The patrol car carrying Dale and Kurt pulled away, and he and Stephen rode to headquarters in a different car. He imagined the two men were responding to a different set of questions from a different detective.

"What brings you out to this part of the country?"

"Stephen and I had business in San Francisco, and my wife is here to ride the Tevis."

This sparked the trooper's interest. "Did she finish?"

"We don't know," Charlie explained. "Those two guys nabbed us on our way back here from San Francisco."

"Where did they take you?" The detective took notes on their impressions of the cabin. "What did they want, ransom?"

"I hope this doesn't sound fishy, officer. We know in a general way where they came from, but we don't know exactly what they expected to gain from kidnapping us. You should be able to get a better answer from them."

"What was your business in San Francisco?"

"A company merger."

That seemed to satisfy the investigator, who assured them, "They were probably looking for ransom then. Did either of them mention Nelson Laidlaw?"

"No, not a thing."

"He was the sniper killed in the casino tonight. He came up out of this side of the Divide. He was in pretty rough shape, according to the owner of the gun shop he robbed. He didn't get much cash there, so he went into the casino looking for money and blabbering about an institute up in Donner Lake. Which is where you're staying."

Charlie let out a long breath. "Then I can see why you're asking about Laidlaw. It's likely there was some connection between him and the two you took into custody tonight, but I certainly couldn't define that exactly."

This much was absolutely true. So he didn't go any further for the moment. He wanted to tell the police the truth, and he wanted to be released as soon as possible to get back to the Institute. It was likely that, now, coming away from the casino with considerable leverage over Celeste, he could negotiate with her to withdraw the new will—before police swarmed the place.

"We'll need a deposition. You going to be in the area for a few days? If so, you can come back to take care of that. We have our hands pretty full right now—robbery, shooting, and a kidnapping—and we're a small force."

When they were out on the street again, Stephen said as quietly as possible, "Jeezus, what an ordeal! I've counted myself dead at least four times since we left San Francisco." They were heading almost unconsciously back toward the casino.

"I know what you mean," Charlie told him, "only I was too scared to keep score like that."

"You didn't act scared," Stephen challenged him.

"Oh, I was. I was. Scared shitless, as your ma says."

"But not too scared to play cards," Stephen pointed out, and Charlie, able to take credit now for at least that, felt his spirits lifting.

"Know why I was scared, Charlie? More scared than I've ever been in my life? I'm going to be a father."

Charlie stopped right there on the sidewalk. "You and Alex?" he asked and then realized it was a stupid question. He really disliked feeling stupid, but these days he didn't seem to be able to escape it for long. He dithered, forgot to offer congratulations, then said the first thing that came to him. "Does Tink know? And she didn't tell me?"

Stephen said simply, "I told her not to." Then, seeing Harrah's a few blocks ahead, he said, "How are we going to get back to Farrell's—or wherever we're going?"

From his trouser pocket Charlie produced the keys to the Plymouth. Stephen looked worried. "Charlie, it's not our car."

"Probably doesn't belong to Kurt or Dale either," Charlie pointed out. "I think we should return it to where it came from."

"The Institute? Why, Charlie? Don't you think it was Celeste who set those goons on us?"

"I don't know exactly who, Stephen. But I think those two being in custody will give us a bit of leverage with her, or whoever is supervising her."

"Leverage?"

"To persuade her to withdraw the new will and back out of contention over AccuGen."

"Oh man, I don't know," Stephen said worriedly. "Didn't we just make a hairy escape? This could get dangerous, and I really don't want to leave an orphan."

"Celeste may be capable of hiring thugs," Charlie granted Stephen that much, "but I don't think she's capable of being dangerous herself."

"I don't know, Charlie," Stephen countered unhappily. "Kurt got pretty nervous when I asked him about that CPAP machine."

Continuous Positive Air Pressure. *Air.*

Stephen's suggestion was like a shaft of clear, cold light. So clear Charlie didn't bother to ponder it. "Right. You could be absolutely right. That's your second brilliant idea tonight—the first one was to get up on your feet in the casino."

"So we shouldn't head back to the Institute," Stephen concluded.

"No. We should. If you're right about what happened to Grant-Worthington, it's just further proof of my assessment of the woman. She's underhanded, but passive in her methods. And she's too timid to be openly aggressive."

"I hope you're right, Charlie. But maybe you've been hanging with Ma too long."

"This is the best, the fastest, way to bring this deal to closure, Stephen. When you can find a truck stop, I'll go in and phone Savage and Messmer. They should be in on this."

13

When I rode out of the Foresthill hold Saturday afternoon, Owen and I were in seventh position. Ten minutes ahead of me were the young red-haired kid and his mother, the three superfits on their horses in three different shades of chestnut, and the mule. It would be a half hour before Owen would see the horses ahead of him, and he chugged along quite amiably. This was the first time I had ridden him more than fifty miles, and over the distance the egotistical attitude he had started the race with had been honed down to something more workmanlike and more beautiful. Now he seemed to be saying, "Yes, I think so. Let's give it a go." His will ran deep, but I was discovering it was malleable.

I had been in the saddle for most of the eleven hours we had raced, and now that the horse and I were alone, I suddenly noticed I was getting tired. The fatigue didn't affect my body so much—my limbs were still in good working order, if you don't count the long chafed patches on the inside of my legs—but the fatigue stirred my thoughts into jumpy disorganization. No sooner did I consider a strategy for catching up to and passing the three superfit men on their chestnuts somewhere up ahead than I began to speculate on Isabel's sudden departure, trying to fathom what she thought had happened to Josh. I considered how the color of the ground under Owen's feet had turned a reddish color and the evergreens were different at this altitude, smaller and bushier than their counterparts farther north. These observations leaped illogically to Stephen and Charlie and why they were not where they were supposed to be, sitting at Farrell's big table and tucking away chicken marengo and wild rice. My thoughts needed disciplining. My hands and legs obeyed me, and the horse kept moving. I just needed to impose mental order.

Owen raised his head when he caught sight of the backside of a chocolate-chestnut horse ahead, the trailing horse in the superfit group. There was little space to pass, and I called out to give the rider notice. He watched Owen coming alongside and said, "Oh, I see he's going to survive his hissies."

"Maybe," I called back. But I didn't keep my lead for even a minute because a hundred yards ahead, the front-runners had packed up around a steep bottleneck. We slowed and then Owen was alongside the chocolate-chestnut horse again. This is how the race proceeded over the seventeen miles between Foresthill and Francisco's. A surge to pass and get ahead and then back to a slower, steadier pace in some intermediate position. I wasn't terribly frustrated because I found that riding in the company of the other riders was somehow soothing. It was not that they weren't racing or that I wasn't racing against them, it was that the trail made its own immutable demands, and we all had to accede.

In the meantime, the desultory conversation and occasional jokes momentarily drew me away from worries that grew when they returned. What was Josh up to that was urgent and maybe dangerous enough to take Isabel out of the race? And why hadn't Charlie and Stephen returned from San Francisco or even phoned Farrell to let him know they'd changed their plans?

The trail had dropped down close to the Middle Fork, taking us past long, rocky rapids and, before a sharp descent, a hydroelectric plant in the distance. We followed the river into the meadow called Francisco's, and when I rode into the checkpoint, I was relieved to see Frankie standing watchfully near the P&R squad. Riders' crews were not allowed to help with the horses at Francisco's, but there was nothing to keep Frankie from walking in from Highway 49 to see that Owen and I had arrived safely for the vet check. She gave me a big wave, just as if we had arrived at the same party and the band was about to play. No hard feelings. That was true to form. Frankie could blow sky-high, and five minutes later her anger would be overtaken by affection for whatever friend—in this case, me—she had just showered with expletives. Now she looked quite fresh. She had had time to wash her face, fix her hair, and put on lipstick. I wondered what I looked like. When I walked Owen past her on my way to the people wearing stethoscopes, she said, "I called Farrell again to ask him if he could go to Robie Park to pick up our trailer."

I wasn't worried about the trailer. I said, "Has Farrell heard anything from Charlie or Stephen?"

"I know they're okay," she reassured me. "And you can't worry about them now."

But I did. I said, "Frankie, you need to keep checking with Farrell. I know and you know there is some bad shit going on at the Institute. I'm worried those people have got to Josh. And I can't figure out what the fuck Charlie and Stephen have run up against."

"You made your choice, Tink. You're staying in the race. So

try to keep you mind on that, just that. You've only got another fifteen miles and what's that? Another hour and forty-five?"

I looked at Owen. Either he was getting taller or I was shrinking. I said, "I can't think," and climbed up on the horse.

"You're tired, sweetie. That's all."

"How do you know?"

"Your foot just had trouble finding the stirrup," she pointed out.

When I left Francisco's in the company of the three men on chestnuts, the sun was low and the air a little cooler. The mule was now just behind us. In an hour or so dark would catch up to all of us. I had been riding all my life and had never ridden in the dark. But I couldn't fret about that because Owen's night vision—any horse's—was better than a human's. And I had other worries to crowd out that one. Josh. Isabel. Stephen. Charlie. The trail along the Middle Fork was nearly level now, a luxury. The horses liked the easy going and the cooler air, and they moved out.

In the dusk we came to Poverty Bar, the deepest moving water on the trail. The crossing was marked by glow sticks floating on a rope strung across the river. At this lovely sight, one of the three chestnut horses, the light chestnut with the blond mane, suddenly asked to be excused. He shied off from the lights in the water, snorting and showing the whites of his eyes.

"Nah, nah," Donald said. "Don't waste yourself, my lad. We still have almost ten miles to go." Eventually, when the horse was left standing unhappily at the river's edge by himself, he put a tentative foot in the water and then splashed nervously across to catch up to his friends.

Owen had played in the river, pawing the water to watch the spray. He had it in mind to get down and roll in the water.

246 • Holly Menino

But I nixed that plan. Considering the distance we had come, he seemed happy and comfortable enough. But a few minutes after we crossed the river he slowed. To my frustration, the three chestnut horses pulled ahead, and yet Owen hung back. I started to go at him, pushing him with my legs and voice. Then I realized what was happening. Owen was "tying up." I popped out of the saddle, loosened the girth, and ran my hand down his flank and over his hindquarters. Sure enough, the muscles were hard. They were seizing up and could nearly paralyze him. Tying up is a metabolic shutdown whose various causes are suggested by the veterinary manuals as "in combination with exercise." Owen had certainly had enough of that.

I wanted to keep the horse moving. If he stopped, the cramping could immobilize him, maybe for hours. "Poor baby, poor baby." Other times when I was trying to get a horse to do something he didn't want to, I said things in the same affectionate voice but didn't mean them. Now my sympathy was as real as his pain. The wiry Ben circled back to me on his chestnut.

"Problems?"

"He's tied up."

Everybody on the trail knew what that meant, and he shook his head sympathetically. "Damn shame. When he looked so good."

"Please don't wait around with me. Could you report this to the vets at Lower Quarry? Ask them—if I haven't turned up in an hour—to send somebody out here with some painkiller."

"Righto. Keep him moving if you can."

Owen was finished. We were out. No question about it. In a way, I was relieved. I could quit the race, and Frankie and I could try to find out what was going on at the Institute or at least find Charlie and Stephen. The only goal remaining was to get the horse to the Lower Quarry vet check, a mile ahead.

He seemed to be able to keep shuffling along. I didn't try to hustle him. I just wanted him to maintain a pace that was more or less comfortable. Although there was still light lingering in the sky, the trail was quite dark, which made it difficult to judge how far we had walked or how far we had to go. But I heard something up ahead.

"Hey, horse!" A figure emerged and slowly defined itself as a blocky young man standing immediately in front of Owen. The three chestnuts had made it into Lower Quarry. In the man's chest pocket was a row of syringes. Without bothering with an introduction, he moved between me and the horse, one hand holding a syringe and the other hand stroking the horse, rubbing his face. He said, "Poor horse. Lousy way for such a good guy to feel, isn't it?" And the needle went in.

We waited for the painkiller to take effect, and the vet said, "Had a number of these today, a few more than usual."

"Do you know why?"

"There's quite a few who think they know and quite a few who will tell you they have the key. Fact of the matter is, once you get past the exertion factor, nobody has been able to put a finger on what the other stuff is—why don't we see if we can get him as far as the hold?"

Lower Quarry was illuminated by lanterns of every variety with lights in every shade of bright. Frankie stood in the glow of one of these lanterns. In the flickering of the lanterns, my friend was her beautiful old self, with her beautiful old spirit. But she was anxious, watching for us, and when she saw Owen, she ran to us.

"He tied up," I explained. She didn't listen to that. She said, "Farrell told me the police called the ranch. They found the rental car. Charlie and Stephen left it somewhere between Truckee and the Institute.

"Nobody in the car?" I asked stupidly. She gave me a frantic look.

"I just told you, Tink. They found the *car.*"

I handed her Owen's reins. "Give me the keys—and pull this goddamn horse. He's done."

If Frankie, rather than me, pulled the horse, I would be disqualified, disgraced, rather than scoring an honorable discharge. But I didn't give a shit.

As if my fear and swearing stirred it, the truck's diesel engine cooperated immediately, clattering into action. The truck's headlights showed me Highway 49's narrow, winding path into the outskirts of Auburn and then up the ramp to I-80. On the four-lane, I relinquished any remaining scrap of patience I had and stomped on the accelerator.

There wasn't much traffic, though the resort developments along the way were filled with tourists who had already made their way up the big road that climbed steadily into the highest peaks. Stephen. Charlie. I was thinking of them in the order they had come to me. I needed to know what they had happened on, why they had left their car. I needed to know they were okay, and I was headed to the Institute to find out. If a trooper had pulled me over for the violation, I would've had to explain that too many things were going unexplained and that before anything else happened that would require an explanation. I was rushing for explanations and for reassurance that Stephen and Charlie were unharmed.

I had the truck blasting up toward Donner Lake and Truckee when the farthest, dimmest sweep of the truck's headlights caught something way across the median and the lanes of opposing travel. A truck and horse trailer, pulled off on the shoulder with its lights still on. Truck and trailer, a familiar combination. But as often happens when something familiar appears in unexpected context, it took me a long moment to recognize that the truck was Farrell's rust bucket, and the trailer was the long one that Isabel and I had hauled out here from Philadelphia. Maybe Farrell's truck had conked out. I didn't want to stop for him, didn't want to lose a moment. I was guilty and impatient at the same time. Goddamn it, Farrell, why, why can't you get your life together the way you have your kitchen together? Why do I have to give you precious minutes?

The next exit was more than fifteen miles ahead, but in places the median was level. I drove ahead until I found a possible path across the grass strip.

Farrell saw headlights coming and stepped out to try to flag this vehicle down before he even recognized it. I pulled off on the shoulder just ahead of him.

"Damn, Tink! What you girls up to now?"

"Goddamn it, Farrell, I'm not a girl, and what I'm up to is all about hurry."

"This has sure been one damn weird day," Farrell commented. "First, Frankie calls to find out if Stephen and Charlie have got back. Then Isabel calls looking for Josh. Then the cops call because Charlie and Stephen ditched the rental car. And I thought the whole lot of you would be partying at the fairgrounds—did you get pulled?"

Baby filled the truck's window, showing her teeth. "Farrell," I pleaded, "shut up. Are you all right? Just tell me that."

"Me? Oh yeah. It's just that this truck has crapped out."

"Have you called the tow truck?" I hoped this would relieve me of rescue duty.

Todd Farrell looked at me like I was a very slow learner. "You know them mobiles don't work out here."

What would it take to hurry the man and his thinking?

"Farrell, it's Stephen. And Charlie, I can't screw around here another minute."

He said, "Wait a minute," and went into the cab of his truck. He switched off the headlights and returned carrying Baby so that she wouldn't run out into the dark road. She was cradled in his arms, not like a lamb in a shepherd's arms but like the baby Jesus, on her back with her legs folded up and her sharp face resting against Farrell's chest. She settled grandly in the front seat, taking up so much space that she crowded Farrell against the door.

"Tink, why don't you just tell me what is going on?"

"Because I don't know." I made this sound as firm as possible.

"Where you going?"

"I'm not sure where I'll have to go. But I'm going to start with the Institute."

"You sure you want to do that?" Farrell was shaking his head. "There's been so much shit going on out there."

"Right, and I just want to be sure that Charlie and Stephen or Isabel and Josh aren't knee-deep in it." We took the exit for Truckee, and when we came off the ramp, I indicated a starkly illuminated truck stop. "Like me to drop you off?"

"Never mind that just now," Farrell told me about his crippled truck. "I think I better go with you. Me and Baby."

Right, I thought ironically. Baby. The perfect search and rescue dog.

When we turned in the private road that led to the Institute, the lights of the building flared against black-cloaked mountains. Another car turned in to the road behind us, which I found uncanny for this time of night. Its headlights lit up the truck cab.

"Who in hell is that?" Farrell wondered.

There was a car already parked in the stone-ringed lot in front of the soaring building. It was a dark blue sedan that had red lights posted on its roof, the kind used by volunteer fire-fighters. I was disappointed that it wasn't Charlie's rental car or the truck Frankie had rented for Josh.

"Doesn't look like any of them are here," I said.

"Well," Farrell insisted, "somebody's here. Better pull in."

The car traveling behind us also pulled in. I slid out of the truck, and the front door of the car beside us opened. Paul Savage stepped out of the driver's seat and stood up, straightening his sport coat. He turned to speak to us, and in the light pouring out of the Institute's faceted glass wall, considered me. I stopped breathing.

"Hello, Tink, he said quietly. There was nothing unkind in his voice or in his face. In fact, it was almost like, "How nice to see you," which he didn't actually say.

I said, "What the fuck are you doing here? Where are Stephen and Charlie?"

Not looking at all surprised, Paul said, "Charlie called an impromptu meeting. On behalf of all of us."

"Hey, Paul, you two know each other?"

"Sure," Paul came back and easily dodged the next question. "I've been working with Stephen and Charlie on the AccuGen deal." He went back into his car for his laptop. "They asked me and Carol Messmer to meet them out here, but Carol couldn't get here tonight."

So Charlie and Stephen would be coming along. This was significant news. I had forgotten or maybe simply never noticed how tactful Paul was. The two men started for the building's amazing front doors, Paul inquiring if Farrell was there for the meeting, and Farrell saying, "No, broke down is all."

Baby watched Farrell walk away and realized she would be left in the truck. She was indignant, furious, and she began barking, whining, scratching at the window. Farrell's sighed and turned back to rescue her. By the time we got to the doors, Baby was already there, and evidently had never been told she wasn't allowed to go somewhere. She trotted into the soaring foyer. The place seemed an even more imaginative architectural exploit from the inside than it looked from the outside. I could imagine esteemed authorities gathered in this reception area to trade brilliant ideas. But the place was oddly quiet now, soundless, in fact. Baby, sniffing the seams where the glass wall met the floor and looking into corners, disappeared down a hallway. When I found enough composure to speak to Paul, I said, "I've been really worried. Frantic."

He smiled. This man I had treated so badly smiled at me. I witnessed this without being quite able to believe it. Farrell, concerned about what trouble Baby might be getting into, hustled silently after the dog. We followed their path into the hall.

Scratching at a door along the hallway and whimpering, Baby interrupted the silence that pervaded the Institute. Farrell behaved as the dog willed him to and opened the door. He stepped back immediately. When we came up beside him we saw what he was staring at. Paul's smile disappeared. In the room were five people observing one another silently. The woman with the streaked-blond hair who had appeared at the Tevis briefing was half-sitting against the edge of a dramatic conference table made of a slice from the trunk of an enormous redwood tree. Seated off to one side were a tall blond man—a professorial person in linen with small rectangular horn-rims—and Celeste. Finally, standing, not leaning, against a wall opposite the two women were Stephen and Charlie. I didn't mind that they didn't rush over to me. I was just relieved to see them, each of them, in such good shape.

"Welcome." This came from the woman braced against the edge of the table. She had exchanged her jeans for a tailored black pantsuit and her boots for three-inch heels, both of which lent her authority.

"Thanks," I said and headed into the room. "Charlie, I have been so—"

He sent me a fierce glance to silence me and with a slight turn of his head, redirected my eyes to the woman who had invited me into the room. Her hand, its heel resting at the level of the tabletop, held a gun. I didn't know enough about guns to know what make or model it was, but I knew enough to recognize it was capable of doing its job. Then I saw that her professorlike partner had laid a handgun carefully on his knee. I saw these people—the woman with the gun, the man with the gun, and Celeste sitting dumbly at the conference table—but I couldn't understand what they were doing or what they were planning to do. It couldn't be real. Maybe fatigue was sabotaging me.

Paul Savage spoke up. "Celeste, what is—"

"Estelle." The woman apparently in charge made this correction with a smirk, she of course being Estelle.

But Paul persisted, guns or no guns. "Celeste, we really need some kind—"

"Celeste is not in a position to speak."

Farrell, hand on Baby's neck to keep her quiet and sizing up the woman with the gun, said in his folksy way, "Estelle, you wouldn't be a Laidlaw, would you?"

Another smirk as she corrected him. "A McCarran."

Perhaps seeing an opening, Charlie said, "Paul, I'm very sorry. Stephen and I had no idea—"

"Uh-uh-uh," Estelle broke in. "No chitchat."

"—what we would walk into here."

How long had he and Stephen been here? They both looked rumpled and tired, probably more tired than I was. I couldn't ask them about that. But since she hadn't aimed the gun at anyone who had spoken to her yet, I tried that.

"I don't understand what's going on here. What is it that you want?"

"I want to get some paperwork out of the way."

That clarified a good deal.

Estelle looked around as if she were taking attendance. "All here? Is this everyone we're expecting this evening?"

I had no idea who else might be on the guest list, and Charlie and Stephen remained quiet.

"How about you?" She nodded at Farrell. "You're the big host, aren't you?"

"How could I be expecting anybody else?" Farrell protested. "I wasn't expecting myself." This was entirely accurate—if I hadn't picked him up because his truck broke down, he wouldn't have been here—but he seemed to assume that he would continue on the same familiar terms with people at the Institute that he always had.

Evidently satisfied, Estelle closed the door of the meeting room.

Then her professor friend took the podium. "This is a very meaningful transaction."

He lost me right there, and I could see Charlie resented having to be his audience. Stephen seemed to be at a remove, analyzing what was being said and what might happen from a perch high above the rest of us.

"This is a wonderful institution—" He waved expansively around to suggest that our immediate environs were actually much larger than anyone in the room. Now I recognized him. I remembered the images Stephen had called up on his computer. This was McCarran's spokesman. "Our Community embraces its mission. But unfortunately our mission has been undermined by the alliances of its leadership."

Now that McCarran was dead, who the hell was he representing? What was he getting at? I tried to catch Celeste's eye. She was looking at the floor.

"Our concern is, of course, the youngsters. Our children need quality education, and the Community has been working for a long time to improve the schools. But this will not be possible as long as Charles Darwin and his ideas are promoted as facts in our schools. It's laughable, isn't it, that the ramblings of a hypochondriac recluse continue to be taught as *science* to our children—children whose young minds are hungry for real knowledge?"

McCarran's professor continued. "We know that the leadership and ownership should be Christian. We made a good-faith offer for AccuGen. But evidently it was not enough. Dr. Grant-Worthington was looking elsewhere for a non-Christian source of capital."

Charlie's eyes were half-closed, his expression wary, and beside him, Stephen was wide-eyed, appalled.

"If the doctor had been wiser and more Christian, none of us would be in the predicament we're in now."

The word *predicament* was accurate. I looked over at Charlie, but he didn't acknowledge this. He said, "How are you going to resolve it?"

"This predicament?" The professor turned his palms toward the ceiling, an ominous gesture. "We have a number of ways," he said. That seemed to implicate the guns. "Some easier to take than others. We'll do whatever is necessary to get what we need and what the doctor's latest will provides for, which is, of course, Christian ownership." This was undisguised extortion. But who in the room had the power to make the bargain he sought? "And unfortunately, while he was well-meaning, Dr. Grant-Worthington wasn't that."

From talking with Josh I knew enough about Grant-Worthington's ideals to know this wasn't exactly straight-line thinking. It caused Farrell to explode.

"The hell you say!"

Either he hadn't registered the precariousness of our situation or he figured that whatever else happened, he would die and so had nothing to lose by speaking out. He was making me afraid, and not only for him. I willed him to be quiet.

"The doctor was the finest Christian I ever met."

"Except that," the spokesman went on gently, "he wasn't a Christian."

"What in hell are you talking about?" Farrell was infuriated not only by the pompous ass in the linen jacket but by the inversion of everything he thought he knew about the Institute. Estelle was tight-lipped.

"Grant-Worthington," the professor stated with punctuated authority, "was a Un-i-tarian."

"Well then," Farrell lapsed into sarcasm, "I guess that settles—"

The door from the hallway burst open, and Isabel charged forward and launched on Estelle.

"You demented bitch!" she screamed. "You killed him. You depraved, you demented . . ." Isabel made contact with her fists and shoulders and knees. She hadn't seen the guns. But Baby had seen her, the veterinarian and public enemy who had been allowed to inhabit her own kitchen all these days. Because a dog can react almost at the same nanosecond it perceives a thing, Baby was immediately on the pair of women, a red-and-white blur with teeth, snarling and not just snapping but tearing into the two bodies. She ripped into an arm she thought was Isabel's. It belonged to Estelle. As Baby's teeth ground in deeper, Estelle involuntarily fired, then lost her grip on the gun. It fell between the brawling women. The Border collie was still slashing with her teeth. Seeing this, I went for the gun. And seeing me in the fray, the professor, who could not shoot without hitting his partner, raised the butt of his gun to smash it down on Isabel or me, whichever one of us came in handy.

In that instant, something remarkable happened. Stephen was behind the professor, locking the linen-suited arms behind the man, inserting a knee into the man's back at kidney level, and twisting his hand until the gun dropped from it. I was there to pick up anything that fell my way. I handed one gun off to Farrell and one to Paul. While I was occupied doing this, Stephen put a hammerlock on the professor and with a couple of wrenching movements put him on the floor. Baby and Isabel were still going at Estelle. She would need hobbling, but in this artistically pristine meeting room, there was no rope.

I said, "Charlie, give me your shirt. And Paul—oh my God, I can't believe you're here in the middle of this—could you give me yours?"

Getting the shirts was easy. Getting Isabel and Baby off Estelle was not. But I tied the bonds on Estelle's feet, shoved Baby off with my foot, then took a few blows from Isabel while I tied the shirt around Estelle's wrists. Charlie got hold of Isabel and drew her away from her victim. She was still yelling and quieted only to assess the bruises she had delivered to Estelle and the bloody wounds Baby had torn. Stephen was using Farrell's shirt and his own to truss up the professor, and Paul rushed out to get to the office and a landline.

It was only then that Isabel said, "I think I've been hit." She cast a clinical eye on her left upper arm and said, "Yup. Get me something for a tourniquet." But she didn't stay with it long enough to tie the belt Charlie gave her. She fainted, and I don't think it was the sight of her own blood that caused this.

Celeste never made a move. She never made a sound. I said, "Don't you dare get out of that chair." She didn't. Because she didn't dare to do anything. It was hard to believe she was the woman who had been such a source of anxiety for Josh. She was like a marionette whose strings had been cut, inert, her face vacant.

When Isabel came to a few minutes later, she was crying. Her bright blue eyes were red in every other respect, and the curls close to her face became damp. "It's not going to happen," she wailed, and except for Paul, all of us knew what that meant.

14

I stayed what was left of Saturday night with Charlie and Stephen at Farrell's. Farrell insisted on opening up a room for Paul Savage, and given the hour and the night's events, Paul had no other recourse. After Paul reached the 911 dispatcher, it took a half hour for the Truckee sheriff to reach the Institute. The rescue squad's ambulance was a minute behind, and two state troopers appeared in the meeting room while an EMT was seeing to Isabel. The troopers confiscated the guns and within a few minutes removed Celeste, Estelle, and her professorial partner.

It took longer for the rescue squad to move Isabel than for the police to put the Institute trio in squad cars because she was crying and fighting them off, insisting she could walk. Finally she fainted a second time and became an easily lifted weight on their stretcher. Farrell sat on the floor with his arms around Baby and his cheek against her shoulder. He and the rest of us were dismissed with orders to reappear and give depositions first thing in the morning.

When we gathered in the kitchen before following those instructions Sunday morning there was time only for coffee and what Farrell called "this damn cold breakfast." Baby was the only one of us who wasn't bedraggled, and she skittered around, making nice with the men and pretending I wasn't there.

"Isn't she something?" Farrell bragged. "And my God, I was terrified. It looked like a pretty sure thing one of those creeps would shoot her."

"It looked like the rest of us stood a pretty fair chance too," Paul commented. "And wasn't what they were saying about Grant-Worthington unbelievable? I mean, he was essentially a scholar of Darwin, and I knew his thoughts on God and Christianity because he was best man at my wedding." He was referring to his second one, which Charlie had mentioned.

"But those *people*," Stephen said the word as if he were saying *pond slime* or *reptiles*, "why was he involved with them?"

"He was involved with Celeste," Farrell said. "Told me she was a member of a church somewhere up in Canada. That was okay with him. I don't think he paid much attention to it. I mean, I don't think he knew how deep he was in."

"At least not until he got the offer for AccuGen from the church." Charlie amended. "He may have figured out that the church had folded other profit-making companies into its nonprofit organization. But whatever he knew, he wasn't going to take their offer over the arrangements with Halefellow. So McCarran decided to take him out."

"Then Laidlaw decided his daddy had made Celeste fire him, and McCarran got it," Farrell explained, "which left Celeste's sister and that guy with the itty-bitty glasses calling the shots. And wasn't Celeste a piece of work last night? Just like one of those dolls on the ventriloquist's lap, only the string to her mouth had come untied. She didn't have anything to say about any of it. Lost all her uppity, didn't she?"

I left police headquarters after giving a deposition and picked up Frankie at the fairgrounds, where she had spent the night in a borrowed bunk in another crew's trailer. When she saw me Frankie said, "Oh dear, Tink. Maybe you better go back to bed and start over."

Frankie herself looked worse than I'd ever seen her. She was sleep-deprived and stiff. There were dim bluish circles under her eyes, her hair needed washing, and most noteworthy, she wasn't wearing lipstick.

We drove to a little hospital in the suburbs north of Auburn. It was new, and the square white columns that supported the roof of its portico were perhaps intended as a gesture toward a traditional Spanish veranda. The hospital had only about sixty beds and not many ways to get lost. Frankie and I had no trouble finding Isabel's room.

Isabel was sleeping and looked pretty small in the hospital bed. But otherwise she looked okay. Some bruises on one side of her face and one hand, a long bandage on one arm, and an IV in the other arm.

Frankie looked Isabel over critically.

"She looks pretty good, don't you think?" I said. "Maybe we should come back later."

"Naw," Isabel protested without opening her eyes. Her next thought came out slowly. "I want you to stay." Then her eyes started leaking tears. She was silently bawling.

Frankie leaned over the bed rail and said, "Isabel, you are supposed to be sedated."

"Yeah," she drawled. "They gave me some Ativan."

"That's supposed to make you feel good. I mean feel okay."

"Yeah, I told 'em it wouldn't." Isabel's face was slick with her tears. Frankie and I knew this was about Josh. We knew he had died, but we didn't know how. Isabel did, and I grieved for her. I'm a sympathetic crier, and I've never been any good at saying things that make people feel better. So I took hold of her hand and tried not to cry. It was difficult to tell what she was thinking.

Frankie tried a new tactic. She put her face down closer to Isabel's and said, "Want to hear about the race?"

Isabel's eyes remained shut, and in spite of her delayed speech, she said quite distinctly, "I don't give a rat's ass about the race," and began actively bawling. Frankie took no notice of this.

"I'm going to tell you about the race. Darwin did not finish."

"Yeah, yeah."

"But Owen did."

Isabel opened her eyes slightly. "Huh?"

"He tied up right after Poverty Bar, and we pulled him," I explained.

"Used to do that all the time. Tie up."

She had never told me Owen had that tendency. If I had known about that, I might have changed my mind about traveling all the way across country with the horse.

"Thought I had it fixed," she murmured.

"We had to pull him," Frankie put in hastily because she wanted to get to her part of the story. "Tink deserted. She left me with Owen to wait for a pull trailer. When I heard there was one coming in, I asked one of the other crew people to hold the horse so that I could meet the truck and trailer. But when I got back, Owen was gone. A group of riders who came in behind Tink left the hold. They trotted past Owen, and he woke up and took off. Tore away from the person holding him and tried to catch up to those other horses, even though he wasn't able to go very fast."

"Figures." Isabel's eyelids closed.

"I had to run after your goddamned horse, maybe a mile. I was stumbling around in the dark, really mad. He could see the trail better than I could. So when I caught him, he pulled me along, tripping and banging my knees. I thought, What the hell, and when we got to a place where the trail dipped down and I was uphill from him, I stopped him—had to fight him to do it—and jumped up on him. It was easier than trying to lead the idiot, and I got to ride across the No-Hands Bridge with the lights and all—very pretty and I was absolutely not scared because I was too tired and bleary to look down."

Isabel grunted.

"So I came up to the back of the fairgrounds and was wandering around looking for the barns where we were supposed to be stabled. I came to a place with lights, and there were a few people sitting at a table. They said congratulations—"

"Oh God," Isabel sighed.

"—and pointed out the way to go. I did what they said and I ended up out in this big arena, standing in these intense lights—and right behind me, here comes this old white-haired guy on that *mule*. I mean, it was a nightmare."

Isabel's chest was heaving again. A nurse, seeing the two of us bent over the bed, came into the room and looked Isabel over. "Still weepy? That arm pretty sore, Doctor?"

The word *doctor* prodded Isabel into a responsible answer. "Yes, it is."

The nurse turned to us and said by way of noting improvement, "When the cops were here early this morning, she was too out of it and upset to make sense. I told them to come back after lunch." Then she looked at her watch. "You're going on four hours now, Doctor. I can get you something more for pain."

"Give me everything you've got." Isabel said quite clearly, and when the nurse had gone, she said, "He knew," and she dropped my hand. "That's why they killed him."

Frankie and I glanced at each other and waited.

"He figured it out about the CPAP machine, that she'd switched the stuff in the canister. Nitrogen. And Celeste caught him fiddling with the connection to the canister."

"Stephen has pointed out that possibility to the police," I told her. But if she took in the information, Isabel didn't acknowledge it.

"So they killed him. And I found him." She stopped because the nurse had brought more painkiller to load into the IV. The nurse let us know that it would take a little time to act and then Isabel would sleep.

"I found him," Isabel resumed when the nurse had gone. "It was so terrible"—she was actively sobbing now—"what they did to him."

I didn't ask her to go further. After seeing what Isabel's arm had looked like before the medics got there, I could pretty well imagine what the gunshot Josh had looked like.

"Where?" I wanted her to stay awake because I hadn't learned whether the police had found his body yet. But my voice sounded too loud.

"The cabin," she said quite particularly. "He took me there once—in the afternoon. I couldn't stay the night—"

"During that week we were resting the horses?"

"I couldn't stay the night because I didn't want the rest of you to know. I wish I had," she bawled. "I wish I'd just said the hell with you. The hell with the rest of you."

"Of course you do," Frankie assured her. "And that's what you should have done."

"He told me that's where he would go if he needed to stay out of their reach. So I knew where to go. That's where I—" she was getting drowsy but fighting sleep. "I think he loved me."

"Yes, absolutely," Frankie said.

"He never questioned his feelings. He didn't know how to question any feelings he had. But it happened so fast and I didn't—I mean, I didn't—I was cold. Why was I like that?"

Neither Frankie nor I responded. Now I really did want to cry. I'd had my share regrets about love but nothing like Isabel had now.

"Now it's not going to happen. He's gone. I lost him." She was drifting off with her sorrowing. "Lost everything."

Although I would wait to say this until I could do it without bawling and Isabel could receive it the same way, she had also found something, in herself. She could take that, go forward with it, and find it sooner when the next opportunity came along. I knew it would. If there was one thing Frankie and I had learned, it is that men are not like streetcars. But they do come along.

Frankie and I walked down into the sunshine. She said, "I've never been any good at recognizing the right one either."

"If Charlie hadn't walked into my life, I probably wouldn't have tried."

"It must be different, though, actually losing one like she has," she speculated. "Very grim. Don't you think?"

"At least you don't have to worry about meeting up with the guy again," I said, making a dark joke about my recent experience.

"Oh, Savage? Wasn't he lovely, just absolutely lovely?"

"Frankie, please." I resented the implication that I had done something so blind and clueless as to let him go.

"Well?" she demanded. "You grew up and he grew up. It's just that neither of you did it in time."

I drove Frankie back to the fairgrounds, and she eased down gingerly from the cab to the truck's running board. "Remind me never to sit on the back of a horse again. I can hardly walk."

I had given the horses only the most perfunctory once-over earlier that morning, and now I went over Owen with both hands, searching for bumps, swellings, and any lingering tension in the muscles of his hindquarters. The water in his bucket was well drawn down, and he was working steadily at the pile of hay in the corner of his stall. When I put my ear against his ribs, his gut was rumbling like Vesuvius. The sound of well-being.

"Did you see this?" Frankie handed me what appeared to be the label off a feed bag. On the back of it, a note was scrawled.

"Hey, ladies from Philadelphia—sorry I don't know your names. Been trying to catch up with you before you ship out. Numbers 106 and 107 are your horses, right? Like to talk to you about buying one or both of them. Cell phone seems to work in town here. My number is 530-555-3558—Tor."

I didn't know what to do about this expression of interest. I doubted that Isabel would part easily from either Darwin or Owen, but that had to be her decision. The immediate problem the note raised, however, was how to respond to Tor without mentioning that Isabel was in the hospital and then answering questions about how that had come about.

"You going to tell her?" Frankie wondered. We were still pondering the situation when Tor materialized in the doorway to the stall.

"Got my note, I see." Even after a grueling, hot hundred miles and a short night there was something merry about this fellow with his lively glance and mischievous smile. "What do you think?"

"Well, you know, these horses don't belong to me," I told him.

"Just along for the ride, then?"

My arrangement with Isabel wasn't all that unusual. He turned to Frankie. "Would they be yours, then? Or maybe it's the little vet?"

Frankie nodded cautiously, and I said, "We'll make sure she sees your note."

"Oh, she's not here then?" Concern flickered briefly in his expression. "It's a hard ride. I hope she didn't—"

At this, Frankie leaned toward him and spoke quietly, as if she were giving up the greatest confidence. "Isabel is," she said meaningfully, "*female*, and you do know what trouble *that* causes."

"Oh," the twinkle returning to his expression, "later then."

"Yes, later," I agreed quickly, thinking that would send him on his way. But Tor lingered to make a close-up assessment of Owen.

"I heard he tied up," he suggested.

"He did." There was no point in lying about what at least ten other people, including one of the ride vets, had seen. But it is a cardinal rule of mine never to talk down a horse. There may be no sale hanging in the balance today, but there could be tomorrow. And in the meantime, the bad word gets around.

"I could fix that, you know," Tor proposed.

"What? His tying up?"

"Right. I know how to condition a horse so he won't do that."

Although it was possible he himself believed that, I didn't. But I held my tongue because challenging him would be the same as talking Owen down.

268 • Holly Menino

"He's going to be complicated," Tor predicted, as if he had already purchased the horse.

I laughed and said, "Certainly is!"

Frankie looked pointedly at her watch and said, "We're off to lunch now with the men. We'll give Isabel your note when we see her this afternoon."

"Great." Now Tor was lingering in front of Darwin's stall. "Be sure now, ladies, to keep those men happy."

"I do strive," Frankie assured him with put-on gaiety. I wondered how she had called that up, because I didn't have an ounce of fun left in me. As soon as we were out of range of Tor's hearing, I said, "Letting go of these horses would be the worst thing Isabel could do for herself right now."

But Frankie was intrigued by entertaining an offer, and as soon as she had settled in the front seat of the truck, she said, "I do wonder if he has any money." I knew she wasn't talking about cash to buy a horse. She was speculating about what she would call real money, and this probably meant she had found Tor at least somewhat attractive.

We went to a table at the back of the Mexican restaurant and found the four men hunkered down behind enormous menus, all of them, that is, except Stephen, who had made his choice, put aside the menu, and substituted as reading matter the local newspaper.

Frankie took an empty chair designated by Farrell and said, "Stephen, is it too early to have a margarita?"

He said, "Yes," automatically and then without looking up from the paper, "Hey, get this. The guy's name was Dawkins."

"Which guy?"

"That slime ball in the linen jacket. The police gave his name as Dawkins, Robert Dawkins."

Savage smiled. Charlie smiled and reached for my hand.

"What's so funny?"

"Dawkins," Charlie explained. "The name of a famous evolutionary biologist."

"Did you learn anything actually important?" I demanded.

"Police did," Farrell said. "Copied all the guts in Stephen's computer."

"About McCarran?"

Stephen nodded. "You'd think they would have done that kind of lookup themselves. But it was like Canada was too far away to bother to look."

Charlie started with his favorite jokey line, "If I were a betting man—"

"Which you are," Frankie thoughtfully supplied the necessary line.

"—I would wager that McCarran sent Celeste down here to set up for taking over AccuGen. He had made money with pharmaceuticals. It was a line of business he knew pretty well, well enough to be aware that being cutting-edge is essential to surviving."

Savage nodded. "AccuGen would have given him all the cutting edge he needed. So he sent Celeste down here to stake his claim. I was the last one to be deposed today, and it seemed pretty clear to me that if our side of the border has anything to say about it, there will be a new investigation of McCarran's finances."

Stephen looked up from the newspaper. "This doesn't say anything about McCarran—or the fact that his own son shot him because—"

"Son?" Frankie interrupted. "But the two of them didn't have the same last name."

"He was the baby of the family," Stephen explained. "After McCarran's second wife divorced him and left with Celeste and her little brother, she must have taken back her maiden name."

When the burritos and chimichangas were delivered, Charlie leaned closer to me to give me what he feared would be bad news. "I'm afraid we can't go home right away, Tink. We'll have to remain in the area for the next several days. Paul may be able to go back and forth from San Francisco, but we're pretty much stuck here."

"I was going to wait until Isabel was in shape to get on a plane for home anyway," I said, "and it will be better for the horses to rest before we ship out. It's a very long ride for them. Farrell, will it be okay with you if we stay on awhile?"

Farrell had said very little, but now he said, "Sure, that part will be fine and dandy. But with the rest of it, I'm purely pickled."

"Meaning what?" Charlie prompted.

"McCarran's dead, right? Celeste is in jail and will probably wind up in jail in Canada. She's holding the mortgage on my place, which means he was probably the one with the note."

"Let me put your mind at ease," Paul intervened in Farrell's analysis. "Celeste isn't holding that note, and McCarran wasn't holding it either. I am."

Farrell looked bewildered. "But I thought—she said she had a friend in real estate who would loan her the money, and from what we figured out this morning, it seemed like McCarran—"

"I'm in real estate," Paul pointed out.

"You loaned Celeste money?" Charlie asked warily.

Paul shrugged. "You're right. I was suckered, but only part-way suckered. I bought the note from her, free and clear."

"But I was paying *her*," Farrell protested.

"Right." Paul smiled then. "It worked the same way as it would if your bank sold your mortgage to another bank."

Farrell looked uncomfortable. "So now what?"

"We can rearrange things," Paul assured him.

"Good," Farrell decided after a pause. "Then maybe I can do something about getting a new truck."

Everybody at the table understood that for Farrell *new* was a relative term. He was mollified, even consoled. His kitchen was safe. His dog was safe. And for another few days he would have guests in the house.

When Frankie and I got up to leave the restaurant, Paul accompanied us to the door. "It's been good to see you again," he told us.

"Oh yes," Frankie gushed, and kept gushing, which made it unnecessary for me to respond.

"And Tink"—he touched my elbow—"an opportunity to banish some old demons, hmm? I wouldn't have missed it for anything."

I absorbed this notion silently. I couldn't think of what to say.

"Tink!" Frankie declared impatiently. "Paul is seeing you off like a gentleman. Aren't you even going to say good-bye?"

I looked up into Paul's face and said, "Yes. Exactly. About the demons."

Farrell, wanting a word with Paul, joined us. "You girls tell Isabel that the sooner she can get herself together, the sooner she can get out of the slammer and back up to the ranch."

Farrell's ranch, however, was probably the furthest thing from Isabel's mind. When we returned to the hospital, she had improved enough to be propped up in bed. Her body, at least, was more elevated. Her spirits hadn't changed much. She wasn't actively weeping. But she looked worn out from as much sobbing she had done, and she watched Frankie and me approach with a sullen glare, or as much of a glare as her dilated pupils would allow. She was zonked and mad, a tough little black-haired cherub looking for some kind of revenge.

Frankie pretended not to notice this. She patted Isabel's knee and said, "How is the arm, sweetie?"

Isabel didn't respond to this. What she said—slowly—was, "I'm going to sell the horses and get out of this goddamned rat race."

Frankie glanced at me worriedly. I mouthed the word *no* about relaying Tor's offer to Isabel because no sooner did I hear what Isabel had to say than I formulated an instantaneous strategy. I wanted to be the one to handle Isabel. She needed taking care of.

"Why would you want to sell them? I thought they acquitted themselves pretty well yesterday."

"If that's what you call tying up." This was tinged with bitterness.

"How much do you think they're worth?" I asked as if I was utterly without a clue as to their value.

"A couple of thousand each. Whatever you can get for them."

"Whatever *I* can get for them?" I actually was a little surprised that she thought I should take care of this for her.

"Yeah, get what you can. But I want them gone by the time I get out of this place."

This was the opening I had been maneuvering toward. "Isabel, you're not going believe this! I think I have the perfect solution for you."

"Yeah?" Her blue eyes had a cynical cast. This didn't worry me. I had seen my strategy, which was based on the perversity of human nature, used by a friend who sold children's show ponies. "What is it, this perfect solution?"

"Tor whatshisname—you know, one of three guys who were

riding those chestnuts—came around today asking about buying both of them, Darwin *and* Owen."

"Owen ties up," she countered suspiciously.

"Tor says he can fix that," I said. Frankie saw I was up to something and kept quiet.

"Oh right," Isabel said with a certain amount of venom. "He's so good, he's such a smart horseman, he can cure a horse that ties up."

"What do you care whether it's true or not? If Tor buys him and can't fix him, he'll still owns the horse. And you keep the money," I said enthusiastically.

Isabel turned her head to look the other way. "No. I don't think so."

"Isabel," I urged, "I have made some very good money on horses I've sold." This was true, but its corollary was also true: I had spent some very good money on the same horses. "My motto—and I try to stick to it—is Never Pass Up An Opportunity To Sell A Horse."

"Why not?" she demanded sourly. "Why not keep the horse until you can get an even higher price for it?"

"Because chances are something will happen to the horse before someone comes along with more spending money. The horse will go down with colic, tear a suspensory ligament, or just plain step in a hole."

"No," she said firmly and closed her eyes. The nurse came in with another loaded syringe, but Frankie motioned for her to hold off.

"Listen, Isabel. You can't pass this up. It's a beautiful opportunity."

She opened her eyes a little and disparaged this. "It's not a real opportunity. He doesn't have the money."

"It's easy enough to find out if he does or doesn't. Just ask your price and see what happens."

"I already know he doesn't have the kind of money I need for even just one of them. These are *made* horses."

"Well, okay, Isabel. I think you're making a mistake, and don't say I never told you—"

"So I sell them," she proposed with a certain amount of rancor, "and what's the first thing that happens? He comes back with them and beats me. Beats me with my own horses."

Not bad, I observed, for somebody who was giving up the rat race.

"You tell Tor I said thank you very much," she commanded primly. "I'm glad he appreciates my horses, but I'm not interested."

The power of reverse psychology. The way that my friend who sold show ponies used it to sell ponies that were safe and perfectly matched to the kids who ended up with them was to offer to let the child's parents see a number of "really stellar" ponies. She would walk past the stall that housed the pony she considered an ideal mount for the child and say nonchalantly, "Nice enough pony. But probably a little too much for your daughter to handle, and probably out of your price range." Inevitably, after enduring demonstrations of two or three other ponies, the parents would insist on looking at the one my friend had put off-limits.

Before we left that afternoon, Isabel asked a fretful question about how her horses would get home to the Brandywine country.

I said, "We'll make it back there with them. You just make it to the plane."

Acknowledgments

Although writing is often called a lonely craft, I find I need a lot of help and need to thank quite a few people for that help. This story has been no exception.

Although it's always tricky to pinpoint the origin of a story, the germ for this one was probably planted when I met Stasia Newell, professional horse trainer and experienced distance rider. Stasia sees and responds to horse behavior with remarkable clarity, and her approach to natural horsemanship, her insights, and her strong opinions are expressed indirectly by several characters in the story. I have absorbed a lot of this without her permission, so it's probably time to fess up and say thank you.

Thanks of a different kind are due to Dr. Pamela Karner. For years my horses have benefited from her tough-minded and practical approach to the science of medicine, and I have often relied on her expertise for my writing. Now that she has emerged as a successful endurance rider, this story centered on endurance makes it absolutely necessary to formally acknowledge her influence. Thanks, Pam.

Kathleen Sweeney, my colleague long ago in publishing, also has experience in the gambling industry. She tutored Charlie about gambling etiquette and advised me on the internal workings of casinos. I owe a similar debt to Claudia, Joe, and Liz Raco of the Christmas Tree Vineyard Lodge in Foresthill, California. Without their hospitality and their knowledge of local roads and trails, I never would have made it to the checkpoints on the Tevis trail. My thanks to all of you.

For longer than I care to admit, my friends Frances and Dean Benson and Caroline and Gerry Cox have been reading over my shoulder as I write. Their reactions and advice are always important, and their support has been invaluable. Of course, I am also very grateful to the two professional readers of my stories, to my agent, Ethan Bassoff—for his diplomacy—and to my editor, Anne Brewer—for her patience and tenacity.

All through my telling of Tink's Sierra Nevada adventure I had on my mind the people who introduced me to the Arabian horse, Maggie Price and Nancy Roeber-Moyer. Maggie, who died several years ago, was a former president of the American Endurance Ride Conference who led a medal-winning team for the U.S. at the World Equestrian Games. Her neighbor Nancy managed their barn and horses, competed up and down the East Coast, and served as the keeper of stories. Looking back on my times with them, I find their generosity with their time and with their lovely horses hard to believe.